LOVE DENIED

Honorable Intentions, Book 1

Rose Phillips

Dragonblade Publishing, Inc. is an imprint of Kathryn Le Veque Novels, Inc.
P.O. Box 7968
La Verne CA 91750
ceo@dragonbladepublishing.com

Produced in the United States of America

First Edition January 2022
Trade Paperback Edition

ARE YOU SIGNED UP FOR DRAGONBLADE'S BLOG?

You'll get the latest news and information on exclusive giveaways, exclusive excerpts, coming releases, sales, free books, cover reveals and more.

Check out our complete list of authors, too!

No spam, no junk. That's a promise!

Sign Up Here

www.dragonbladepublishing.com

Dearest Reader;

Thank you for your support of a small press. At Dragonblade Publishing, we strive to bring you the highest quality Historical Romance from some of the best authors in the business. Without your support, there is no 'us', so we sincerely hope you adore these stories and find some new favorite authors along the way.

Happy Reading!

CEO, Dragonblade Publishing

Let me not to the marriage of true minds
Admit impediments. Love is not love
Which alters when it alteration finds,
Or bends with the remover to remove.
O no, it is an ever-fixed mark
That looks on tempests and is never shaken;
It is the star to every wandering bark,
Whose worth's unknown, although his height be taken.
Love's not Time's fool, though rosy lips and cheeks
Within his bending sickle's compass come;
Love alters not with his brief hours and weeks,
But bears it out even to the edge of doom.
If this be error and upon me proved,
I never writ, nor no man ever loved.

—Shakespeare, "Sonnet 116"

CHAPTER ONE

*Life's but a walking shadow, a poor player that struts and frets
his hour upon the stage and then is heard no more.*

—Shakespeare, *Macbeth*

NICHOLAS TUGGED THE bridle, pulling Taurus to a stop, and then slid from the stallion. Relief coursed through his cramped legs. He let the reins drop and brushed at his jacket and trousers, the rising dust tickling his nose, its chalky residue lingering on his tongue. He straightened, rolling his shoulders, and tension rippled down his spine until the muscles in his lower back contracted and released.

The domed roof of the addition to the manse rose above the tree line, the pearl marble gleaming in the sun. It reminded him of the folly, once his pride and joy. His dream of architecture long gone, he wondered if the sight of the folly would still bring pleasure. He glanced in its direction, but it was well hidden by the forest, cloistered from the world as he'd hoped when he'd first envisioned it.

Taurus, nostrils flaring, snorted, blowing a warm stream of air across Nicholas's face. He'd ridden him too hard. He patted the stallion's neck, the hair moist beneath his hand. "You're a good man." A few feet off the main drive, the bridge beckoned. He left the horse, knowing it would wait where it stood.

Stubborn but loyal. Like Catherine. He scanned the ground for a small rock. Scrub grass and a few pebbles but nothing worthy of a wish.

His boots clicked against the wood. He stopped midway. It was impossible to tell if the lake was well stocked with fish. There was no sign of movement beneath the surface, but it was a deep lake. He couldn't remember the last time he'd held a rod. Such indulgences were probably now and forever relegated to the past. There would be no hours to waste, no idle time to fill. Not that there'd been for years, but he'd always thought leisurely activities would enrich his life once again. And Catherine's. All dreams included Catherine.

Reaching up, Nicholas ripped the epaulet from his shoulder, clutching it in his fist. He raised it to his mouth and kissed his curled fingers, the rough metallic threads coarse against his lips. "To simple pleasures." The gold braid plopped ungracefully into the lake, tilting awkwardly as it absorbed water. He watched the epaulet sink, wishing it took his shame with it, wanting to bury the last four years under the silt and sludge at the bottom. If only it were that easy.

The special license tucked inside his jacket brought some comfort. He traced its stiff outline, his heart lightening at the promise it held. The far end of the bridge beckoned. It would be so easy to cross it and follow the path to Stratton Hall. To see Catherine. To hold her in his arms again. He drew his shoulders back and pivoted. He knew too well how to stiffen his resolve as well as his back. Pleasure must be delayed for duty. Catherine would have to wait.

The rising specter of Woodfield Park summoned. It was time to face Daniel.

THE DOVE SHIFTED uncomfortably from foot to foot, eyeing

Catherine with suspicious curiosity.

"You've nothing to fear from me," she said.

It cocked its head, blinking rapidly, dark eyes judging. A warm breeze swept through the enclosure, and Catherine brushed at an escaped tendril drifting across her eyes. Startled by her unexpected movement, the dove flitted away with a fluttering coo. She fought foolish disappointment. Perhaps the gentle bird would come again tomorrow.

For Catherine would return. Drawn here, despite many resolutions to cease the daily ritual, she liked the quiet solitude, although peace remained elusive. Perhaps it would always remain so, for atonement for their sins could only be granted by one person. And she feared he would not be forgiving. Leaves rustled restlessly, and sparrows chirruped a litany to her musings.

She drifted around the tomb, her hand trailing along the stone, its surface cool despite the warm day. She stopped at the rosebush. It was a fledgling, but someday its blossoms would spill color over the bland gray. Yellow, like sunshine on a cloudy day. Daniel would like that.

His laughter still echoed off the rock walls. They'd used to play here as children. Daniel had loved to scare the stuffing out of her. He would hoot with triumphant glee and fall to the ground with her brother, both boys holding their sides, rejoicing at her fright. Life had been so unfettered then.

Odd how someone can be so vibrant, so infused with life, one day, then the next day cease to exist.

She knelt at the head of the tomb and pushed at the loose soil, unearthing dankness as she molded it to support the base of the struggling scrub. Frustration rose anew, and she slapped at the dirt. She had wanted to be at the service, needed to be there to say goodbye. As Daniel's intended, she'd assumed it was her prerogative. Instead, her protestations had been hushed with mumbles about delicate sensibilities, and quicker than she'd been able to argue, certainly sooner than she could ever have anticipated, the deed had been done. Roses were all she had left to offer him.

Pressing her forehead against the unforgiving limestone did not stop the inevitable question. *Why? Oh, Daniel, why?*

"Catherine?"

She froze. Surely the voice was the whisper of the breeze, simply her imagination running rampant once again.

"Catherine?"

His deep baritone sent familiar shivers down her back. Nicholas. No flight of fancy, then. He was here. How many times had she dreamed of him these last four years? How often had she longed for him? She pushed her head harder against the stone, the pressure providing no easement to the flood of emotion. Nicholas. Home at last. But she could no longer have him. She had burned that bridge and could offer no palatable explanation for casting him aside. He would never forgive her.

He touched her, and heat radiated where his hand rested on her shoulder. Still, she could not lift her face. She did not wish to see her betrayal reflected in his eyes. He brushed his hand softly, comfortingly, along her arm. A shudder shimmied throughout her body. *Oh, Nicholas. I am so sorry.*

"Catherine, my love," he said quietly as he continued the gentle caress. "It does my heart good to know that Daniel has had you to mourn him in my absence."

She had not shed any tears since they'd found Daniel's body, but they threatened now. She wiped at her eyes, angry at her weakness. This was not the time. She reached up and placed her hand upon his, gathering strength to face what she must. Stiffening her spine, she looked up. The tenderness softening his eyes was almost her undoing. Inhaling deeply, she shook off her self-pity. It was too late for regrets. She removed her hand, and he gallantly offered his, assisting her to her feet.

"Nicholas." So much needed to be said, yet no words came. She wanted to reach out, to trace the sharp edges of his cheekbones, to feel him, to know he was truly here. But she'd surrendered that right.

He smiled hesitantly and then pulled her close, smelling of horse and the sweat and dust of the road. She wrapped her arms around him, grateful for this moment. Perhaps he had forgiven her? No, not Nicholas. He would not excuse such a transgression. His chin rested on the top of her head.

"I find it difficult to believe my brother lies here," Nicholas said quietly.

She released her grip and shifted in his arms until they faced Daniel's burial plot together. "I still cannot believe it. I keep expecting him to jump out and frighten me."

"He did love to give you a start. So did that rascal of a brother of yours. Two peas in a pod, that pair."

Nicholas chuckled, the light rumble from his chest rippling against her back. She turned to him, pleased he could rejoice in the familial relationship among them all. No greater truth had been spoken. Laurence and Daniel. Their brothers. She had never before known a more compatible duo.

He kissed her forehead and released her, glancing around the cemetery as if he too thought Daniel might appear. His gaze rested on the mausoleum that dominated the graveyard. It was a monolithic, classical structure, built ten years ago when Lady Woodfield had died. A frown creased his brow.

"Why is Daniel not with Mother?" Nicholas asked. "She adored him. They should be together."

"I don't know. I am not privy to your father's decision-making. I was not even allowed to attend his service." It was difficult to keep the bitterness from her tone.

"You were not allowed?" His brows relaxed. "No, of course not. It is not a realm for women, is it? I regret I was not here to insist upon your presence. Goodbyes are important."

He reached out and swiped a gloved thumb along her cheek. His sympathy would be her ruin.

She concentrated on the somber limestone. "Daniel hated being cooped up. Loved to be outside. This is more fitting. He can hear the howl of wind and the patter of rain. He will smell the roses when they bloom."

"Ah, always the romantic, my Catherine. You see poetry even in this lonely tomb. Come, let us leave this melancholy for a time and see me home. Father is not expecting me until the end of the month, so it shall be a surprise."

She stopped. "You've not been to the house?"

His eyes darkened to indigo. "I have seen too much death over the last few years not to accept its heavy hand, but I must confess, I am struggling with Daniel's. I found I had to see for myself that my brother truly had been put to his rest before I saw Father. I left Taurus at the stables and climbed directly up here."

He reached for her, and she could not resist the lure.

"It was the mercy of the angels that led you here today to comfort me in this validation of Daniel's death. Come." He tugged her hand, and she obediently followed him out the gate and down the worn path toward the manse.

"It was no small feat to manage. I was torn by my obligation to my men and by my duty to Father. That aside, applications had to be made to see it through," Nicholas explained as they strolled hand in hand.

He slipped easily into conversation with her, sharing as though she was a comrade and not...not what? What was she? What had she ever been? What would she become?

"...Father's influence was absolutely critical. I have no doubt I'd still be on the continent if not for his connections. Still, the timing is awkward, and I return with no end of guilt."

She'd missed his explanation. No matter. Soon he would not share confidences. Not when he found out. She needed to tell him before anyone else had a chance.

"Nicholas," she began but faltered.

"Well, home at last." He pulled his gaze from the tall columns of the portico and stared at her as if seeing her fully for the first time. "Oh, Catherine, you dress in full mourning. If I didn't know better, I'd say you are wearing widow's weeds."

Her eyes welled, his sad face blurring. "Nicholas..."

He pulled her close, kissing the top of her head. "You do him honor to mourn him so. I do not deserve so loving a woman."

She could say nothing. How could she? She inhaled deeply, memorizing his scent, wondering if he would ever allow her near him again.

"Come." He held her back, at arm's length. "Let's go see Father."

"No." She would not give that old man the chance to slay her again. Not that she could tell Nicholas that. "This is your time with your family." She touched his cheek, knowing it would be the last intimate touch afforded her. "Please forgive me." His brow furrowed in question.

She spun around and ran down the sweep until she was around the bend and out of sight. Only then did she slow her walk, trying to catch her shortened breath as she cut off the main drive to the path that led to her father's estate. Crossing the footbridge at the base of the smaller of the two lakes that bordered their properties, she paused. Woodfield Park sat on a hill in the distance, and the pavilion rooftops of the new entrance and library were visible over the crest of the trees. It was hard to believe Nicholas was here. Four long years and he was finally home.

"Please forgive me," she whispered again, then turned away from the home she would never share with him, to resume her lonely existence at Stratton Hall.

CHAPTER TWO

*I did never know so full a voice issue from so empty a heart: but
the saying is true "The empty vessel makes the greatest sound."*

—Shakespeare, *Henry V*

NICHOLAS WATCHED CATHERINE flee, resisting the impulse to
chase her. She had not been expecting him and, no doubt,
was feeling overwhelmed. After all, it had been four years since
they'd last laid eyes on each other. And she'd been through much
in the last few months. Facing Daniel's death without Nicholas's
support would have been difficult. Her brother must be equally
devastated. Laurence had been more brother to Daniel than
Nicholas had been himself.

He continued staring until she disappeared around the curv-
ing sweep, strategically planted shrubbery hiding her from view.
Running a hand through his hair, he tugged at the windswept
tangle with a frustrated jerk. This was not how he'd imagined his
homecoming. He certainly had not spent his nights envisioning
Catherine running from him.

He turned and faced the manse. She was right. It was best
that he see his father alone. In all honesty, he had hoped to use
her as a bulwark. Not fair, but he would have preferred entering
the austere building with her by his side. Well, there was nothing
to be done about it. He crossed the drive. The colonnade blocked

the sun, and he shook a sudden chill from his shoulders.

Before he could take the last few steps, the door swung open. Of course it did. A groom would have given them word, and they would be watching for him. Years of looking over his shoulder for the enemy had dulled the memory of what it was like to anticipate time with family and friends. Except his older brother was no more. He shook his head, rolling his neck to free the grasping tension.

Fredericks, dressed impeccably in somber black, his shock of white hair as untamed as ever, stood just inside the threshold. While his face was impassively schooled, there was a twinkle in those milky blue eyes. Nicholas took the last few steps and clasped his bony shoulder.

"Fredericks, old man, good to see you." He meant it. Fredericks was a fixture at Woodfield. He'd been in the employ of Nicholas's grandfather, and Nicholas would swear the man had been ancient even then.

Fredericks's eyes crinkled in response. "Lord Walford, it is good to see you safely home."

Nicholas stiffened at the effusive welcome. *Damn. Damn. Damn. Lord Walford.* It didn't feel right. He was Sinclair. Daniel was damn Lord Walford!

"I am sorry, my lord. For your loss."

The old man had always been able to read minds. He and Daniel could get away with nothing under the butler's watchful eye.

"As am I, Fredericks. As am I." He squeezed Fredericks's shoulder lightly, then dropped his hand and scanned the foyer. "Father?" His voice echoed in the cavern of the hall.

"In the library, my lord." Fredericks's voice reverted to its customary detachment.

He tried not to wince at the deference. It was not Fredericks's fault that Nicholas now wore the title that Daniel had shed with his death. Instead, Nicholas nodded. "I will see myself in."

"As you wish, my lord."

"As I wish?" he muttered, walking past the first column, tugging at his gloves. "Nothing is as I wish." He yanked off the second glove as he reached the library door, then hesitated, girding his loins. What must his father be feeling? They had not parted on good terms, and now he'd come back as heir. He knocked but did not wait for permission to enter.

Nothing had changed in the years he'd been gone. The library remained a masterpiece of architecture, affirmation of the earl's masculinity and affluence in every line, in every piece of furniture. His father sat in one of the overstuffed chairs by the south fire—a fire that burned despite the temperate July afternoon. His crown of gray hair just visible over the high chair, he did not turn around.

"Father?"

No response. *Damn him.* Nicholas tossed his gloves on a side table.

"Father," he repeated, suddenly uncertain. "Am I welcome in your home?"

Silence ensued. He was about to leave when the low, familiar rumble finally answered. "It is soon to be your home, isn't it?"

Nicholas hesitated. Just how did one respond to that? He took a calming breath. He had lived through much more than this. So much more. Refusing to cringe before one man when he had not cowered before an army, he headed toward the brandy on the opposite side of the room to put some distance between them. Grabbing the decanter, he poured far more than a finger, threw it back, and then refilled it. He gripped the ends of the mahogany stand, gazing into the dark, amber contents of the glass.

Steady, old boy. Steady.

Standing tall, he snatched the tumbler and walked toward the fire before flinging himself into the chair a few feet from his father. Petulantly refusing to make eye contact, he instead stared at the flames. The silence in the room was suffocating, and he ran his fingers around his collar, trying to loosen its choke. He raised his glass, ready to toss the contents down his throat, seeking surcease to the stifling stillness.

"Did you become a drunkard as a soldier?"

Lowering the glass, Nicholas almost laughed at the absurdity of the question. He had not touched alcohol on the continent until Badajoz. Drink was many a soldier's escape, but it was also their downfall. An officer needed his wits about him to survive in the shifting tides of war. No. Liquor was not a vice for Nicholas. Could the man not see that *he* drove him to imbibe?

"You took your time coming home. Your brother has been dead more than three months, and you finally elect to make an appearance."

The fire snapped, a hiss escaping the wood as Nicholas counted his way to a calm and reasoned response. He watched the shooting sparks, the falling embers. He would never please his father. That had been clear many years ago.

"I had to seek permission, as you well know. Sell the commission. Wait for my second to arrive. It was not easy, nigh on impossible…" The luxury of returning this quickly to Woodfield Park was due solely to Nicholas's father's dirty work. In the middle of war, it would have been inconceivable if it were not for the formidable Lord Albert Woodfield calling in markers and, no doubt, bribing old cronies. Nicholas pinched the bridge of his nose as if it could stem the tide of emotions battling inside him. He was formidable too, on the field, yet somehow his father still made him feel like a young boy in small clothes, as if he had dallied on his way home and was late for evening dinner.

Hidden behind the walled arm of the chair, his father merely grunted in response. Nicholas tossed back the contents, its coursing warmth providing no comfort, and set the glass on the side table. What was the point? He was too road weary to play his father's games. He began to push from the chair.

"Sit down, boy." His father's voice was quiet, but it might as well have been a bellow, such strength did it toss his way.

He lowered back into the plush cushioning, irritation prickling at the ingrained submission to the man's command.

"I know well your accomplishments on the continent. Wellesley has kept me apprised of your every move."

What the hell did that mean? Was that convoluted praise? He had not missed this. This parlaying where he did not recognize when he scored a point or when he was in forfeiture. The fire snapped, shooting a burst of warmth in his direction.

"Bloody hot in here," he said.

"Watch your mouth. You're not out on some campaign with your ruffians. This is your sire you're talking to."

Nicholas flushed with embarrassment and anger. How did the man get under his skin so? He whirled to attack but instead choked. The man leaning forward in the chair was not his father. It was some elderly impostor. While his father had always been in good health, he'd leaned toward the rotund. Now jowls hung slack, and his eyes, even in profile, were drooping hound-dog pouches. His jacket hung loosely around his frame. He must be down a good three stone. Had Daniel's death taken such a toll?

"Get that gleam out of your eye. I'm not dead yet."

Any sympathy Nicholas might have felt was swept away. "I daresay Satan himself is not looking forward to your arrival."

His father twisted toward him, glaring, although Nicholas could swear he saw a twitch of his lips. However, if the man felt the urge to smile, he did not pursue it.

"My heart failed me. Temporarily, mind you. I'm getting stronger every day and will soon be back to full health."

"Was it…" He could not ask the question, was not yet ready to talk about it. He had seen men strewn about the field, pure cannon fodder, yet he was not prepared to speak of his brother's death.

"No." His father saved them from another awkward silence. "It ceased beating before."

Nicholas pushed from the chair, grabbed his glass, and headed straight back to the brandy. He could not resist the distraction. Truthfully, he wanted to drown himself in it. When had *this* world turned upside down? Would it have done so had he stayed?

He dismissed the thought; his actions did not determine the hands of fate. After pulling out the stop, he tipped the amber liquid into his glass.

"Wouldn't mind a bit myself, boy."

He grabbed another glass and poured some for his father, handed it to him, and retook his seat. They both stared at the fire, the quiet surprisingly bordering on companionable. Tilting his glass, he swirled the brandy but found he did not want a sip.

"The estate needs some tending," his father said, finally breaking the silence. "Been neglected for a while. Even before my heart played its game. I was at Parliament and didn't realize Daniel wasn't pulling his weight here. Brownlee didn't tell me of it either. Then the man left to deal with family business. I've sent him word of your return and demanded he come back." He took a mouthful of brandy and started coughing. Nicholas instinctively leaned forward even as the old man waved him off. "I'm not dying, and don't you think it. Just haven't taken a sip since…" His voice trailed off.

Well, there it was again. Time to face what lay unspoken between them.

"How did it happen?" Not knowing the details had haunted his daylight and dark hours since hearing of Daniel's death. He knew there'd been a hunting accident. The shot had been fatal. That was all his father's letter had stated, other than the fact that it was essential Nicholas come home. Of course, his father had neglected to mention his heart too. It would seem the man was reticent to have Nicholas privy to anything of importance.

Silence blanketed the room once again as they both nursed their drinks. Nicholas waited, fighting impatience. His father always weighed his words first—a trait he had oft admired, but it made his teeth grind now. He was glad he'd worn his collar unadorned during the ride. Heat was growing around the hearth, and he didn't think he could abide being trussed up in a tight cravat. Even so, he pawed at his shirt, opening it further.

"Bloody fool," Nicholas's father said.

Was he referring to Nicholas?

"He went to the park for a hunt."

Daniel. But the earl rarely cursed. And never in front of the boys. Despite his own tendency for profanity, Nicholas was oddly disconcerted by it but said nothing.

"A hero's death would have been preferable. No, he was chasing grouse when he met his maker." His father took a small sip.

Nicholas waited, watching.

"He'd fired but one shot. Hadn't even the satisfaction of a successful shoot before getting himself killed."

The earl tossed back the entire contents of the glass, choking only slightly this time. The old man held it out toward Nicholas, the crystal trembling in his hand. Nicholas took it, dutifully refilled it, and passed it back before retaking his seat. His father gripped it tightly, his hand shaking as he raised it to his lips. Nicholas waited, but his father shared no more.

"Who shot him, Father? Who the hell shot him in his own park?"

Just when he thought he would scream at the lack of response, his father responded. A simple answer, but the world tilted on its axis. Nicholas knew in that moment that nothing in his life would ever be the same again.

"Laurence."

Laurence? Dear God. Catherine! No wonder she was not herself. No wonder she had begged forgiveness. Her brother had killed his. Accident or not, her brother had *killed* his. It was inconceivable. Laurence loved Daniel like family.

"How?" The question caught in Nicholas's throat, sounding strangled, but his father understood well enough.

"Damned if I know. I was still weak when it happened, and I've yet to comprehend it." He took a drink before continuing. "It seems they bet that one could best the other in a single day's count. Somehow, Laurence's shot went wrong. He did not see Daniel." He finished the rest of his brandy in a single gulp, wiping with irritation at a dribble on his chin.

"But April? It's the wrong season." It was all his mind could grasp hold of. Hunting season did not commence until next month.

"You think I didn't know that? Even as feeble as I was at the time?" His father glared at Nicholas. "You think I did not pursue this? Did not investigate?"

Chagrined by his father's chastisement, Nicholas stared again at the flames. Of course the earl would have ordered a thorough examination. He was a hard man but not without integrity and, perhaps, some feeling. Besides, family was family.

"Laurence?" Nicholas asked.

"Fled. He knew I could not stand to have him about. The man who ruined my son, who put an end to my dreams." His father spat out the words.

Nicholas could not withhold his gasp. Laurence? Was he insinuating deliberation in the act?

"Don't be a fool, boy. To the army." His father looked at him, disdain clear on his face. "You cannot possibly think that coxcomb could have purposefully hurt anyone." He slammed his glass on the side table. "No. He feared my wrath. Feared repercussion and ran like a cur with his tail between his legs. Maybe the army will make a man of him." He grunted. "Don't know how that boy came from the loins of Stratton."

The Lord of Woodfield Park leaned back in his chair, disappearing once again behind its plush side. Nicholas recognized the move. He would get no more information. His father had said all he intended to say, and Nicholas was dismissed. Grateful for the discharge, he quietly left the room without looking back.

CHAPTER THREE

Some rise by sin, and some by virtue fall.

—Shakespeare, *Measure for Measure*

CATHERINE EMERGED FROM the dense copse of trees and approached Stratton Hall. The setting sun was partially hidden behind the old manse, and the weathered red sandstone building was magical in its departing rays. She'd lingered in the woods, the comfort of the familiar path calming her pinging nerves. It was done by now. Nicholas knew. Although cowardly, she was glad that she did not have to see his face when he heard. Nor confront his immediate wrath, for he would never understand.

She walked slowly across the lawn. Other than the dining room on the west side and the kitchens at the back, to the east, the house had changed little since the sixteenth century. A central structure encased by two wings, it was imposing but nothing like Woodfield Park. Stratton Hall was not grand. No whimsical additions, only practical ones. She would reside here for all her days. What else was there to do? She had given her heart long ago and could not, would not, settle for another.

A sigh escaped before she could quell it. What was done could not be undone. She tugged the ribbons at her chin and removed her bonnet, letting it dangle by its shallow brim on the edge of her fingers. No one was about. Her father had left to spend time with friends in Worcestershire. He disappeared a lot lately, no doubt escaping the somber mood of the hall. All laughter had ceased the day Daniel was killed. And all hope for the Strattons had departed with Laurence. Lord how she missed Laurence's cheerful presence.

The hall was not a grand entrance but a serviceable room, its high-beamed ceiling echoing voices of days long ago. She laid her hat on the weathered table, its etched surface testimony to the many meals that had been eaten on it once upon a time. She ran a finger along one of the grooves. *We come. We go.*

The walls were adorned with hunting trophies, the activity a tradition passed down through the ages and a nasty habit her father continued after his grand tour. He was proud of each and every one, but Catherine found the glossy-eyed wildlife somewhat unnerving. However, she'd made peace with a buck on the far wall. She walked to him now, holding his gaze. He was too high to pet, but she'd always imagined stroking him when she was a child. She felt the urge to do so now.

"What do you say, my friend? Can you bear to watch me grow old? To never hear again the sound of children gracing these halls?" She turned at the discreet cough. "Edwards."

"Miss Baring. I worried I would have to send out a search party for you."

It was good to know that someone cared. "Well, at least you know which path to follow," she replied, struggling to keep her smile and remain cheerful. "You won't need to fret anymore. I won't be straying far now."

He did not alter his expression, but she saw understanding in those dark eyes. "Lord Walford is home, then?"

"Yes, he is. And he is the perfect picture of health. Praise God that he has walked from the continent unscathed."

The butler bowed his head. "Amen." Then he picked up her bonnet, brushing at some unseen speck of dust. "You must be hungry, Miss Baring. You have been gone the better part of the day. I shall have Mary prepare you something."

"Thank you. Tell her to keep it simple. Some cheese and bread will suffice. And some preserve. You know how I must have a sweet. I'll take it in my room."

She headed for the stairs at the end of the hall, then stopped and turned around. "Oh, and Edwards, I would so love a bath if the boys are not too busy."

"For certain, miss."

Her legs felt heavy as she ascended the stairs. She stopped in the landing where the stained glass shimmered in the fading light, its beauty as captivating as ever. The collage of color depicted a hero, triumphant in battle, holding up his arms in jubilation. She fought tears. Nicholas was home. Finally home. But she could feel no victory. Nor must he.

Shaking her head, she took the last few steps to the next floor before drifting down the long hallway. She loved that she was at the end, far away from the rest of the family. It was always her refuge, and she hoped to find succor there this evening.

Her shoulders dropped when she entered the room. There was no need to pretend here. She did not even have to face a lady's maid. They kept a simple staff. One of the downstairs girls helped when she needed assistance, which was seldom in the last few years.

After removing each glove, finger by finger, she laid them over the edge of her dressing table and then sat down. She unbuckled her walking boots and drew off each one before setting them under the table, out of the way. Next, she untied her garters and listlessly peeled off each stocking, wriggling her toes. One thing she'd learned through Daniel's death was that the mundane daily routines and rituals brought comfort.

At the sound of a light tap, she dropped the dress back over her legs, tucking her toes under and out of sight. "Enter."

The boys dragged in a large copper tub and placed it before the fireplace.

"Would you like the fire lit?" one asked.

"No, Samuel. It's warm enough this evening. I shall be fine."

He tipped his cap in deference and departed with his twin brother, Sampson, to get water. They were so alike, and hardly boys anymore. Only a few years younger than her four-and-twenty, they always seemed so much more youthful. Not to mention Edwards always referred to his sons as "the boys." Said he named them as he had so they'd both come running when he hollered, "Sam!" Half the work, he'd say with a grin.

She waited as the boys made multiple trips to fill the tub. No fancy additions here. No separate bathing rooms or water closets. She still had to visit the back garden or use the pot under the bed. It was not an arduous existence by any means, but she was not enfolded in the lap of luxury. Not for lack of means. Her mother had died giving her life, and the house had lacked a woman's influence her whole life. Her father's two greatest passions were politics and hunting. Updating his home did not enter into his thinking. Except here. He gave her carte blanche with her own room. Her large, canopied bed dominated the room, its luxurious deep-blue velvet a contrast to the rich, creamy silk walls. The plush furniture cushions were wrapped in cerulean chintz. She always felt afloat, the room her own whimsical sky, her sanctuary.

Sadie brought in the simple dinner as the boys finished topping up the bath with hot water. "Would you like assistance, miss?"

Sadie wanted to be her personal maid, but Catherine did not see the need for such attention at Stratton Hall. Unfortunately, Sadie knew that Catherine had planned on taking her to Woodfield. She'd been quite excited about finally taking on that role and thrilled at the thought of living in a great manse. It would seem the dreams of many had died in the woods that day.

"I shall be fine, thank you." Catherine had no energy left to force a smile.

Sadie nodded solemnly but didn't say anything. Catherine usually enjoyed Sadie's bantering comments but, today, was grateful for her silence. Sadie placed a small pile of drying cloths near the tub and closed the door as she left. Catherine moved to it and lowered the latch. It was not something she usually did, but she wanted no interruptions.

She disrobed, placing each item carefully over the chairs, then settled into the tub. The hot water helped leach some of the anxiety from her bones. If only it could have the same effect upon her mind. As she sunk lower, her knees popped into the cooler air, but her shoulders were comfortably immersed. The dull gray dress mocked her from where it was draped. *"Oh, Catherine, you dress in full mourning. If I didn't know better, I'd say you are wearing widow's weeds."* She should have said something then. He should have heard it from her. She was such a coward! She closed her eyes to block out her clothing and to hide from her room, the blues too reminiscent of the changing colors of Nicholas's eyes.

She had done what she'd had to. Revisiting all the reasons she'd accepted Daniel's proposal would bring no alternative to light. She'd known what she was giving up when she'd agreed to it. If faced with the same dilemma again, she would make the same choice. She sat up abruptly, pain twisting her insides, and splashed water on her face. There it was. She would make the same choice, for it was the only one. She swiped at her eyes and lay back against the tub, staring up at the ceiling.

Then why did it now feel so wrong?

CHAPTER FOUR

Haply I think on thee, and then my state,
Like to the lark at break of day arising
From sullen earth, sings hymns at heaven's gate.

—Shakespeare, "Sonnet 29"

THE DOOR REVERBERATED despite Nicholas's valiant effort not to slam it, although a part of him unkindly hoped the old man jumped in his chair. The vastness of the atrium mirrored his sense of hollowness, his heels clicking on the floor as he moved to the marble stairs dominating the hall. He paused at their base, feeling oddly disoriented.

"Sir? Forgive me…I do apologize. My lord?"

Fredericks's cheeks reddened, and absurdly, Nicholas wanted to laugh. He'd never seen the weathered face disconcerted, and it happened now because Fredericks had forgotten to address him as a peer? It was a sobriquet as far as Nicholas was concerned. He himself could not digest that he now owned the title.

"Fredericks, when have I ever stood on ceremony in this house?" He resisted the urge to laugh, afraid he might not be able to stop.

Fredericks thrust his chin toward the stairwell. "The east wing has been prepared for your convenience."

"The east wing?"

"Aye, my lord. Your father requested it. He remains comfortable on the first floor."

Did he want to stay in the lord's chambers? He would not be displacing his father. The man had never lived in that wing. The earl had commissioned it as part of the upgrade for his wife. Nicholas's mother had not lived to see its completion. That was when his father had taken over the old state suite on the ground floor. Did conceding to this designation indicate Nicholas was complacent with this new role? He shook his head. Was there truly a choice? What the hell did he care? He'd been sleeping on camp beds in tents for years. He should be grateful for the comfort of a large bed and four walls.

"Thank you. No need to accompany me. I've not been gone so long that I've forgotten my way." No, but he'd lost his way. He set his leaden foot on the first step, hesitating at the sound of a cough, easily heard despite its polite subtleness. He turned, and if possible, Fredericks's cheeks were ruddier.

"Fredericks?"

"My lord, you did not come with your man. May I send Isaac to attend you?"

Nicholas's weary brain could not place the name, but Fredericks appeared eager, so Nicholas acquiesced. He had been wearing army attire too long not to need some assistance reentering civilian mode.

He continued up the stairs, paused at the division, then headed right where he would have normally gone left. Reaching the top, he stood at the iron balustrade. The rail encircled the entire atrium, a full gallery walkway. He watched as Fredericks scooted beneath the stairwell and disappeared from sight.

Nicholas had been in his early teen years when Wyatt had built the east wing, including this grand entranceway. The man was innovative—absolutely brilliant. Watching Wyatt had inspired a passion for architecture in Nicholas. A love he had not been able to pursue except for the folly. And now? Was there place for such passion as an only son? He thought of his men. Of the aftermath of too many battles. He thought of Daniel. Alas, real life tended to get in the way of aspirations, of dreams.

Shaking off the shadow of gloom, he left the balcony and entered the large chamber, leaving the door ajar so the hall light could spill into the quarters. Nothing had changed. As with the library, his father's money and virility permeated the room. Rich, mahogany paneling and dark, puce curtains drawn over the tall windows added to its luxurious formality. Each piece of furniture, chosen for its workmanship and attention to detail, was designed with the comfort of a large man in mind. Well, he didn't have his father's girth—scratch that—his father's girth of days gone by, but he did have his height. He sunk into the voluminous framed chair set before the mantel. His father certainly strayed from austere when it came to his personal comfort. The chair was as well padded as those in the room below.

The hearth sat empty. It was too warm this evening for a fire, and he was grateful Fredericks did not presume his father's desire for heat would be his. He did wonder why the man had not drawn the curtains back to let the remaining light of day into the room. Instead, several candles flickered on the mantel, making the dark grate an abyss for Nicholas's thoughts.

Four years. He'd left to prove he was an independent man. A man worthy of his father's esteem. Deserving of Catherine's love. All he had found out for sure was that life was fragile and, for a certainty, finite. What he had done was throw away four precious years. Years with Daniel. Years with Catherine. He ran his hand over his face. What use, regrets?

"My lord?"

Isaac. Garishly overadorned, he stood in the doorway, staring at Nicholas expectantly. Of course the name had struck a vague cord of memory—his brother's valet. *Had been* his brother's valet. Isaac had been a gnat since childhood, always hovering about. Now a full-blown popinjay, he was the last thing Nicholas wanted in his room. He was about to send the man packing when he recalled that Isaac was also Fredericks's grandson.

All energy seeped from Nicholas, and weariness took its place. Lord, he had no patience with men who were more concerned about the turn of their collars than they were about the state of the world, but he could not insult Fredericks. Besides, Nicholas's man had been wounded at Badajoz and would not be arriving at Woodfield until he was well enough to travel. Laying his head against the back of the chair, Nicholas surrendered. What had happened to his introspection of moments ago? Life was finite. What harm could it do?

"Enter," Nicholas said.

"I took the liberty, my lord, of unpacking your bag."

Nicholas grunted.

"Oh, you are quite welcome, my lord," Isaac continued as if Nicholas had expressed some form of pleasure, "although I have sent most of it to be laundered. Your items were in despairingly poor condition. I cannot imagine how horrific the war must have been when you could not even maintain basic standards of hygiene."

"Is."

"Pardon, my lord?"

"*Is*, damn it!" He turned in his chair and scowled at Isaac. "The war *is*, not *was*. It didn't end just because I abandoned it."

Isaac's cheerful countenance fell. He may have dressed like an aging dandy, but he still had the face of a lad, a bloody cherub actually; his cheeks remained as round as a youth's, with a crop of golden curls to boot. Nicholas felt like he'd just kicked a puppy.

"Bloody hell." He ran a hand through his hair, his fingers tangling in resisting knots. "You are right. I am in need of laundering myself. How is the bath? Any improvements?"

The valet brightened. "Well, my lord, the water runs clear these days, but we have yet to master the hot stopcock. Oh, we can get it hot right enough, but as it draws on the rainwater, we still have problems with the little extras that crawl in."

Nicholas could swear the man shivered. He almost laughed out loud. Well, he'd be grateful for a warm bath, little, crawling extras and all. A knock sounded at the door.

"Come in, lads, come in," Isaac chirped, comfortably back in control.

Four young men entered, each carrying a steaming bucket of water. Isaac ushered them through the door on the left. Hot water splashed into the tub. Nicholas's muscles ached in response to its lure.

Standing, he reached to his waist and loosened his whip sash, letting it fall to the floor. What need had he of it anymore? Methodically, he unbuttoned his jacket. After shaking it from his shoulders, he held it in one hand. How many nights had he done thus, wondering if the morrow would be the last time he would don it again? He ran a hand over the remaining epaulet. Advancement came quickly in war. What had he gained? Was he a man now? Would Catherine see him as worthy? *Was* he worthy?

He threw the jacket to the chair. Had he learned nothing? He had seen men, with life and hope in their hearts, slaughtered like cattle. Worse, he had watched other men, good ones with women and children waiting at home for them, desecrate the living. Badajoz. He must never forget those lessons.

He ripped off his waistcoat, drew the shirt over his head, and then sat down to pull off his boots as the servants exited. All except Isaac, who quickly knelt to remove the second gaiter.

"Thank you, Isaac. If you could have Nan send up something in about an hour. That will be all."

"Oh…but…my lord," Isaac veritably stammered, "I would see to your toilette."

His toilette? For years he had existed in squalid conditions, always taking the hardest assignments. His toilette! He was anxious to enjoy an honest-to-goodness hot bath, but he did not need any assistance to cleanse himself.

He rose. "Thank you, but that will be all." A flash of guilt at the valet's crestfallen expression forced a concession. "I will need assistance in the days to come. I stopped in London and was told that a certain Brummell has taken the town by storm and that the most fashionable of men follow his dictate."

Isaac bobbed his head enthusiastically. "Yes, though I hold to the old form of color. He is terribly stark, my lord," he said and, catching his criticism, added, "but quite dashing."

"Well…yes." Nicholas was not sure how to respond, fashion never having been a priority for him. "Stark will do, I think. I am in mourning." Besides, he'd already been to the tailor. His new garments would be arriving within a week. Quick attention was one of the advantages to having gained a title.

He strode toward his bath but stopped abruptly, his shoulders stiffening at the hound on his heels. "Thank you, Isaac. You are dismissed for the evening." He waited in the doorway until the outer door clicked shut.

Finally alone, he shed his trousers, small clothes, and stockings, and stepped into the large tub—another joy of having an oversize father. He relaxed into the steaming water, tension easing from his fully immersed shoulders. How many nights had he dreamed of such an extravagance?

Candlelight flickered in the spigots. The cold ran clean because it was from the cistern. The hot was still a problem. Well, it would be one of the challenges he could pick at, when he had the time. When he had the time. What did his time look like? For years, it had not been his own. Now he had full control. What would command his time? His father had indicated that the estate was neglected. That Brownlee was on leave. For how long? And what of the tenants? Would they remember him? Why had Brownlee not managed better? Daniel surely would not have stood in the land steward's way.

He grabbed the round of soap and swiped it over his body. The scents of cinnamon and orange tickled his nose as he swirled it into his hair, hair that was becoming far longer than he was accustomed to, and massaged his scalp. It was a luxurious indulgence. After ducking under the water for a rinse, he resurfaced spurting like a whale. He wiped the excess moisture from his face, then settled back to let the warmth of the bath work its magic.

If he had not been near Lisbon when he'd received word, he might still be on the continent. With so many ships in the water, it had been a simple task to return to British soil once the second captain had arrived to assume Nicholas's duty. He'd lingered in London for a single night's rest, just long enough to see to some ordering. Clothing. A ring for Catherine. A visit to the Doctors' Commons—that had proven to be a tonic for his flagging vitality, and he had left immediately. Anxious to be home, to see her in the flesh, he'd ridden hard. Poor Taurus. He hoped the horse was being indulged in the stable.

He closed his eyes and smiled. Catherine. Four long years. Years that had proven nothing except his love for one woman. She was so eloquent, so beautiful. Her burgundy hair had been pinned up today and covered by a bonnet, one strand hanging enticingly by her ear. He could still see her hair as it had been on the day he'd left, its richness undulating in waves. Her green eyes had been clouded that morning, but when she was happy, they were like the moss by the stable. Catherine.

He must find a way to embrace this new title. For her. For them.

Dawn's dew kissed the window, the rising sun a bleeding watercolor behind its misty sheen. Nicholas had never been one to tarry in the morning, and for certain, years of army routine had conditioned him to an early rise. He must have slept deeply, since for the first time in recent memory, no dreams had haunted him through the night.

He leaped from the bed, grinning like a bloody Cheshire cat. He, always the more somber of the two brothers, felt like a youth in the first bloom of love. How early would Catherine arise? Was she already awake? Was she as anxious to see him as he was to hold her in his arms again? He wiped at the window, and the forest that lay between their properties blurred even more. *Well, dear brother, I shall graciously accept this gift you have left me, this chance to finally begin a life with Catherine.*

A dark, navy velvet banyan lay over the chair, replacing his discarded clothing. He pulled it on. The cherub certainly did not neglect his duty. He must have crept back in. Any other night, Nicholas would surely have heard him. A slight tap sounded at the door. Like clockwork. It would seem the man had some of his grandfather's second sense.

At least he had the wisdom to wait for permission.

"Enter."

"Good morning, my lord."

Isaac was in full feather this morning. His peacock-blue jacket and breeches, and the contrasting waistcoat of canary yellow, would rival any bird that may be up and about this early morning. He waved vigorously toward the hallway, and a young maid came in bearing a tray with two steaming pots. She stopped abruptly, her eyes widening, cheeks blushing.

"Ahem, my lord." Isaac stared pointedly at Nicholas's midriff.

He had not buttoned the damn robe, and it hung open to his waist. He yanked it closed, smiling apologetically at the poor girl as he clumsily looped the frogs. He'd never been one to assume servants were blind nor to have little care for their feelings. Nan had taught him better than that.

"My apologies," he said.

The maid giggled nervously and deposited the tray on the table by the window.

"That will be all," Isaac said brusquely, strolling over to the table, removing a cup, and setting it upright. "I did not know your preference, my lord. Fredericks said you favored tea, but I understand that coffee is more popular on the peninsula." He raised an eyebrow in question.

"Your grandsire is correct."

The man flushed at the familial reference. Odd. The valet

could not possibly be ashamed of the connection. Fredericks was a landmark. Hell, he was more family than…well, damn family! Surely the popinjay knew that? Nicholas pressed thumb and forefinger to his temple, trying to dislodge the ponderings. What did he care? His man would be here before long. The situation was temporary. This colorful bird would fly free of his chambers soon enough.

"I did not develop a taste for coffee and have longed for one of Nan's brews," he continued by way of concession. Nan had been with them almost as long as Fredericks. Everyone called her Cook, but she was more to him than that. She was his Nan.

Taking the cup, too restless to sit, he took a sip. Ah. Pure ambrosia. He had thought of her tea on many a cold morning. Isaac's chatter interrupted the pleasurable moment.

"…and he says you don't have a thing to eat until you are done riding."

Nicholas shook his head, confused. "Who says?"

"Fredericks. You were not listening were you? Your thoughts were elsewhere, perhaps? Well, never mind. I'm not here to be heard, only to make sure you are clean and presentable." He looked him up and down, and more clucking ensued. "It is as I thought. Too small. Far too small. Whatever will we do?"

"We? About what?"

"Your attire. Your ensemble. Whatever will you wear today?"

"Just give me what I had on my back yesterday. It will do for another day."

"Absolutely not. It was feculent." The man actually sniffed in disgust. "Besides," he continued, brushing off impending interruption with a wave of his hand, "it has all been sent to be laundered."

"Then just bring me some of my old riding clothes."

"Oh, much of it has been discarded. I went through it myself when I heard of your imminent arrival. Much too out of fashion, not fit for your new position."

Well, the little shit!

"Regardless," he continued, either oblivious to or unconcerned with Nicholas's rising irritation, "it would not fit you now. You have grown quite...bulky. Your thighs, my lord, and your arms—they are far thicker than when you left."

"Digging trenches does tend to do that to one's arms and thighs." Did the man live wrapped in cotton, unaware of what was happening on the continent, what real men did for a living, for their very survival?

The valet noticed nothing of the sarcasm; he did not come up for air. "I think your father's old breeches might do in a pinch, the ones before he attained his...hmm...girth, and I believe you just might get away with one of your old shirts, although the fit will be quite snug." He tapped his finger against his chin. "Your father's jacket will be too large. Well, his old ones will be, his new ones too small. You'll just have to do without a jacket until dinner." Isaac circled him. "Yes, that will do. What think you, my lord?"

"Just get me some clothes," he growled with little impact on Isaac. The irritating dandy merely smiled, then strolled from the room, closing the door softly behind him. Nicholas refilled his cup and toasted the air. "Welcome home, old boy. Welcome home."

CHAPTER FIVE

*Thou wouldst as soon go kindle fire with snow as seek to
quench the fire of love with words.*

—Shakespeare, *Two Gentlemen of Verona*

THOUGHTS OF WHAT could have been, what should have been, haunted the long, dark hours. As dawn's hue brought shape to the furniture in Catherine's room, she arose and took care of her toilette. She dressed quickly but lingered in front of her mirror. Her forest-green riding habit was becoming, accentuating her eyes, highlighting her cascade of dark hair, its strands gleaming claret in the rising sun that caught the glass.

Who was she? Who was this woman who had given up the only man she could ever love for another who had also owned a piece of her heart since first memory? She scowled and stood straighter. *Stuff and nonsense!* She knew who she was—a woman who had done what had needed done. Out of love. She would do no differently if the hands of time could be wound back. Yesterday's despair did not revoke that stark fact. Why must she continue to revisit this as though a different ending might result?

She shook her head, brushing at the soft fabric of her skirt. Besides, what did it matter? She could no more undo anything than she could fly. And there was nowhere to run, nowhere to hide. She must face Nicholas. His censure. His disappointment.

She must witness the pain wrought by her actions. A light scratch broke through her grim thoughts, and she opened the door to find a startled Sadie about to depart.

"Oh! You're awake, Miss Baring!" The maid flushed. "I was trying to be quiet, thought you might still be abed," she stammered.

While Catherine was no idler, she did not usually depart the hall at this hour. She smiled, trying to ease the jittery girl. Sadie was so anxious to please.

"Up and about, as you can see, and I do appreciate that you are available at such an hour. I shall enjoy a change of clothes when I return," she said before heading down the corridor.

"Yes, miss," a more cheerful Sadie replied. Catherine heard the click of her bedroom door as she reached the stairwell. *We all need to be needed*, she thought ruefully. What was to be her role in the years to come? Her father would continue to use her as his housekeeper and hostess. When he was gone, would Laurence? Would Laurence even return?

She took the stairs swiftly, running from such dark ruminations. Life would unfold as it would. Edwards must have overheard her speaking with Sadie, as he waited at the bottom of the stairs.

"Star is ready, Miss Baring. We gave her feed early, and she is anxious for some exercise." He handed her a well-worn pair of riding gloves.

Edwards was perceptive, as always. Of course, he'd been party to arranging many a morning ride to meet Nicholas. Perhaps he just assumed she would slip back into her old routines. If only that were true. This was likely to be her last early-morning ride, at least in the direction she planned on heading. The lingering mists of her dream life would disappear with the stark reality of day.

"Thank you." She exited the open door, pulling on her gloves as she descended the steps. Yes. Her old routine. In the year before his departure, she'd used to meet Nicholas at the large lake every morning. They had been friends for an eternity, comfortable companions. In that last year, her twenty-first, they'd discovered something entirely different with one another. The new flame that had ignited between them had only deepened their connection.

Of course, she'd known long before that summer that she was irrevocably in love with Nicholas, that no other could ever take his place, although she'd never shared that with him. He'd finally declared his feelings for her at the same time he'd shared he had purchased a commission and would be leaving for the continent. She had railed and stormed, but he'd been adamant. It had been for her. For them. He was four years her senior, and it had been time he made something of himself. He could not offer her great wealth or a title. The least she deserved was to be married to a man of honor. He did not want her to hang on to the arm of a second son who lived off the profits of the heir.

Tobias waited at the stable, grinning, holding Star's bridle. As he was Mary's grandson, Catherine had watched him grow up and ease comfortably into the role of a hardworking young man. His pleasure must come from anticipating her need; surely he did not remember her escapades of four years ago. He would have been only eleven. More likely, Mary had shared Catherine's eager anticipation to meet Nicholas each morning. The cook did have a tendency toward gossip. Catherine shook off the embarrassment. There would be nothing of a tryst in this visit. She simply, and perhaps foolishly, needed to go to the lake this morning. If only to see Nicholas one last time without others standing witness. She did not doubt he would be there.

Tobias took her hand and assisted her onto the mounting block. From there, she easily threw herself onto the mare. She stroked Star's luxurious chestnut coat, reaching over to touch the soft white blotch on the horse's forehead. She'd always done so before a ride, to connect with the lovely girl, and for a little luck. A wish upon a star. What she would have given for wishes to be so easily granted.

"Thank you, Tobias."

He tipped his cap, and she left the yard and headed down the path toward the first lake. Nicholas's property bordered on her father's with two lakes. The smaller was set back slightly from the main road. It was man-made and well stocked, mostly used as a diversion for houseguests of Woodfield Park.

The first lake was larger, nestled closer to the hillside, with a wonderful, cascading waterfall feeding it throughout the year. Its waters were fresh and clear, spectacular in all weather. This morning, the sun sparkled, dappling the water in a dance. A stark contrast to the churning dread inside her.

When planning the folly, Nicholas had shared his vision. She had sat with him by the waters as he'd designed and sketched the structure, soliciting her opinion throughout the project. That was when she'd known he was the best life had to offer, and she'd felt exceedingly blessed. That he would seek her opinion, and remodel according to her advice, affirmed he'd respected her as a person long before he'd loved her as a woman. She sighed. Now he must feel neither for her.

She followed the path around the lake, halting a few feet from the pavilion. It was a wonderful, classically styled building, its columns and dome a mirror of the new porte cochere and library of the main house. It should have been outlandish and out of place, but Nicholas had had the foresight to plan landscaping as well. They'd conferred on this at length. She loved gardening. The columns were rich with the blooms of violet clematis; rosebushes, abundant with butter blossoms, adorned the steps; and shrubbery abounded—all softening the blunt white structure.

How many times had she gone here to meet Nicholas? How many times had she come over the past four years to remember him? It was here Daniel had found her and proposed. He'd known she was at her most vulnerable when wrapped in reminiscences and had worked it to his advantage.

The memory should have drawn anger, but no ire flourished in her breast. Daniel was a charming scoundrel, always had been, and he'd done it for love. Could one ever begrudge that emotion? It was impossible for her to renounce it, although perhaps things might have turned out differently had she spurned him. Instead, she'd accepted his love as truth and acted in the best interest of their families.

She dismounted, leaving Star to graze. There was no need to tie the horse, as she would not leave. This was familiar territory to the mare, and she always waited patiently.

There was no sign of Nicholas. Well, that in and of itself was telling, was it not? If he did not come today, then he had truly severed her from his life. She could not blame him one whit. No, she could not fault him at all. Yet she would be forever tormented by his rejection, rightful or not.

She drifted up the steps of the folly, caressing the flower petals as she went. They were vibrant velvet, four years of growth obscuring the pillars with their beauty. She opened the oversize wooden door and entered the vast chamber. Nicholas had not wanted to break up the majestic interior.

Its lushness still made her happy. Nicholas had adhered to the barren beauty of classical structures but had furnished the space like a Turkish palace—plush carpets, comfortable settees, and extra wide chaise lounges abounded. Sheets of sheer curtains billowed in the breeze that flowed freely through the upper arches. The tall main windows remained fast against the weather, but he'd cleverly included arcs of open space at their tops, unimpeded by glass. He'd wanted the building to remain fresh at all times. Fresh as their newfound love. She smiled at the memory of his declaration.

"Catherine."

Not a declaration but a prayer. His voice was reverent. Did she imagine it? She turned. He had come, his silhouette tall against the morning sun, his face hidden in the shadow.

She bit her lip to stop the trembling.

He entered, his dark shape transforming into defined features much as her furniture had done in the early light. His eyes were indigo with emotion. Was he angry? Forgiving? Full of love? No, he was tense. So, not here to grant her absolution.

"Nicholas," she started, not quite sure what she could say to make him understand. No words came.

In a few quick strides, he was with her, taking her into his arms and seizing her mouth with his. She surrendered easily, relishing his attack. Oh, how she had dreamed of this. The reunion of her fantasies. He was not gentle, and she was glad of it. He was angry. He was needy. So was she. She met his every volley, craving this as much as he did.

He shuffled backward with her until her legs hit furniture, and they buckled upon a chaise. His weight was a comfort, the hardness pressing against her stomach a joyous relief. She wanted to shout in triumph. He wanted her. He loved her. He must, *must* have forgiven her! Her kisses became feverish as she pushed at his open shirt, her hands caressing his warm chest. She whimpered. For so long she'd imagined touching him again.

"Catherine," he murmured, grabbing her hand and pressing it to his heart. "My Catherine, my love." He raised her hand and kissed it with such aching veneration that tears blurred her vision.

"How I have yearned to be with you again. How memories of you have sustained me through endless nights." His eyes darkened further. "Picturing you here at the folly kept me going. Knowing that you had yet to know the pleasure of our joining ensured I did not capitulate in battle. I knew I must come home to you. That you waited for me to fulfill my promise of loving you." He rested against her neck, gently nuzzling.

Oh yes, she'd waited. She'd longed. She had spent each night lighting a candle and praying for him. That he come home safely. That he come home to her. That, after his worldly experience, she would still be enough.

How many nights had she dreamed of this? She ran her hand through his hair, relishing the familiar feel of the thick strands, of his breath on her neck, of the spicy scent of him. The last thing she wanted was to shatter the moment, but she needed to know for sure, needed to hear the words. "You forgive me?" she asked quietly, going still, hope and fear mingling.

He raised his head and stared at her. His brow furrowed, and her heart skipped a beat. "Forgive you, my love? There is nothing to forgive. I don't fully understand what happened, but I know if there is blame, it rests entirely upon his shoulders." He kissed her forehead and then pulled back again, locking gazes. "His actions are not yours. I do not forgive you, because there is nothing to forgive."

"I didn't think you would understand. I love you so. I never stopped, even when…" Her voice caught in her throat. No words could express her relief, her joy. So, instead, she pulled his head down and lost herself in a kiss that left her panting with need.

She touched his face, tracing his sharp cheekbone down to the slight cleft in his chin, not knowing what to ask.

"Nicholas? I want…" She wanted more of him. She wanted all of him.

"Shh, my love, I know. I need more too. We've waited so long."

Grateful she did not have to give voice to her rapacious thoughts, she rested her head back on the cushion. He sat up, and she mewled at the loss. A smile lit his face.

"Hush, Cat. You'll be well sated soon." He tugged at his shirt, swiftly pulling it over his head.

She gasped. A puckered ridge bisected his stomach. She reached out, tracing it with her finger, wanting to weep at the pain he must have endured with such a wound. Saddened she had not known he'd been hurt, had not been there to tend to him. He grabbed her hand.

"I told you I would bring back a souvenir." He grinned.

"How can you be so cavalier, you blackguard?" She tried to swat him with her other hand, but he caught it before she could strike. He took both her hands in one of his, stretched them over her head, then leaned in and stole another kiss.

"Blackguard, is it?" He licked a path down her neck, pausing at the high collar of her riding habit.

She giggled at his growl.

"I prefer your pretty, little dresses, the ones that show me those wonderful creamy..." His voice trailed as he nuzzled her breasts through the lightweight wool.

"Oh, but my wandering soldier, this is so much more convenient," she purred as she pushed at him, shrugged out of her jacket, and reached for the first clasp on the front of her bodice. Stretching out beside her on the spacious lounge, resting on his elbow, he eyed her fingers working at the second eyelet. His grin was slow, evil, and absolutely delicious.

"Miss Baring, let me assist you with that." He knelt, unhurriedly undoing the long line.

Catherine brushed the dark locks from his forehead. She loved his hair like this. It curled in abandonment, rebel locks falling where they chose. She tucked a strand behind his ear as he reached the end of the row and pulled her frock apart. Despite despairing that he would never see it, she had worn her most delicate chemise.

His contented sigh sang in her heart. He took a nipple in his mouth despite the silk barrier. She groaned, and he moaned in response. Abandoning her breast, he gripped her neckline and tore the delicate fabric, ripping it down the center. There was no embarrassment, only a ripple of excitement at the sounds of the rent and his labored breathing. They both watched the hand he trailed languidly down to her stomach.

"Oh, Catherine." His eyes shimmered, their sadness a window to the regret of lost years.

"Hush," she whispered, tapping a finger against his cheek, "there is only here and now. Only us as we are meant to be."

He turned his head and kissed her finger. Then, without another word, his mouth resumed its pleasuring, nurturing the exposed bud. She cried out at the exquisite pain, and he pulled back, his face filled with concern.

"I'm sorry. Perhaps we should not...I mean..." He ran a hand through his hair. "It's just…I have waited too long. I have dreamed for so—"

She drew him back, holding him to her chest. "As have I."

The muscles in his back eased as she rubbed him slowly, his skin hot beneath her hands. He suckled with renewed ardor, and she arched her back. Switching attention, he fondled the abandoned breast as he nurtured the other. She squirmed with need. He slid sensuously down her body, pressing a trail of kisses to her stomach, growling in frustration when he reached her skirt. She felt his aggravation, her need equal. Sitting up slightly, she slipped the bodice and chemise off her shoulders, wriggling until she shed the entire ensemble. She lay back on the plush settee, closing her eyes, suddenly embarrassed by her brazenness now that she was naked.

She'd never fully disrobed for Nicholas before. They had played around the perimeter of lovemaking, but never once in their dalliances had she ever fully bared herself. Nor had he. Was he appalled at her wantonness? She dared a glance from under the cover of her eyelashes.

"My love," he whispered.

He, too, had closed his eyes, his face pinched, looking discomforted. She was about to reach for her skirt, embarrassment warming her face, when he opened his eyes, his slow perusal from toe to face a caress over her body. When his fiery gaze reached hers, all trepidation deserted her, replaced by shivers of excitement.

"I have dreamed of this." He swept her body with indigo awe. "But it was never as beautiful—" His voice caught in his throat.

She wanted to shout in triumph. She wanted to weep. Four years. So many barriers. Yet here they lay, bared in love. Well, no, not quite bared. He had only removed his shirt. Feeling a fresh rush of boldness, she pulled at his breeches.

"So my little Cat is no more immune to this dark draw than I." His eyes twinkled, playfulness replacing solemnity.

It was her turn. She licked a slow path across his chest, taking his nipple and reciprocating the pleasure. He moaned and fumbled for his placard, frantically undoing its buttons. She murmured her approval as he sat up fully, methodically yanking at his boots, and tossing them to the floor. Quicker than she would have thought possible, he stood, squirmed out of his breeches, and pulled off his stockings.

He turned to her, his glorious form highlighted in the beams of light that crossed the room. Oh, but he was magnificent. He was bigger than she remembered—distracted by his scar, she'd not fully registered the change in his physique—his arms bulged with muscle, his abdomen rippled, his strength a powerful aphrodisiac. And his…what did you call it? She had touched it. Felt its strength beneath her hands. But always under cover. Now it was fully exposed, superb, and absolutely intimidating.

He smiled wickedly, crawled onto the chaise, leaned in, and took her mouth in a passionate siege. When she was senseless, he leaned back on his heels, stroking her breasts soothingly, sensuously with one hand. He took himself in hand with the other, languidly stroking up and down.

"It, too, has thought only of you. It, too, is full of love for you." It glistened, crying for her, and her body wept in response.

"Let me give you pleasure. Let us be as we were destined to be." He paused midstroke, waiting.

"Nicholas, my love." It was all she could manage, and she hoped it said it all. He was everything she wanted in life. All she needed. He *was* her life.

CHAPTER SIX

A dream itself is but a shadow.

—Shakespeare, *Hamlet*

NICHOLAS STARED AT Catherine. He'd never seen anything so splendid. His staff ached, and he squeezed it tightly, trying to distract it. He didn't want to spend quickly like a schoolboy. He wanted to revel in each moment, wanted to savor every inch of this woman who gazed at him with such love.

Except she was not gazing at him lovingly now. Instead, she was fixated on a certain part of him. He pulled at his cock one last time, fighting a satisfied smirk as her eyes grew rounder. She was intimidated. Nervous. He wanted to crow, so exultant was he at her naivete. It wasn't that he didn't have faith in her, but four years was an unbearably long time. And she was always a spirited girl. Correction. Woman. She was all woman now.

He tugged at the laces of her riding boot, and her gaze shifted to his as he slowly pulled off the shoe, keeping eye contact as he removed the second one. He hoped she could see that her love was returned tenfold. That he, too, had waited. There'd been no one since their year together. Her twenty-first summer.

"Share your thoughts?" she whispered, her vulnerability a sweet balm to his soul. Innocence had not caressed his days of late. His throat tightened with longing for lost years, so he merely smiled, saying nothing.

Silk stockings drew a delicate line of temptation, and his hand willingly followed it. And she'd worn a sheer chemise. Not so innocent in intent. That pleased him, and the last drop of doubt trickled away. She truly wanted this. He unhooked a garter, lazily unrolled it, and then repeated the procedure with her left one. Throwing it to the ground, he moved lower, tasting her calf, her knee, her thigh.

"Nicholas?" Her voice was louder, almost strident.

He pressed a kiss to her soft flesh and glanced up. She was uneasy. And excited. A filly ready for a confident hand. "Come, Cat. You have felt me beneath your hands as I have you." He stroked her gently, approaching her core with each successive swipe.

"Yes, but…but I have never seen you."

She squirmed as his thumb found what it was seeking.

"Oh!" Flushed a delicious pink, she tried to wriggle away, but his weight held her fast. "And…"

She began to pant, short breathy little sighs, so he increased the pressure, the speed. "And?" he teased.

"…you have never seen me!"

"Nor have I tasted you."

She gasped as he replaced his thumb with his mouth. If she made any further sound, he did not hear it. The rushing of his blood filled his ears and blocked all noise as he inhaled deeply. Pure heaven. His thumb resumed its dance as he relished each inch of her. When release vibrated through her body, it echoed in his—as sweet for him as he hoped it was for her.

He rested his head against her thigh for a moment before kissing his way back up her body. Rising on his elbows, he studied her. Eyes closed, her furrowed brow was softened by the hint of a smile. He kissed her lightly, and she looked at him, her eyes a virtual forest of variegated green. Woods he could get lost in. Was lost in. Would remain lost in forever.

"Oh," she sighed, her hands caressing his face. "That was…"

"That was just the beginning," he said, pressing his forehead to hers and moving his hips. She stiffened. Perhaps he was asking too much? Expecting too much, too soon?

He pulled back. "We do not need to—"

She put her finger to his mouth. "Yes, we do."

Still, he hesitated. But she wrapped her legs around his thighs, snugging him in place. He nudged, and she smiled in timid encouragement. Settling back on his elbows, he abandoned all chivalrous considerations and prodded for admittance, not able to resist looking down to see their bodies melding. She inhaled sharply, so he withdrew abruptly, glancing up, expecting distress again.

Instead, she shook her head, still smiling. "It's new to me. That's all."

He advanced again, this time meeting her barrier. He'd never been with a virgin, but there was no doubt he had reached her maidenhead. It was unlike anything he'd ever felt. He faltered, not wanting to cause her pain.

"I'm not fragile. I won't break." She seemed unsure even as she egged him on.

He kissed her noble nose. "That's my girl." His Cat did not shy away from a challenge. Thank God, for he did not wish to stop.

She lifted her hips, providing encouragement and easier access. He pulled out, then reentered with full strength. Her barricade gave way, and she whimpered as he nested himself fully. Her breath rasped in his ears. He worried he was crushing her, but he found himself unable to lift his own weight. He could easily spend right now. But he'd waited too long to let go with such readiness. He wanted to bask in this union as he had luxuriated in tasting her body.

She wriggled beneath him, and his rod twitched in response. He chuckled against her neck. Their bodies were as in accord as their hearts. Rising onto an elbow, he traced her lips with his thumb. Lips that tilted in a devious smirk.

"I would have it all, Nicholas," she dared with the impertinence he so adored.

He withdrew and reentered, still cautious. She flinched slightly, but her smile grew to a grin, and her eyebrows arched high.

"Is that the best you can do, soldier?" She rested the back of her hand upon her forehead, feigning dismay.

He growled playfully, thrusting more forcefully. Her body clutched his. It was too much sensation for restraint, so he let the momentum build. She met him each time, and he thought he would lose his mind with pleasure. But no. Not until she reached her heights. He did not want to go it alone.

"Look at me."

She opened her eyes. and he almost lost control at the sensual storm brewing in their depths.

"Come for me. Give me everything you have saved for me all these years. Come, my love. My fiery Cat. For me." He adjusted himself so that he could reach between them, his thumb encouraging her to leap into the chasm.

She cried out in climax, lightning flashing through those jungle eyes. He held her gaze, stroking one more time, releasing his need, his pent-up emotions pouring into her. Into the woman he loved. Home at last.

CHAPTER SEVEN

So foul and fair a day I have not seen.

—Shakespeare, *Macbeth*

NICHOLAS HANDED THE reins of both horses to the stable boy, then he and Catherine walked slowly along the path to the house. Content in their silence, they'd no need for words. Their bodies had spoken for them at the folly. Her hand comfortably enclosed in his, two had become one. There was no going back. Their joining was for life. He was not sure he'd ever known such satisfaction.

Woodfield Park came into view. In many a horrific moment on the battlefield, he'd thought he'd never see it again. He certainly had not thought he'd return to it as heir. He'd left to make a better life for Catherine, to become someone worthy of her admiration. He had sold his commission at a commendable profit, but it paled in comparison to his father's wealth. Wealth that would someday become his. The thought was so bittersweet he fought the weight of guilty melancholy. He'd not asked for this. All he desired stood right beside him, and he would never lose sight of that.

Stone crunched beneath his feet as they left the grassy path and stepped onto the drive. Catherine gripped his hand tighter, her tension suddenly palpable, although she did not say a word.

She hesitated when they reached the front steps. As she stood in the shade of the great archway, her body was brittle with resistance. Was that panic in her eyes? Ridiculous. They'd grown up together. She had run these halls in her youth, as wild a firebrand as their brothers.

"Come my, love," he cajoled. "He barks, but he does not actually bite."

"Oh, he bites. Make no mistake. He wounds severely with those jowls."

He squeezed her hand in encouragement. What was this? She'd never feared his father before.

"Come. I would have you with me when I tell him our good news."

"No, I leave it to you to enter the lion's den." She raised his gloveless hand to her mouth, kissing him with utmost chivalry. "I will go tell Daniel. He'll whoop in celebration. I should like to hear it echo off those old stone walls."

What could he say to that? He watched her leave the sweep and disappear from view. She had loved Daniel too. He sent a small prayer of thanks skyward, grateful Daniel had had someone who loved him these last few years, someone to mourn him when he'd passed from this life.

He took the stairs, shrugging off the draping gloom with each step. He'd dreamed of this day for years, enacted it in his mind during the long, interminable weeks of waiting, during the endless nights and the excruciating days of digging trenches that would, in the end, hold their dead. Today was about living. Today his life began anew.

Fredericks opened the door as he reached it, but Nicholas had nothing to hand him. He'd not worn gloves nor hat nor jacket. He'd never dressed shabbier on the home front, and yet Catherine did not seem to mind at all. He grinned. Fredericks beamed back. The old dog. He'd seen her. Them. Together. What a champion for love was their Fredericks! He clapped the old man on the shoulder.

"You have seen your new mistress in your spying, have you?" His laughter resounded in the vast marble chamber, and the sound further buoyed his spirits.

"A man could not wish for better," Fredericks responded.

Was he speaking metaphorically, personally, or directly to Nicholas? What did it matter? Nicholas was in perfect accord.

"Father?" he asked.

"In the breakfast room, my lord."

Nicholas headed past the first column, turning left down into the corridor. He passed the dining and billiards rooms, took a deep breath, and entered the next door. His father sat at the foot of the table, staring toward the window. Nicholas glanced in that direction. Catherine's gown flitted between trees on the path to the family cemetery.

"Father," he acknowledged before waving out the attending footmen and moving to the sideboard to fill his plate. The roll top of the silver server slid smoothly back. He dug into the mountain of bacon, shoveling a pile on his plate, and grabbed some rolls. Their fresh scent incited an anticipatory rumbling in his stomach. Beneath another lid, he discovered smoked herring. He could not remember the last time he'd enjoyed such a feast at this hour. He scooped a small bowl of marmalade from the tiered dumbwaiter and headed to the table. It seemed he had worked up an appetite.

"Wipe that grin off your face, lad. You are no pimpled youth in the bloom of first love. You cannot choose the first chit who crosses your path."

The verbal slap smarted as much as any physical one Nicholas had ever received from the man. "You are out of bounds, sir!" Nicholas slammed his plate on the table. He was not about to stay and let him denigrate Catherine.

His father merely gestured in dismissal. "Sit down. Sit down, boy, and eat."

Nicholas stared at the mound of food, his appetite deserting him.

"Surely an old man's words are not so distressing that you are unable to enjoy a meal?" His father tore at a roll and returned his attention back to his own plate.

Nicholas pulled out the chair with reluctance and sat down, a glimpse out the window showing no further movement. Catherine must be at the graveyard. What did it matter what his father said? His life was waiting. Waiting for him up on that hill.

He speared a piece of herring, chewing ferociously, taking out his frustration on the dead fish. His father said nothing as he worked aggressively through the entire plate. When he was finished, he placed his napkin on the table and swiveled to face his sire. It was best to be done with it, regardless of the old man's opinion.

"Catherine has agreed to be my wife."

His father patted his lips and laid the linen to the side. "It has been four years," his father began, but Nicholas cut him off.

"Four long years, and I have thought of her every single minute."

His father was silent for a moment, his blue eyes sharp in the haggard flesh surrounding them. He finally cleared his throat and raised an eyebrow. "But has she thought only of you?"

He pushed from the table, upsetting his chair. "What the hell do you mean by that…sir?"

Unperturbed, his father made a great show of ruminating.

Nicholas's patience quickly came to an end. "I asked—"

"I know what you asked. It's difficult to find the right words to tell your son he has been betrayed. That the woman he *thinks* he loves was betrothed to another."

Betrothed to another? His Catherine? With no word from her mouth? He shook his head at such nonsense. "You lie, sir!"

His father reddened, and his knuckles whitened as he gripped the table. "How dare you doubt my integrity. If you were not newly home, not unaware of the happenings here, I would have you horsewhipped for your effrontery!"

Nicholas was not impressed by the show of indignation, yet his pulse accelerated nonetheless. Something was definitely afoot.

"Your little childhood friend was set to be married to someone else. Do not let her innocent face convince you otherwise. Clearly she is most anxious to better herself. Otherwise, she would have waited for you. Instead, she agreed to marry for an earldom."

Nicholas swallowed the bile of anger lodged in his throat and tried to digest his father's words. Surely he was misinformed? What had just occurred at the folly, the love that had cocooned him in its warmth, could not be a mirage? No, this bitter, old man had a hidden agenda. He always did. "You are mistaken."

His father's features sank further into a hound-dog sag. "I know it for a certainty, son."

Son? Bloody hell. When was the last time Nicholas had been called that? The familial sobriquet, so quietly spoken, somehow gave credence to his father's words. Disbelief warred with the dread of certainty, fogging his brain. "Who?" he finally managed to choke out.

The old man pushed from the table and slowly stood. Then he took a step toward Nicholas, lifting his hand as if to touch his shoulder, but he dropped it to his side. "Have you not figured it out yet?"

Nicholas waited, a cold statue.

His father shook his head as if in disbelief. Then he calmly shattered Nicholas's world. "Your brother. The girl wanted a title. So she wanted Daniel." He shuffled from the breakfast room.

Daniel? Catherine had been betrothed to Daniel? No! She would not do that to him. To them. His stomach clenched, and he fought the urge to vomit. He knew from the imperious surety of his father's countenance that it was the truth. Catherine had been betrothed to Daniel. How could she betray him so? He stormed from the room, determined to find the answer.

CHAPTER EIGHT

In rage deaf as the sea, hasty as fire.

—Shakespeare, *Richard II*

CATHERINE PINCHED THE single faded bloom. She had hoped for a profusion when she'd planted the bush, but it seemed to be struggling. The summer had been mild to date, so there was no reason for it to flounder so. She smelled the dying blossom. Ah, how she loved the sweet perfume of roses. They all did. That was why Nicholas had wanted it in abundance at the folly.

She walked around the stone, basking in the late-morning sun. Nicholas. A flush caressed her cheeks with its warmth. She could not comprehend how she'd allowed their rendezvous to go so far, yet she felt no regret. He had claimed her this very morning. He'd forgiven her and made her his own.

She laid down the limp rose on the top of the tomb. "Daniel, I am to be married. I know you are so happy for us." She fought tears. How she wished she could see Daniel's face light with that wicked smile, hear him shout in merriment.

"It appears you placed your bet on the wrong horse," Nicholas said from behind her.

She wiped at her eyes and turned to face him. He was fuming. It must not have gone well with His Lordship. Not that she was surprised. The old man had a dark soul, always seeking companionship for his misery.

"I beg your pardon?" she asked, not sure she'd heard him correctly. She brushed her fingers against her skirt, holding on to the soft folds like they'd anchor her against the storm of his black gaze, keep her grounded while he delivered whatever bad news his father had sent.

"It would seem you chose the wrong viscount for the win. Of course, you could not have known at the time that I would become a viscount. Which makes it all the more sullied, doesn't it?" He stood ramrod straight, another monument in the small enclosure.

Catherine couldn't process what he was saying. Had his father threatened his title? His inheritance? Denied permission to wed? Did he...did they...need permission at their age? She stepped toward him.

He raised his hand sharply, and she stopped as if struck. He was furious. At her! What had happened?

"Were you or were you not betrothed to Daniel?"

She stared at him. Had he not already forgiven her that sin? "Nicholas, I—"

"Cease," he barked, cutting her off abruptly. "I do not need to hear it. It is written all over your face." He ran a hand through his hair.

The anguish darkening his eyes pierced her soul. She moved toward him, but he took a step back.

"Damnation, Catherine. How could you?"

Oh, my dear Lord, how could she have hurt him so? How could he not have known? "But you forgave—"

"I forgave? I forgave! I absolved you of the sins of your murderous brother. I had no idea you played whore for a title!"

Anger rose, fierce and ugly. She stepped closer and slapped him with all the force she could muster. "How dare you!" To call what had transpired between her and Daniel such a thing was utter blasphemy.

He grabbed her hand and held it to the welt that was rapidly rising on his cheek, his glare a full tempest now. "As my be-trothed"—his voice dripped with hardened sarcasm on the last word—"I should show you just who has the harder hand in this relationship."

She yanked her hand free, appalled at what she'd done and sickened by his threat. "You may save the back of your hand for your wife." She rubbed her sullied palm on her skirt. "I absolve you of all obligation." She marched past him toward the exit.

"But you are not absolved, Miss Baring."

She froze at the tone of his voice, the icy chill trickling down her spine.

"You are not pardoned. You are not forgiven. But nor am I lacking in honor, despite the fact that I have recently discovered that the woman I have pined for over the past four years is a harlot. No, I stand by my word, unlike others currently in my presence."

She spun around, speechless. How could he be so cruel? How could he say such things of her? She could find no answers in his angry stare, so she turned away again.

"We will be wed in the morning. Bring your maid to witness. I will send the carriage at nine," he said, his voice calm, cold, assured—the voice of a commander who expected to be obeyed.

She did not grace him with a refusal. She could not face him again. Instead, she fled from the burial grounds, more afraid than she'd ever been during those childhood pranks.

IT SEEMED A bleak start to mornings was to be the norm. Catherine rolled, pulling the coverlet over her head. This was to be the happiest day of her life. She'd planned it over and over for four years. She groaned. How had it come to this…this…agonizing charade?

She had shed tears throughout the night. The tears that had

not flown for Daniel cascaded at the death of a dream. No, it was worse than the loss of that fantasy. It was the decimation of hope. The utter destruction of love. Her eyes burned, the welling threatening to begin anew. She threw off the covers in anger. Enough! She jumped from the bed and shuffled to the window, aware but uncaring about her bare feet on the cold floor.

The weather mirrored her mood, the forest beyond the drive obscured by a dense fog and the sky veiled in threatening clouds. Let it shed her tears, for she was done. *Accept the things you cannot change.* That was what her father always said.

She had pondered many rebuttals through the long night but, in the end, knew she would not reject the marriage. She'd given herself to Nicholas long before yesterday. If this was her only recourse to having him in her life, then she would acquiesce. Although it was a painful truth, she could not see the years ahead without him.

A light tap, and the door opened a fraction. Sadie's round face peeked in, flushing when she made direct eye contact with Catherine.

"Come in, come in," she said. It seemed that, today, Sadie's aspirations of becoming a personal maid were about to see fruition. Catherine refused to leave Stratton Hall without an ally.

"Would you like something to eat, Miss Baring?"

"No, thank you."

Sadie bobbed, her face trying to mask her excitement. It was not every day one's mistress got married. To one of the richest men in the district. To a man who felt obligated only because he'd taken her mistress's virginity.

Catherine shook her head angrily. He had not robbed her. He'd taken it with genuine affection, and she had given that most precious gift willingly. Wantonly. She shivered at the thought. It was what he'd accused her of being. A whore. She'd certainly proven it with him.

Sadie picked up the riding habit Catherine had shed to the floor last night. The girl started brushing fervently at the garment.

"Sadie." Catherine bit back a bark; her tension was not the maid's fault. It was not even Nicholas's. She'd strayed from their preordained path. He had every right to his anger and every right to the absolute fury he'd demonstrated yesterday. There was naught to be done about it. She would never be able to tell him why she'd betrayed him, for he would never understand it. How could he when she barely did herself? Besides, regardless of how it had all come to pass, it was betrayal. There was no way to soften that dreadful reality. Marrying him now was her penance.

"I don't know what to wear," she confessed. What did one wear to a ceremony that sealed the demise of a heart's desire?

Sadie oblivious to the reality of the day ahead, her face brightened. "Oh, Miss Baring! You said nothing, so in the circumstance that you might not have thought about it—being so swept away by Lord Walford's impatience—I took the liberty to ready your outfit." She hesitated. "But we can quickly get anything you want ready. The iron is to the fire, waiting."

"I am sure that whatever you have chosen is fine."

Sadie was disappointed, but Catherine just could not fake enthusiasm. She'd longed for this day. Now she dreaded it.

"Would you like a full bath, Miss Baring?"

Why not? She had the time, although she hated to make everyone work so hard this early in the morning. At least she was the only soul they had to wait upon. She'd sent an urgent message to her father last night but doubted he would be able to respond in a timely manner.

He certainly could not be here in time to…to what? To stop the wedding? To intercede? To demand it be the marriage of her dreams? She almost snorted. The marriage of her dreams had evaporated with the frenetic acceptance of Daniel's proposal. What had she been thinking? To be Nicholas's sister by marriage would have been unbearable. This consequence was a lesser one. She hoped. He'd been so angry. Surely, in time, that would pass and he would find marriage to her tolerable?

While waiting for the twins to finish filling the tub, Catherine sat by the fireplace, wondering what Laurence would say about this new tangle she'd managed to put herself in. When the boys finally left, Sadie took Catherine's wrapper and gown and held her hand as she stepped into the tub.

"Just leave the linen, Sadie. A little calm before the storm, if I may."

Sadie lay the toweling on a nearby chair and quietly slipped from the room.

Catherine slid down into the warm water, the smell of jasmine infusing each breath. It was such an exotic scent, one that promised lands unknown. Lives unknown. Dreams unknown. She inhaled deeply again, but further whimsical thoughts eluded her, dampened by the pressing truth. At the folly, her dreams had once again been within her grasp. A fleeting moment of utter happiness.

She sighed heavily. She'd always known the consequences of her decision to wed Daniel. She ducked under the water, then brushed the wet strands of hair off her face and stared at the embers in the grate. This was life. Real. Not some perfume-inspired, romantic vision. Today she faced her fate. Today the love of her life would stand before the church and declare fealty. Today her dreams died.

CHAPTER NINE

*He that is strucken blind cannot forget the precious treasure of
his eyesight lost.*

—Shakespeare, *Romeo and Juliet*

NICHOLAS STARED DOWN at the gardens. The rain gained
momentum, pelting the glass. Perfect. Bloody perfect. It
seemed the heavens concurred with his mood. He sipped brandy.
Its cherry flavor was not as satisfying as the cognac in his father's
rooms, but it would do. When was the last time he'd partaken of
a spirit so early in the morning? For that matter, when was the
last time he had spent a night drinking?

After Badajoz. After the carnage. After witnessing the pillage.
He'd drunk. He had tried to drown out the noise of death, of
terror.

He tossed back the contents of his glass. Had *tried* to drown it
out. He would forever hear the cries. Forever resent the
overwhelming sense of helplessness both during the attack and in
the aftermath.

He turned from the window and set his glass on the table.
What was done was done. Then as now. He rolled his shoulders
and stretched. He suspected this was not the last of long nights.
Tonight she would be in his home. She would be his legally, but
would she ever truly be his? Had she ever been?

What had possessed him to force the marriage? He ran a hand down his face. The question had haunted him throughout the night. Why? Why had he not accepted her absolution? After all, she'd betrayed him. His gut churned. She'd been prepared to marry his brother. For the role of countess? The Catherine he held in his heart did not worship society, did not covet a title. What the hell had happened?

"My lord?"

Nicholas bit back a curse. Would the man never stop creeping up on him? "Isaac?"

"Fredericks has instructed the coachmen. The carriage will leave shortly. Should we not be getting you ready for this day?" The damned coxcomb clapped his hands together twice, like Nicholas was some dog to command.

"Yes, I would think *we* should," Nicholas drawled, but the man seemed immune to sarcasm. He sighed. There was no need to take out his frustration on his brother's valet. He pulled on his stockings and donned his trousers, and acknowledging the freshly laundered shirt as it slipped over his head, he tucked it into his waistband. Isaac's efficiency at least allowed Nicholas to go to chapel in fresh linen.

"Sit, sit," Isaac insisted. The valet's arm, wrapped in a vivid apple-green jacket, flapped toward a chair.

Nicholas sat where directed, in front of the mirror, watching as Isaac dramatically folded a large white square of muslin, moving behind him and choking him with the cloth. When he tried to pull at it, the man actually had the audacity to tut-tut and slap his hand away. From a military campaign to chastisement from a popinjay? If he wasn't so disheartened with the downward spiral of his life, he might actually laugh.

Endless minutes later, as the starched linen poked at his chin, the slight sense of amusement departed. He looked ridiculous.

"What the hell is this? This isn't mine." He pulled at its confinement.

"But it is all the rage. You need to wear it thus. Brummel says it is high fashion, and this is a special day. You should be fashionable." The man fussed with Nicholas's neck, making cooing sounds as he adjusted the cravat.

"It is a bloody stupid rage. Damnably uncomfortable thing. Besides, it isn't bloody well mine." He tugged it off, tossing it on the dressing table. The crushed linen lay there, oddly forlorn, an abject blossom curled upon itself. He stared at it. *Damn.* It was Daniel's. Was he forever destined for his brother's discards? He grabbed the cloth and threw it to the floor.

"Never bring me one of his items again." He ignored the valet's intake of breath as Nicholas stormed from the room.

He stopped at the sound of voices below and peered over the rail as Fredericks invited the guests into the drawing room. For the first time since hearing the news of Catherine's deceit, his spirits lifted. He had sent word but had not thought Thornwood could make it in time, that he would even think the urgent request worthy of consideration. It had been years since they'd chummed at school.

Darting down the steps, Nicholas slowed as he entered the drawing room. Thornwood turned and smiled. Nicholas strode toward him.

"It is bloody good to see a familiar face," he said as he pumped Thornwood's hand.

Thornwood grinned, his long mop bouncing against his collar, looking much like he had when the two of them had run the halls of Eton. He grabbed Nicholas's shoulder and squeezed. "You may have been among strangers these last years, but we have remembered you here. Tales of your exploits have been celebrated at home."

Nicholas fought to keep his face placid, although he wanted to shout a response. Celebration? Of destruction? Death? Loneliness? War was a barren, soulless landscape, but those safe at home saw it as a bloody Benjamin West painting. "I am no Nelson at Trafalgar."

"No," Thornwood responded, dragging out the simple word

as he eyed him. "*You* are very much alive, despite your daring acts."

He waved the statement away impatiently. "I have no doubt reports of my role in Spain are greatly exaggerated." Movement by the front window caught his eye, and Thornwood followed his glance.

"Oh, yes, my wife."

Their lack of comfort was palpable. Was it his request? Or was there something else at play? He rolled his shoulders again. What did it matter? No couple could be more awkward than him and Catherine.

"May I present Lady Thornwood?"

Dutifully, the woman joined them. Her smile seemed tentative, but her beauty and dignity shone superbly. Thornwood was a lucky man.

"My lady." Nicholas bowed, and she returned the courtesy with a graceful curtsy.

"Please, my lord, Elizabeth. If you have known my husband since youth, then consider me a childhood friend also." Her smile became inviting, friendly. The knots in his shoulders unraveled further.

"You are too kind…Elizabeth. Then you must call me Nicholas."

Her blue eyes lit with pleasure. "Nicholas it is."

Her warmth wrapped around him. Thornwood had found an absolute peach.

"May I offer my felicitations?"

"Thank you," he replied, harsh reality stripping the moment of her kind spirit.

Thornwood slapped him on the shoulder. "So you are finally ready for the shackles of matrimony!"

He chuckled as his wife gasped, "Richard!"

"It seems I am," Nicholas responded, glancing apologetically in Lady Thornwood's direction. "I am grateful you were able to accede to my request on such short notice."

"There is little excitement in the country, is there, Elizabeth? How could we resist?"

Perhaps it was his imagination, or it was his heightened sensitivity this day, but he was sure Lady Thornwood flinched. She glanced at the floor but not before he caught the sadness in her eyes. He recognized the ache of loneliness. It had been his companion for four long years.

"Your betrothed?" Lady Thornwood asked, her gaze once again steady.

"She will meet us at the chapel." He did not answer her question. He knew the woman wanted to know more, perhaps why she had been asked to stand witness to a stranger, but he could not tell her that despite his anger, his disgust, he could not allow their marriage to be witnessed only by servants. He could not bring himself to belittle Catherine to that degree or desecrate their vows in so deliberate a manner.

Lady Thornwood's eyebrows tilted in query, but she asked nothing further. Fredericks announced the carriage. They exited the room only to find the butler standing there holding out a tan waistcoat, with a dark-blue jacket tossed over the other arm. The man did not have to say a word. His censure at Nicholas's state of undress was clear in his expression. Nicholas had forgotten himself. He was no beast to go out as such to the church, and he would need to apologize to Lady Thornwood for such disrespect.

He slipped into the waistcoat, quickly buttoning it up, trying not to think of its owner. For he knew without a doubt it was his brother's. Fredericks helped him into the too-snug jacket, then shifted him around to tie a simple neck cloth.

"It must be your excitement, my lord, making you forget yourself."

Nicholas did not answer.

Fredericks brushed at his shoulders and straightened his lapels. "Not that I blame you, my lord," Fredericks continued quietly. "Miss Baring is a diamond of the first water. We are pleased she will become our mistress. She is just the breath of fresh air this old house needs." He stared, his milky blue eyes piercing. "She is still the girl you left, son."

He wished it were true. The girl he'd fallen in love with would not have considered such treason. For that was what it was. She'd switched her allegiance and willfully breached his trust. "You'd do well to remember your place, Fredericks," he said brusquely. He turned from the melancholy in the old man's eyes and strode to the door. Damn Fredericks for defending a traitor.

Lord and Lady Thornwood had already been handed into their carriage. His carriage was harnessed behind theirs and ready to go, but he did not want to ride alone. He climbed into Thornwood's conveyance. Neither of the couple commented on his improved appearance. A blanket of silence settled as they made their way to the small village chapel. When the carriage came to a halt, Thornwood hopped out, quickly reaching in for his wife before the footman arrived. She seemed hesitant as she took his hand but then smiled brightly at her husband. Nicholas shook his head. He must stop projecting his own trepidation on the couple.

He alighted, the gray morning no brighter for the last hour, although the rain had abated. The carriage he'd sent for Catherine sat on the roadway, its driver's cap pulled down as the man dozed. His neck tingled as he let his shoulders relax. She had come.

The Reverend Jonathon Wilson stood on the landing, his tiny frame dwarfed by the chapel. He flew down the few steps, his cassock billowing behind. "My lord! We were beginning to think..." His voice trailed as he obviously registered the grave insult he was about to speak, and he fretted with his cravat, his head small amid the fold of white cotton.

The man was here on short notice only because of Nicholas's new title, the same title that had enabled him to quickly get a special license while passing through London. He felt a pang of guilt. While it may conflict with well-founded religious beliefs, the clergy knew on which side their bread was buttered. One could not woo the souls of others if one did not have a congregation, and a congregation's existence rested upon the whims of its benefactors, the nobles.

"I apologize, but I awaited my dear friends as witnesses. One cannot pledge under God without appropriate attesters to proclaim the worth of the union."

The reverend took stock of Nicholas's companions and, no doubt noting their rich appointments, nodded enthusiastically. "Quite right, my lord. Quite right."

Yes, no doubt about it, the man knew where to toss his hat. Nicholas frowned at his own cynicism. Did his dark mood know no bounds? Mr. Wilson had always been a sincere, dedicated member of the clergy. He shook his head, trying to refocus on the moment. "Lord and Lady Thornwood, may I present the Reverend Jonathon Wilson."

The trio conversed pleasantly about the changing weather before they looked at him expectantly. He swept his arm, gesturing for them to ascend. It was time to get the deed done.

They entered the vestibule. and he froze in the entranceway. He'd imagined many things for this day, but this was not one. Catherine stood, so stiff and pale that he wondered briefly if she was ill. He wanted to go to her and wrap her in his warmth, bring her home, and nurse her. He shook his head, trying to dislodge the image. She had brought this on herself. He pushed his aching heart aside.

"Catherine." He hadn't meant to say it so caustically.

"Nicholas."

Her voice was hollow, void of emotion. Dear Lord, did he want this? Did he want the shell of Catherine? Had she given her core to Daniel? He tempered a growl. *Daniel be damned!* She was his. Had always been his. He could not foresee a future without her in it; he had dreamed of her for too long. Besides, he had compromised her without care to the consequences. She might, even now, be carrying his child.

"Lady Thornwood, may I present Miss Catherine Baring, my affianced."

Catherine's eyes darkened, unexpectedly glimmering with unshed tears. He swallowed, his throat void of moisture. *Damn. This charade should not be so difficult.*

He cleared his throat. "Lady Thornwood has graciously agreed to stand witness this day."

"Thank you, my lady." Catherine's voice was barely audible, a storm of confusion washing her eyes with changing shades of green.

He did not blame her. After all, he'd bullied her into using her maid. But that had been in anger. Degradation was not something he wished upon her. He was grateful Thornwood had actually brought his wife. Rumor had it Thornwood spent much of his time in London with a mistress, while his wife lived contentedly in the country. Perhaps not so blindly content if his senses weren't misleading him. Well, no matter; Thornwood had brought her this day. Moreover, she was lovely in every sense. Catherine would be well represented.

The reverend shuffled uncomfortably, awaiting Nicholas's direction. Dedicated and astute. He must remember to reward the man amply for his forbearing and discretion. Nicholas nodded.

"Well, shall we begin?" Mr. Wilson's smile was no longer hesitant. He turned to Catherine, beaming. "Get thee ready for giving away, and I shall hightail it to the front to receive you." He chuckled and sprinted toward the front of the chapel.

Nicholas hadn't thought of that. Sometime before that debacle at the cemetery, she had mentioned her father was not at home. Was she to walk down the aisle alone? She stood quietly, focused on her feet. He could not see her so abandoned.

Nan and Fredericks sat quietly side by side on the last bench. How had they managed to get here so quickly? Catherine's young maid sat beside them. The valet respected no such propriety. He should be sitting with the other servants, but dressed in an abundant splendor of greens and orange and clasping his hands expectantly, he sat in the second pew. The man was irksome but did not act without enthusiasm. Nicholas shook his head at the fleeting thought. No, he could not allow the man to give Catherine away.

"Thornwood." He hesitated. Thornwood must already know something was amiss. What would he make of this new request?

"It would be my pleasure," Thornwood interceded as he raised his arm for Catherine.

Nicholas avoided looking at Catherine, turned, and strolled down the aisle to join the reverend. He didn't want to see her anger, her censure, or worse, the shadows of disappointment. When he reached the altar, he pivoted toward the vestibule, waiting for the inevitable sadness that would walk his way. He stared at the cold tiled floor. He had faced battle, had faced death. He did not want to face the demise of his dreams.

CHAPTER TEN

My conscience hath a thousand several tongues, and every tongue brings in a several tale, and every tale condemns me for a villain.

—Shakespeare, *Richard III*

S HE SOMEHOW MANAGED to speak the simple vows and write the marriage lines in the register without her shaky legs giving way and without looking directly at Nicholas. Afterward, as they all stood awkwardly in the vestry, he invited his guests to Woodfield for a wedding breakfast. She wished he had not. Elizabeth Thornwood seemed pleasant enough, but the woman regarded her with such commiseration that Catherine struggled for composure. She wanted to cling to the offer of feminine fealty; however, she'd made her bed, and she must now, quite literally, lie in it. Would he even want her to?

"If you continue to worry that lip, our guests will think we are anxious for them to leave." Nicholas's voice was gruff with anger.

She hadn't realized she was biting her bottom lip. It was a habit long embedded. She released it as he stared at her mouth. They were alone in the carriage, the Thornwoods riding comfortably in their own. She ran her tongue along her lower lip, tasting blood. She'd bitten down hard.

"For Christ's sake, Catherine. Have some mercy."

He turned to the window. What had she done now? He sounded so bitter. Well, he'd forced this, had he not?

"Mercy? As you have shown me?"

The carriage jolted, hitting a rut in the road, and she fell from her seat. He caught her before her knees hit the floor. Gripping her arms tightly, he pulled her close. She inhaled deeply. Nicholas. Clean. Crisp. Delicious Nicholas.

He nuzzled her hair, then froze for a second before depositing her unceremoniously back on her seat. Momentarily baffled by the sudden abandonment, she looked to him. He stared out the window, his mouth tightened in a grim line. No mercy. She could not live like this. What had she done?

CATHERINE CLIMBED THE stairs, the weight of the day making each step leaden. Breakfast, which seemed a disaster, had been the brightest spot in the day. Both couples had worked hard to maintain an air of celebration, but it had been labor for all and, in the end, reeked of superficiality. Nicholas had graciously invited the Thornwoods to stay, but they'd claimed a need to get home to their children and had not lingered. She had no doubt they'd just wanted to escape the gloom that had continued to drape heavily despite all efforts to lift it.

She'd been relieved at their departure until she'd turned to Nicholas and found his face expressionless. Before she could gather her wits and try to breach his defenses, he'd excused himself to check on tenants. He had yet to return. She'd dressed for dinner and waited in the drawing room for over an hour with only the ticking of the longcase clock in the front hall to keep her company. If Nicholas's father was at home, he had not put in an appearance. It was just as well Lord Woodfield had not shown. She was not yet ready to beard that particular lion in his own den.

Pausing at the top of the stairs, she looked down at the grand atrium. Fredericks had finally come to usher her to the dining room. She had been mortified walking across that vast expanse of marble as the beautiful but coffin-like clock had chimed for a third time, trailing the butler like a small child. He had dismissed the footmen and served her himself. Such a considerate man, although his sympathy added to the overwhelming weight of the day. She'd eaten little of the multicourse meal Nan had kindly prepared. Hopefully the servants would enjoy it. Someone might as well have a little pleasure this day.

Running her hand along the rail as she walked to her room, she kept her eyes on the foyer below, refusing to glance at his bedroom door as she passed it. She'd been to her room earlier to change for dinner. Nicholas, efficient as always, had seen her things brought from Stratton Hall. She reached the front of the house and entered her room.

"Ah, Lady Walford!" Sadie, her face beaming, was clearly excited to use the new address. "We need to get you into something special." The girl had the grace to blush, although her eyes twinkled with enthusiasm.

"Sadie," Catherine began, then stumbled. She could not bear to share her shame. "That would be lovely." She hoped her face did not betray the desolation that caged her heart.

Sadie clapped her hands in glee. "I found this tucked in the back of your dressing room."

She had forgotten it. Sophia had insisted she purchase a beautiful nightgown. Sophia was special. A widow who had taken Catherine under her wing these last few years, she was exotic and sophisticated. Worldly. Everything Catherine was not. Sophia had fallen in love with the notion of a lonely girl waiting for her man to return from war to marry her. They'd had a wonderful time visiting a dressmaker and planning her trousseau.

The white silk was soft, delicate, and sheer. So fragile. She traced the subtle rosebuds embroidered around the neckline. How many times had she held it thus, thinking of Nicholas's fingers following their path? Tears welled, but she fought them, quickly pivoting and giving her back to Sadie. Sadie dutifully undid the row of buttons and then pulled the dress from Catherine's shoulders. Catherine removed her undergarments and stockings and took the nightgown from Sadie before slipping it over her head. The gossamer fabric whisked against her skin. She shivered as she sat down in front of the mirror. Sadie reached for the hairbrush, and Catherine grabbed her wrist.

"No," she snapped.

Sadie's eyes widened in the mirror, those large blueberries genuinely startled. Catherine inhaled deeply, trying to calm her emotions, and softened her tone. "I wish to be alone. That is all."

Disappointment washed Sadie's face, then she blushed again. *Good. Let her think it is maidenly shyness that requires the solitude.*

"I will await your summons in the morning, Miss Bar...Lady Walford."

She could not fault the girl's genuine desire to please.

"Thank you," she said, sighing in relief as the door clicked behind the young maid. She stared at herself in the mirror while she plucked the pins out of her partially piled hair, then picked up the brush.

"And who are you?" she asked, drawing the brush through her long locks. "A daughter." She stroked her mane. "A sister." She swept through once again, combing away thoughts of Laurence. "A lover." She hesitated. Well, she had been for a moment. One incredible moment in time. "A wife." She brushed down, hitting a mat. Yanking pulled painfully at her roots. Frustrated, she threw down the brush.

"A wife," she muttered in disgust, pushing from the dressing table and moving to the door on the north side. A door she had dared not touch earlier. She opened it, fully expecting Nicholas's private quarters. Instead, she found a lovely sitting room. It mirrored the high-ceilinged library below. Beautiful bow windows with cushioned seating graced the semicircle of glass. Two fireplaces dominated, one against her wall and one against the far wall. The fire on her side was lit, chasing dampness from the room. She was grateful for it, as the temperature had plummeted with the rain and the flimsy gown was certainly not going to keep her warm. She stared at the door to the left of the other fireplace, which must lead to Nicholas's chamber. Was he in there? She held her breath and listened but heard nothing.

A lovely mahogany bookcase graced each side of the fireplace. She ran her hands along the books and pulled one at random. She did not care what it was, so long as it occupied the hours of waiting. For wait she would. Nicholas must face his own decision. She was not going to let him run away from this commitment. Escape had been offered, but he had chosen to sentence her to marriage. If she was to wear these shackles, then he, too, would feel the cold manacles.

NICHOLAS ENTERED THE kitchen, feeling like the wayward boy of his youth. It had been years since he'd avoided the main entrance, hoping to evade confrontation with his father. Of course, it was not solely his father he wished to avoid this night, although both his sire and Catherine must have long gone to bed. He shook the rain from his overcoat before shrugging it off his shoulders.

"Let me, child." Nan's face appeared out of the shadows.

"I thought you too young for senility."

She slapped him lightly on the arm as she drew off his coat. "I am not the one who has lost their mind." She clucked, grabbed his gloves, and set them side by side on a small stool before standing on tiptoe and hanging the coat on a peg. "I've not been out in this weather till the wee hours of the morning."

Reaching over her head, he hung his hat on the remaining free dowel. He rolled his shoulders and gave her a quick peck on the cheek. "It's not yet midnight, Nan. The night is young." He wished he meant it. In truth, he was weary to the bone.

Nan merely muttered something incomprehensible and moved to the large fireplace. She poked at the logs, and the flames jumped to life. A few more jabs, and she nodded her satisfaction, then turned to him, hands on hips.

"You may be lord of the manor now, lad, but don't expect no special treatment from me. Sit down and warm your hide." She gestured to a wooden-back chair by the fire.

Under his breath, Nicholas chuckled mirthlessly at her insolence. Nan had never minced her words. His mother had refused to hire a governess yet had seldom found the time herself to be with him and Daniel. So as young boys, they'd spent much of their time around Nan's skirt. Even in their adolescent years, they'd hung out in the kitchens when home. The old cook had always ensured there was food ready to fill their endlessly hungry, growing bodies. She'd also accepted the both of them, no matter what their state, unconditionally and with no questions asked.

He obediently sat, grateful for the warmth and the gruff caring. He rubbed his hands together, the tingling burn familiar from his days on campaign. Lord of the manor. He almost laughed. Not yet. Perhaps not ever. Should a lord not feel some power? Some control?

"I am guessing you've not had a bit of food since this morn." She shoved a plate into his hand. He stared at the cold meat and cheese. A large slab of bread sat on the edge. His stomach growled in appreciation.

He took a bite of the bread while Nan sat down on the chair opposite him, picked up a skein of wool, and began knitting. She said not a word, the needles clicking softly as he wolfed down the food. When he was done, he set the plate on the floor and reached up his arms in a stretch. Lord, but his body ached. It was time to head upstairs to bed. He began to rise.

"I love that lass too." Nan's voice was low, quiet, the needles clacking loudly in comparison.

He lowered back onto the chair, the chains of guilt holding him captive.

"I remember the little sprite lighting up our halls. A wee angel running alongside you three devils." Nan stared at the fire, chuckling in remembrance. Then, setting her knitting on her lap, she stared at him, her eyes narrowing, her forehead wrinkling. "Tonight she wandered this house like it was a mausoleum. And it might just as well have been."

He did not like the image, but he would not tell Nan that. Instead, he held her gaze, refusing the shame she was serving up along with the meal. She shook her head and picked up the needles, pulling at the skein to release some yarn.

"Catherine looked beautiful this evening. She has always been a lovely girl, but she made a special effort." Nan yanked fiercely at the wool, then heaving a sigh, rested the wool on her lap again, her angry gaze softening to sad. "The lass sat alone in the drawing room before dinner. She sat alone in that great dining room *for* dinner. Heavens knows she ate like a bird. Your father didn't leave his rooms at all, now did he? Although, perhaps that was a mercy for the poor child."

He rose.

Nan reached out and grabbed his hand. "There has been too much loss in this family. So much to mourn. Catherine has shared all of it with us. She was family long before you fell for her beautiful soul. She has earned more respect than she has received from either of the two lords of this manor."

Remorse rose like bile. He'd not thought what this day might be like for Catherine, had only thought of his own pain. He patted Nan's hand, then slipped his from it.

"Thank you for the meal. It's good to see you again." He headed toward the hall, pausing at Nan's voice, her disappointment in him clear in the tone.

"Lad, she has gone to bed lonely on her wedding night. Go to her. Sort out your anger in the light of day. Give her the love she needs, the love she deserves, in the night."

NICHOLAS WALKED THE long corridor from the kitchen and paused at Daniel's study. His study now. His sire kept a suite of rooms beyond the library, rarely venturing to this side of the house, and would not lay claim to this lair. It was definitely Nicholas's now. He reached for the doorknob, then dropped his hand. He was not yet ready to face it.

He turned left, into the hallway, wider now that he was in the main house, and glanced at the breakfast room. Would he share it in the morning with Catherine? Make idle conversation as though nothing was amiss? No, such ostensible behavior was beyond them both.

After moving further down the hall, he stopped at the dining room. He stared at the long mahogany table, a lengthy shadow in the dark room. Catherine had sat alone eating her wedding dinner. Nan said she'd not eaten much. Was that what he wanted? For her to suffer as he was suffering? He leaned back against the doorway, staring into the darkness. The worst kind of loneliness was the one felt when surrounded by others. He knew it well and did not wish that upon Catherine.

He pushed from the door and entered the atrium. Fredericks stood ready. Did the man ever sleep?

"I have left my things with Nan," Nicholas said.

Fredericks nodded, but his face expressed his feelings clearly. "You'll not be wanting a brandy at this hour, I'm sure, my lord. Your wife has gone to bed these many hours past."

Fredericks's word choice and emphasis were not lost on Nicholas. While Fredericks kept his tone neutral, his censure was unmistakable. He would not accept such belligerence from others, but Fredericks had been with him since birth, encouraging him to be the best man he could be despite his father's censure. Like Nan, the old man had known Catherine through the years. He could not fault either's loyalty to her.

He moved toward the west stairwell.

"I will summon Isaac forthwith."

Nicholas stiffened. He did not want to listen to the canary chirping, was far too weary for it. He bit back a like comment. Fredericks did not need to hear such dismissal of his grandson. Blood was blood, after all.

"I have done for myself many a year, Fredericks. Let him go to bed. Although, I *do* need more brandy in my room. Preferably some of the earl's stock."

He did not care to see Fredericks's response, so he quickly took the stairs and rounded the gallery to his bedroom, hesitating for a moment. Two doors down lay Catherine. Had she lain awake waiting for him? Did she yet stare at the ceiling, wondering if he would come this night? His abrupt laugh was startling in the stillness. She despised him. How could she not after what he'd forced upon her?

The warmth of a fire greeted him. He rolled his head from side to side, then reached back with one hand, massaging the nape of his neck. He surveyed the room, his eyes landing on the large poster bed—a bed meant to be shared—and shifted quickly away. There was no sign Daniel had ever occupied it. Finally a corner of the world that did not hold his memory. This room was all Lord Woodfield. A thought that would normally be distasteful but now brought relief.

Nicholas thought briefly of his father. Nicholas had invited him to the wedding, but the earl had declined. He'd claimed faltering health, but the disdain in his expression had said otherwise. In truth, Nicholas could not blame his sire. To see one woman betrothed to both sons—well, he'd no idea what that must be like. He could not fathom the thought himself. How could he possibly understand the workings of the mind of a curmudgeonly old man?

Nicholas tossed his jacket on a chair, unbuttoned his waistcoat, and slipped it off, then stood in front of the fireplace. A chill chased up his spine. He had all but forgotten the wet, cold day, but his body remembered it well enough. A light tap at the door, and Fredericks quietly ushered in several footmen with hot water, which was soon splashing in Nicholas's dressing room. Ah, Fredericks. Such an efficient man.

He pulled his shirt over his head in anticipation of the bath. A slight gasp caught his attention. The young maid from the other morning stood in the doorway, as red-faced as she had been when she'd held her tray of tea. He grabbed his banyan and pulled it on, fumbling with the damn frogs, the satin loops elusive. The heat of embarrassment raced up his neck. He was always respectful of the innocent, servant or no.

"By the fire will be fine, um…"

"Kate," she supplied, giggling as she set the tray on the table by the chair. She made a fuss of arranging the brandy and wine with their accompanying glasses before facing him again. "If you should need anything else, my lord." She let the offer drift as she walked by him, stopped to trickle her hand down his arm, then glanced over her shoulder as she exited.

The chit was propositioning him! He shook his head. So much for innocence. Grabbing the decanter, he poured a stout brandy and, sinking into the voluptuous chair, rubbed his neck again with his free hand while replaying the awkward scene. The girl was definitely offering to dally with him. On his wedding night! When had he become such a scoundrel that she felt the freedom to do so? Did everyone see him as a lowly cur now? He threw back the entire contents of the glass, only registering after he swallowed that it was, indeed, the fine cognac from his father's stash.

The familiar, discreet cough drew his attention.

"My lord? If you need nothing else?"

He did not turn to Fredericks. No doubt, disapproval still ruled his bushy eyebrows.

"No, Fredericks. That will be all."

"Very well, my lord."

There was no sound of movement. Nicholas was not surprised; it was inevitable. He could command an army, but he couldn't seem to manage the staff. He sighed dramatically. "What is it, Fredericks?"

Fredericks took his time, a pregnant moment of silence, followed by that distinctive clearing of his throat. "Problems can be more easily sorted through in the light of day." The old man hesitated before continuing. "The night, my lord, the night is what makes those problems worth working through. The night is for love."

Nicholas stared at the fire. A few seconds later, the door tacitly closed.

CHAPTER ELEVEN

Excellent wretch! Perdition catch my soul, but I do love thee!
And when I love thee not, chaos is come again.

—Shakespeare, *Othello*

NICHOLAS STEPPED FROM the tub, listlessly drying himself. The bath had chased the chill from his bones. He'd spent the day visiting tenants and recording a growing list of needs throughout the park. He hoped Brownlee returned soon. He needed to talk with the man, and the sooner, the better. He could not fathom why Brownlee and Daniel had allowed things to become so neglected. He understood that his father had been battling health issues. But Daniel? What had preoccupied him? Catherine? *Damn!* He brusquely looped each frog on his banyan and marched across the room to their shared sitting room. Had she loved Daniel with equal distraction?

He yanked open the door and stopped, immobilized by the scene before him.

The fire, diminished to embers, glowed brightly enough to illuminate Catherine. She lay sprawled, for there was no other word for it, on the sofa. He swallowed over the lump in his throat, his cock stiffening, and moved cautiously forward. Dear God in heaven, how was he to resist? Her burgundy locks spread upon the cushion in a halo. Her face serene, she was the visage of an angel.

But her body! Oh, her body made a mockery of that thought. It would tempt the devil himself. He stepped closer. The translucent fabric draped over perfection. Mesmerized, he watched the slight rise and fall of her breasts. His breath reached for syncopation.

He moved nearer, needing to feel her breath against his, needing to smell her essence. He stumbled, cursing silently lest he wake her. He bent and picked up a leather-bound book, squinting to read the title. *Coelebs in Search of a Wife*. He almost laughed aloud. He had not read the book, did not read tripe, but his Catherine was a romantic at heart.

She whimpered in her sleep, rolling onto her side, raising her arm over her ear as though to block out his thoughts. Did she know he was standing here drinking her in? She was so incredibly beautiful. In the eyes of the law, she now belonged to him. But would she ever truly be his?

Muttering at his asinine lamenting, he laid the book on the table at the end of the sofa. He might not be the husband of her dreams, of his own dreams for that matter, but he could not let her spend the remainder of her wedding night on this uncomfortable sofa. Her day had been miserable enough, and he was to blame for that. He slipped his hands under her warm, lithe body and lifted her against his chest. She snuggled closely. He inhaled deeply, pressing a kiss to her head. Jasmine. Would he ever smell that without thought of her?

The door to her bedroom was ajar, so he moved easily into her chamber and gently laid her upon the bed. She mewled when he let her go. His body screamed in response as memories of his Cat at the folly tumbled through his mind. Nicholas leaned in for a last kiss, brushing lightly against her lips. She would never be his, and he needed to accept that sooner rather than later. Yet he did not resist when she wrapped her arms around his shoulders and pulled him tight.

"Oh, Nicholas." Her tongue slipped into his mouth, nursing

his yearning to have one last moment.

He groaned. Catherine. Four long years. She was supposed to be his pot of gold waiting for him at the end of a dark and dismal rainbow. He took her in, tasting, assailing her with his desire, alternately soothing her and trying to swallow her whole. Her body responded, bucking, her eyes still closed.

"Catherine." Her name came out more growl than warning.

"Mmm, Nicholas."

She squirmed beneath him, and he could take no more. Yanking at the fragile fabric, he positioned himself.

"Tell me you want this."

"Mmm" was her only answer as she tugged at his robe.

He entered her abruptly, then caught himself, recalling the pain he'd caused her at the folly. He lay still, trying to regulate his breathing so he could proceed with caution. She pushed her hips against him, and he was lost. Blind need would dictate this night.

Withdrawing slowly was sweet agony, sinking back in intoxicating. Catherine moaned, encouraging him by rubbing her hands up and down his back. He repeated the ploy, then lost control, pummeling mindlessly. She squirmed beneath him, adjusting, stroking and sobbing in turn. He was at his peak, ready to release, but she had not yet gone and he could not leave her behind. He reached between them and rolled that precious pearl. Her body responded immediately, and the last of his restraint left. He pumped as she milked, their cries mingled in pain and ecstasy.

I love you. It was all he could think as her softness, her warmth, encased him. *I love you despite what you have done to me.* He pressed his forehead to her neck, choking back the pain.

CATHERINE CURLED INTO him, and he did not have the stamina to disengage and go to his room as he ought to. Her regulated breathing soothed him into a shallow sleep, during which he surfaced throughout the night to the scent of jasmine and the lingering musk of sex only to drift off again.

Now he lay restless. First light could not be far away. He stretched his arm, then rested it gently across her shoulders, stroking her softly, not wanting to wake her but needing to touch her. He had thought of nothing but her since he'd left for the continent. Surely they could overcome the years in between.

He nuzzled her glorious mane, his body's interest reigniting. She murmured, running her hand down his chest, then rolled from him, drawing her knees up and pulling the covers over her shoulders. So much for rekindling passion.

Nicholas eased from the bed. He needed to think. That was impossible when he was near Catherine. He grabbed his robe and stepped into the adjoining room. Pulling it on as he strode through the now darkened area, he headed straight for his chamber. Someone had stoked the fire, as embers still lit his room well enough for him to locate the brandy decanter and a glass. He moved to the door, entering cautiously into the hallway. No moon shimmered to light the way. It did not matter. He knew every corner of this house.

Descending the stairs, he went down the hallway he'd come through earlier in the evening. When he'd been heavy with despair. Did he now hope? He shook his head. He was always a man of reason, yet he could make no sense of his emotions. The girl bewitched him. No, the *woman* bedeviled him. For she was every inch a woman and twice as lethal as the girl he'd left behind.

He stopped before reaching the servants' corridor to the kitchen and faced the door. Just a door. Just a study. It might be Pandora's Box, but after what had happened upstairs tonight, he must face reality. It was time. For both their sakes. Perhaps he owed it to Daniel too. Nicholas felt, for a certainty, that the truth lay beyond this door.

It was easy to locate the large desk in front of the window. He put the glass and decanter down on it. It took him a few minutes of fumbling to illuminate the room. He cursed his idiocy for not doing so in the faint light of his chambers and carrying the lantern with him. It seemed he'd left all sense back on the continent. What had he been thinking to take Catherine while she'd slept? Would she even remember their joining? That perfect moment of coming together?

A hint of honey wafted in the air as the flame blossomed. He grabbed the candlestick, sweeping the room with its light. The study was a pigsty—piles of books, stacks of paper, and discarded rubbish. It was a miracle he'd not gone ass over tip when he'd come in. Clearly the servants had not touched anything in months. He wiped a finger across the books on the desk and rubbed the thick dust between his thumb and forefinger, his nose tickling in response. It seemed nothing had been disturbed since Daniel's death. Nicholas fought the shiver that threatened. He was no stranger to death. He certainly would not be unnerved by his brother. In life or death. *Ah, Daniel, what were you about?*

He sat down and pulled the chair closer to the desk. Where to start? Reaching for the brandy, he poured two fingers and tossed back the contents, the slow burn pooling comfortably in his stomach. He refilled his glass and stared at the stack of books, moving the lantern to better read the titles. It was a varied and extensive collection of law books and treatises. *Commentaries on the Laws of England. Considerations on Criminal Law. A General Introduction to the Common, Civil, and Canon Law in Three Parts.* He tapped each title as he read it. Had Daniel been trying to discern a legal issue? Had he been in some sort of trouble? Nicholas dismissed the thought immediately. Daniel was no rebel or criminal. Perhaps an estate issue?

Nicholas sipped the second drink, the fine cognac warming his blood, while he sifted through the mounds of paper. Separating renter needs from bill collection requests, he wondered how all these receipts were now so long overdue. He recognized some of the renter names from his day's ride around the estate. It was clear they had not exaggerated the neglect.

Finally, satisfied that the notes were at least haphazardly organized, he leaned back, running his hands through his hair. When had first light begun? He gazed around the room. It would take more than one foray to fully sort the mess. He pushed back the chair. Perhaps he should go see if Catherine remembered the night? If she felt as uncontrollably drawn to him as he was to her?

When he turned, his leg hit a handle on the right side of the desk. Running a soothing hand over his knee, he opened the offending drawer. Stacks of envelopes, tied neatly in red ribbons, lay in an orderly fashion. They looked far too personal for him to deal with right now. He only wanted to return upstairs and pick up where he'd left off. He was about to shut the drawer when he registered the address sticking out to the left of the ribbon. *To Nicholas.* Bloody hell! He slammed the drawer shut, his stomach lurching.

He'd spent the last few days despising Daniel, yet here was evidence that Daniel had thought of him. That he'd reached out to him. Written to him. Why had he not sent them? Nicholas rested his head in his hands, massaging his temples. Was he meant to read them? Did he even want to know Daniel's thoughts, what he wanted to say to Nicholas? His breathing filled the room, whispering back at him, as he struggled to gain control of his emotions.

Could he ever fully embrace Catherine without understanding what the hell had happened while he'd been on the continent? Despite the fact that he would hate every revelation, he needed to know. Maybe there was no depth to the missives. Perhaps they were as light and playful as Daniel had always been. Would that not also provide comfort?

He pulled open the drawer and took out the first stack of letters. He picked at the frayed edge, and his heart sank as the ribbon unwound and fell to the desk. *To Nicholas Sinclair. March 7, 1808.* He traced Daniel's handwriting before sifting through the pile. He noted that the top date was the earliest. The remainder of the letters were dated later and in sequence. He pushed the drawer closed, gently this time, and stared at the envelope. He ran his hands through his hair, tugging the ends, the pain keeping him focused on this moment, this decision. He could easily take them upstairs to the fire. He was under no obligation to read them.

He grabbed the knife, broke the seal, and carefully unfolded the paper.

My Dearest Brother,

It has been a month since we last talked, yet it feels an eternity. How is it I did not appreciate you when you were here? Truly, it encapsulates my selfishness. Father is badgering me to be the man you are. I fear I cannot be that man. Will never be that man. In truth, I'm not sure I want to be. It seems to me there is far too much weight upon the shoulders of a man who takes command.

The remainder spoke of the demands of the estate and the continuing impatience of his father. Nothing surprising in any of it. Nicholas tore open the next letter.

I am humbled by all you do. By all you are. I sit here, a prince in the making, knowing I am unworthy of royal velvets. I am cloaked in deceit. No one will want me near. I am a fraud. And you, my dearest brother, will hate me most of all. You are good and strong and true. I am none of those things. Please forgive me.

Nicholas let the letter fall to his lap. He had not known his brother to be insecure. What had happened in Nicholas's absence that had made Daniel judge himself so harshly? He was the more carefree of the two of them. Had Father pressed him so hard? Had he belittled him to the point of depression? His sire had always been a demanding ass.

Picking up the letter, Nicholas quickly finished it and grabbed several more. Reluctantly, he opened the last one from the first bundle and stared at his name on the envelope, pausing on the date script. *April 4, 1811.* A year before Daniel's death. Nicholas's brother had written these. To him. He raised the envelope to his nose. It smelled of paper. What had he expected? That he could smell Daniel? Irritated with the whimsical notion, Nicholas ripped open the packet.

> *My Dearest Brother,*
>
> *While I know you fight the enemy and live a life of strife and woe, I cannot help but want to tell you my news. I am in love. Oh, I find I must repeat that. I—am—in—love. It is true. Your brother, Daniel Sinclair, Viscount Walford, someday Earl of Woodfield, is head over heels in love!*
>
> *I will not bore you with the details, but suffice it to say I am excited, enthralled, and absolutely 100 percent enamored. It is the oddest thing. It has been right beneath my nose the entire time. Someone familiar has turned into the most exquisite, enticing person I have ever met. It is difficult for me to remember my manners and keep my hands to myself! Newfound love in old places. Who would have thought it?*

Nicholas crumpled the letter. He could read no more. Daniel had fallen for Catherine. And Catherine had agreed to be Daniel's wife. It would seem their love had been reciprocal. Nicholas was a fool. He snuffed the candle and stomped from the room, running up the stairs that were now clearly visible. He entered his chamber and dressed quickly. Blast his romantic intentions! Confound the bloody war! Curse his love for Catherine! She had given her heart to another. They had both been damned by life's interfering circumstance.

CHAPTER TWELVE

The miserable have no other medicine but only hope.

—Shakespeare, *Measure for Measure*

CATHERINE CLAWED TOWARD the warmth. Her body resisted, trying to nestle deeper into delicious slumber, but the glow beyond her eyelids beckoned. Blinking awake, she squinted until her eyes adjusted. Glorious rays basked the room in effulgent light. It must surely be the refraction from her heart. She rolled away from the beams to gaze at…emptiness.

Her joy plummeted. Had she imagined Nicholas? She grabbed the pillow and held it to her face. *Please let it be real. Don't let it have been a dream.* She inhaled deeply, fighting a rising sob. Pulling the pillow back, she stared at it and then pressed it back into her face, inhaling deeply once again. He had definitely been here. She hugged the soft down tightly to her chest.

Pushing aside the clutter of sleep and panic, she began an inventory. No clothes. With the sheet clutched to her chest, she rolled over and scanned the floor. A silken cocoon of fabric lay on the carpet. She flopped onto her back and slid her hand down her body until she reached her inner thighs. She could not fight the grin, although she felt entirely foolish sharing it with the ceiling. It certainly had been no dream.

Nicholas had loved her last night. Passionately. He'd come to her on their wedding night. He must have found some forgiveness. She was not so naive as to think all was forgotten. They must talk and sort through his hurt so that he might fully accept her as his wife. She knew him too well to believe he no longer held some amount of anger. But *he* had offered the olive branch. Oh, how she loved him.

A tentative tap at the door pulled her from her romantic reverie. Was it Nicholas begging admittance from the sitting room?

"Yes?"

"'Tis Sadie, my lady."

She fought disappointment. Why would he knock at his wife's door? This was his house. He did not need permission to go where he pleased. Sunshine filled the windows, washing the room in light. It was late morning. Likely, he was taking care of estate business. Lord knew it had held no interest for Daniel.

She sat up and pulled at the coverlet. "Come, Sadie."

Catherine sighed as chocolate wafted her way. When was the last time she'd greeted the morning with such a treat? Nicholas must have remembered her fondness for the addicting bitter brew of hot chocolate.

Sadie settled the tray on the nightstand, poured a cup, and handed it to Catherine. She raised it, sniffing, relishing the memories it brought forth: sitting in the kitchen with Nan when the boys had ostracized her from their circle; Nicholas taking her to Nan to have some minor wound tended to—usually one she'd gotten trying to keep up with the boys; in the later years, stealing alone time with Nicholas in the kitchen, sitting beside him, sipping the warm liquid, while Nan knitted endlessly on the other side of the fire.

She laughed at Sadie's curled-up nose.

"Cook says you adore the stuff." Sadie sniffed and shook her head disbelievingly. "Said it would start your day off with a smile."

"And she was correct. Please thank Nan for me," Catherine

said, hiding her disappointment. Nan had remembered. Not Nicholas. Two disappointments in as many minutes. No need to mind. Nicholas was a busy man with an estate to attend. Such attention to detail was trivial. Fighting the lure of self-pity, she sipped, swallowing over the newfound lump in her throat. She tried to relish the sweet edge given to the bitter brew. Good old Nan had even remembered to mellow it with sugar. Nan knew how to soften everything.

Sadie flitted about the room, chattering while she straightened here, rearranged there, although the room was perfectly tidy. She paused at the discarded nightgown, then bent to pick it up. Her sharp intake of breath at the rent in the fabric made Catherine cringe. Did she think Nicholas had had to use violence to seduce his new bride?

"Sadie," she began, stumbling, not knowing what to say. She owed the girl no explanation. She was a married woman, and what happened behind these doors was no one's business. Still, staff did gossip. "Sadie…"

"Oh, my lady, it is truly sad I am for this beautiful dressing gown."

She held it up as embarrassment began a quick journey up Catherine's neck, reaching her cheeks in a heated flush.

"I don't think it can be saved." She threw it over her arm and grinned with no sign of the embarrassment from the night before in the her twinkling eyes. "My lord must have been right anxious for his wedding night."

Catherine raised a hand to her own burning cheeks, grateful Sadie could no longer see them. The girl had entered the dressing room with the torn garment. Catherine sipped her chocolate, contemplating the maid's words. Anxious? Not so impatient that he'd stayed the day with her. Nor come home to share dinner or the evening. Still, she had felt his need. Felt his want and desire mingle with her own. He'd come to her last night. That had been no fantasy. Her tender womanhood was testimony to that fact. It was a beginning. A step. A place from where they could start to rebuild their relationship.

There was another tap at the door, and before she could respond, Sadie flew from the dressing room.

"A minute, sirs!" She sailed over, grabbed the cup, and put it on the nightstand, then unceremoniously, yanked the bedding over Catherine's shoulders. "You may enter."

She was impressed with Sadie's command of the men as they marched in with buckets of steaming water before disappearing into her dressing room. It has been the right decision to bring the girl with her. She was clearly already comfortable with her position, and her familiar company was appreciated.

After the men disappeared, Sadie ushered Catherine to the rear of the dressing room. The large bath was positioned far enough back from the expansive window, for privacy. Catherine sank into the tub, her muscles relaxing in the warmth.

Sadie swirled the water with her hands. "Is it temperate enough, my lady?"

"It is absolutely perfect."

Sadie turned off the spigot that was spewing cold water. "They say the other one will bring hot water but it's not yet perfected. Can you imagine it, Miss Baring? Oh! Please forgive me."

"Sadie, it is perfectly fine. I have been Lady Walford for less than a day. I am impressed it has taken you until now to slip the name you are accustomed to." She was not used to such fawning. Stratton Hall did not stand on formality, and she did not want Sadie to think she'd lost the warmth of her family home when she'd become Lady Walford.

"Can you please open the drapes? I wish to linger for a while but not in the dark. It is a glorious day. I would like to see it."

Sadie pulled back the fabric, exposing a picture-perfect view. Catherine could see the fountain in the center of the courtyard. She'd used to love sitting on its edge, listening to the endless fall of water. Nicholas had pushed her in a time or two. For that matter, so had Daniel and Laurence. Oh, Dear Lord, where was

Laurence now? He'd left for the colonies with such haste, in such despair. Where was her beloved brother now?

"A small breakfast in my room would be lovely." She might as well. She had certainly missed sharing this morning's meal with Nicholas. He had always been an early riser and hungry as a bear. He'd be long done. "Would you mind attending to that?"

Sadie beamed. "Of course, my lady. I know all the things you love. I shall go speak with Cook and have it for you shortly," she said and ran from the room.

Catherine sunk into the luxuriously deep tub, only the blue sky now visible. Laurence. What would he think of Nicholas's return? Would Laurence be happy for her? His pain was so profound she did not think her happiness would enter into his world. Daniel's death had driven Laurence to enlist in Upper Canada. He was not prepared to live in such a wild land, nor was he born to be a soldier. And now that they were at war, surely it was suicide. Suicide. She ducked her head under the water to wash away the taint of the word.

Laurence. Daniel. Nicholas. The men in her life. The boys they had been, the men they had become, defining the woman she was. Perhaps if she'd had a woman in her life, they wouldn't have had such influence on her. She sat up, stroking wet locks from her face, staring out at the trees beyond the spray of water. What did any of that matter now? Their lives had been altered in those woods the day Daniel had died. What did fate intend?

She lay back against the sloped copper, staring at the high ceiling. She mourned the loss of Daniel every day. Laurence's absence was an endless ache. Yet because of the tragedy, Nicholas had come home. Alive. To her? This morning, her heart had dared to hope.

She closed her eyes and relived each touch. Nicholas had loved her with his body. *Please let his heart follow suit.*

CHAPTER THIRTEEN

So we grow together, like to a double cherry, seeming parted,
but yet an union in partition.

—Shakespeare, *A Midsummer Night's Dream*

NICHOLAS RESISTED THE temptation to enter through the kitchen again. While it seemed he was currently incapable of facing his wife in the drawing room, or from across the dinner table, he *was* the next master of this estate and needed to behave as such. Fredericks greeted him, taking his hat and gloves. No need for a coat today. The weather was quite amenable.

Fredericks brushed at the felt, handing the topper and gloves to a nearby footman before turning back to Nicholas. "My lord—"

"Well, it's about time you got home! I've enjoyed far richer conversation with a scarecrow than I have this evening with my Catherine. Where in blazes were you? I would think a man who pined for my daughter so strongly that he had to marry her posthaste would at least have a care that she is in need of a little company during her dinner."

Despite the chastisement, Nicholas could not suppress a grin. Baron Stratton was everything Nicholas's father was not. Tall and lean, he was in fabulously good shape for a man past his prime. His dark-auburn hair had a few streaks of gray that seemed only to lend credence to his ever-present confidence. Jovial as always, he slapped Nicholas on the shoulder.

"While I'd like to take you to task for claiming her so quickly, I, too, was young once"—he leaned in conspiratorially—"and I loved her mother with the same distracted passion you have for my little kitten." Stratton laughed, throwing his arm around Nicholas's shoulders, pulling him toward the drawing room. "I found a sad lass when I arrived, although she put on a brave front and did not share a word about her melancholy. I've no doubt the return of her groom will be cheering." Stratton pushed open the door, and his arm still firmly keeping Nicholas alongside, they swept into the room.

Catherine sat by the fire on the settee, opposite his father. Head bent, she continued with her stitching. Was she avoiding him or his sire? No doubt both. Without hesitation, Stratton led him toward the duo.

"I pulled your father from those infernal rooms that he claims are his respite. His escape would be a more appropriate description. Come out and face the world is what I say. The good, the bad, and the abhorrently ugly. We're all in it together." He squeezed Nicholas's shoulder and finally released him, then marched toward Nicholas's father. After a brief, muffled conversation, his father rose and, without a so much as a glance in his direction, trailed Stratton out the door.

"My lord?" Fredericks's voice startled the silence. "A small repast and a bracer?" His face remained expressionless as he handed Nicholas a laden plate and a glass, but his eyes twinkled with delight. The man clearly knew what had transpired the eve before. No bowing to nobility here and no offense meant. Fredericks was simply a man pleased for those he cared about. Nicholas wanted to rejoice at the thought of resuming life in such domestic comfort, but as the door clicked behind Fredericks, he became achingly aware that he was alone with Catherine.

He stared at the small meat sandwiches on the plate, grasping the glass of Madeira tightly in his other hand. If Catherine were not sitting so stiffly, he would have believed her to be lost in her needlepoint. He wanted to reach out and massage her shoulders or have her remove the knots from his neck. No Madeira could relax him the way she could. No magic could possess him the way her look could. As if reading his mind, she glanced up at him, a slight flush pinking her cheeks.

She was wary. No doubt about it. But there was also optimism. Her eyes glimmered sage, hinting of anticipation. *Damn.* He should not have gone to her last night. He'd known it to be folly, but he'd been unable to resist the allure of her sweet body. Now that he'd read Daniel's words, he knew it for the madness it had been. No good could come of pretending all was as it should be.

He took the chair his father had vacated, laying the food on the side table. His glass caught a reflection of the flame from the table lamp. He swirled the tumbler's contents until the thick red liquid coated the sides, dulling the glow. Stillness resounded off the walls, yet he could not find words to break it nor the fortitude to look up for that matter. Instead, he concentrated on the wine, lifting it to his nose, but its smoky spice, usually so enticing, soured his stomach.

"Lord Woodfield seems much improved." She waited for him to comment. Focusing on her hands, which clutched the embroidery frame too tightly, he could feel her growing trepidation. Still, no words came to him. Only silence, piercing and loud. He reached for a sandwich before almost choking on it as he swallowed it whole.

"Catherine," he started. *Catherine, what? You have been my beacon through dismal years, but in truth, you were a pirate's light leading me to shipwreck? I have longed for you, but you have longed for my brother?* He ran his hand through his hair. He wanted her so. Would always want her. But he did not know what to say to bridge the gulf between them, the chasm created by her betrayal.

"Nicholas?"

His stomach clenched at the plea in her voice. *Damnation,* he could add no more guilt to his heaping plateful. He laid the glass on the side table and stood. "Catherine," he started again, finally looking at her.

Those white knuckles grasping the frame on her lap were the only visible indication of her stress. She smiled uncertainly, eyebrows lifting, hopeful. It was the Catherine he remembered, the Catherine he'd envisioned on many a long, lonely night. He shook his head. The reality was that it was now the face of the woman his brother had loved. The face of the woman who'd agreed to marry his brother. Anger percolated, dark and bitter.

"Catherine," he bit out, fighting back the heated words that threatened, "have a good evening." He strode from the drawing room before civility was lost.

SHE COULDN'T MOVE. Couldn't put down her needlepoint. Couldn't stand up. Couldn't follow him out that door and up those stairs. Had last night meant nothing? She'd known he would still hold some anger, but he'd barely hung on to basic courtesy.

"Catherine?"

A flush of heat sealed her mortification. How much had her father overheard? Did he understand the ramifications in the spare words exchanged?

He strode to the sofa and sat beside her. The concern that warmed his eyes to a dark moss undid her; tears pricked, and his face blurred. She wiped angrily at her eyes. She'd made her bed. This was not her father's doing but her own. She could not run to dear Papa to fix things. She was not a child.

"Papa," she began, ready to explain it was her fault, that she alone bore the blame of the sad state of her marriage. Instead, tears trickled.

"Ah, kitten." He pulled her close, wrapping his arms around her. He smelled of tobacco and wool, of Stratton Hall, of home.

She began to quietly weep. He petted her head, whisking kisses across her forehead. The gesture, so familiar from childhood, broke all her restraint, and she assaulted them both with the impact of her unleashed emotions.

She clung to her father, wishing she were an infant once again with a woe easily soothed by his kind words. Though he murmured the same comfort against her temples, she knew he would never again be able to solve her problems. At this moment, she so wanted to be that little girl, but she would never be again. She choked down another sob. She was a woman now. A woman who must face the truths in her life.

She pulled away. He reached into his jacket and took out his handkerchief, dabbing carefully at her eyes. Then he lifted her chin and smiled. She could not help but respond in kind, though it felt fragile and false.

"Oh, kitten," he said, swiping his thumb along her cheek. "I came expecting the best." He swept back her sodden, stray locks. "Most fathers would be angry with the expedient nuptials, but I was filled with satisfaction. My little girl has waited for so long." His forehead furrowed with deepening lines; he awaited the explanation.

She didn't know how to account for Nicholas's dismissal without damning him in her father's eyes. Despite his behavior, he did not deserve that. He had not been a part of the goings-on at Woodfield Park. Besides, her father was not oblivious to the years in between.

His eyes darkened further, and he inhaled deeply. "It is Daniel."

She nodded. It was so much more. He knew that. It was love. Fear. Betrayal. Yes, it was Daniel. He would forever stand between her and Nicholas.

He blew out his breath forcefully, and his eyebrows gathered in a storm, not so much angry—more frustrated. "Did I not tell you? Did I not tell you no good could come of it?"

"Papa," she started, but the argument was old, and she had no energy to renew it.

"Papa, nothing. You care too much for too many people. I should have interceded. I should have stopped you. I was selfish. We were all selfish."

The pain in his eyes was too much. She touched his cheek. "No. It was all done in love. All of it. You cannot regret love."

He placed his hand on hers, pressing the weight of their combined hands against his rough skin. "You love so deeply. I was sure Nick would see that. Thought he had recognized it when I'd gotten your message."

She did not want him to be angry with Nicholas. To hate him. The burden of guilt was hers alone to bear.

"He has been through much. It is Nicholas who has lost. He has lost his youth to war. He has lost his brother." She hesitated, but she wanted her father to see she was no longer a little girl, that she was a woman facing a woman's consequence. "He has lost the dream girl of boyhood. That girl betrayed him. Gave herself to another."

Her father stiffened beneath her hand.

She patted his cheek. "Figuratively speaking, Papa. You of all people know that."

He clasped her hand and moved it to his lips. "Ah, kitten, he must know the treasure he has in you."

A father's love. Was there anything more true? She managed a smile. "I have not yet convinced him of my devotion. But I assure you, I will dedicate my days to it."

He released her hand, his face radiating a renewed optimism she wished she could reflect.

"You will tempt him, I've no doubt. He has never been able to resist your company." He glanced around the room, his mood visibly dampening. "It is difficult for me to leave you, to know that these walls are now your home. One crotchety old man to contend with here would be bad enough, but now with Nicholas so…" He did not finish his thought. Instead, he pulled her close and hugged her tightly.

"Stratton Hall will always be your home." He pushed her away, firmly holding her arms. They stared at each other, her eyes welling again despite the desire to remain strong.

He pressed a quick kiss to her forehead before rising and heading for the door. When he reached it, he turned. "Your home. Always. No questions asked."

CHAPTER FOURTEEN

A stage where every man must play a part, and mine a sad one.

—Shakespeare, *The Merchant of Venice*

NICHOLAS TOOK THE stairs two at a time, refusing to glance over the balustrade. If Catherine dared follow, he didn't want to see her face. He was fully aware of the pain he'd just caused. He entered his chambers and leaned back against the door, accidently banging his head on the wood. *Damn!* He'd had to do it. It was no different from the battlefield—better it be quick than prolonged.

Pushing from the door, he rubbed the back of his head. The war was far less complicated than the home front. He sat in front of the barren fireplace, pulling at his boot. He paused and sighed. How could he even compare the two? The continent may have been more straightforward, but here, at least, only one life had been lost. Well, physically. He yanked off the boot and threw it at the fire screen.

"Lord Walford, let me!" Isaac squealed in dismay, throwing himself at Nicholas's feet, quickly and adeptly removing the second boot. Where had the cherub been hiding?

"Your clothes arrived today," he said, standing, his blond curls bouncing in enthusiasm as he clapped his hands. "Oh, my lord, you do have exquisite taste! A mite somber but absolutely elegant."

Ah, he'd been in the dressing room. It was good the London tailor had been expeditious. Nicholas could do with a change of clothes, and he certainly did not trust Isaac to find him anything suitable. Even Nicholas's batman would do better navigating fashion, which was praise that would make Langdon laugh. Nicholas was looking forward to his arrival, although he worried about how Langdon fared. The surgeons had tried to save his arm but in the end had had to cut it below the elbow. Nicholas prayed no infection had set in. Although he'd hated to leave the man, there'd been no choice, for Langdon was not fit to travel. He had been by Nicholas's side throughout the four years. He missed Langdon's jovial companionship, not to mention his lack of zeal when it came to a man's wardrobe.

"My lord, it's early. Shall I select one of the new jackets and you can rejoin belowstairs? Surely Lord Stratton would like a game in the billiards room." The man's eagerness was palpable. Nicholas felt like a doll to be dressed.

"I have no wish to see Stratton or anyone else for that matter." He stood, stretching, trying to roll the tension from his shoulders. "That will be all."

"Oh…but…my lord—"

A quick knock at the door provided a welcome reprieve. Isaac scuttled over, opening it to his grandfather. Fredericks did not acknowledge his grandson; instead, he looked directly at Nicholas.

"Your father wishes to see you, my lord."

"Well, you can tell my father to—" An abrupt cough from Fredericks, simultaneous with a sharp intake of breath from Isaac, cut Nicholas short. He absorbed Fredericks's censure and the valet's shock. *Damn.* Nicholas was to be an earl. It was past time he started behaving like one. "Tell Lord Woodfield I will be down shortly."

Fredericks closed the door, and Isaac ran and grabbed the discarded Hessians. Nicholas flicked away Isaac's hands and tugged them on himself, then sat back in the chair. Was there no peace to be had in this house? What did the old man want now?

"Get me a brandy, would you?" A little fortification would not go amiss.

"But your father waits."

Nicholas glanced up, ready to give the cherub a lashing, but the man appeared genuinely distressed. Nicholas laid his head back on the plush velvet and sighed. "Lord Woodfield will not meet his maker due to my lingering here a few minutes longer."

"Oh, yes, my lord. Perhaps not." Isaac ran to the table and quickly poured the drink, scooting back and pressing it into Nicholas's hand. "But he is formidable when he is angry. My lord hated it so. He was always morose after a visit with the earl."

Nicholas sipped the brandy. So his brother had continued to feel the old man's ire. Daniel had always been sensitive to their father's moods. Nicholas never had gotten it. The old man could be an absolute ass, but he loved his oldest son. Daniel was the image of their mother—all light and goodness, playful, and full of joy. One could say what one wanted about the earl, but he had loved his wife. He'd never sought another woman to fill Nicholas's mother's role, despite the fact that he'd had two boys needing tending. Fredericks's expectant face flashed before Nicholas. He stood. The damn butler held more sway over him than his own father. *That is what you get when you hand the rearing of your children over to the servants.*

Not wanting to alert Catherine to his presence, he descended cautiously. No sound came from the drawing room. Perhaps she had left for her chambers, although he had not heard her. He paused by the doors. Was she still in there, sitting quietly with her sewing? Had she accepted that their marriage was a shallow imitation of what it should have been? He shook his head. She must know it to be true.

Striding past the library, he ducked around the stairwell to the door hidden behind it. His father's sanctuary. Nicholas rapped three sharp taps. A muffled noise was response enough for him to open the door and enter the main retiring room. His father stood by the far window, the drapes drawn back, the night black beyond the pane. The old man's shoulders were slumped, his tall frame oddly fragile. *Damn and blast.* Nicholas did not want to feel pity.

"Father?"

"You married the chit despite my warning."

Nicholas stared at the blurred reflection in the window and waited, refusing to rise to the bait.

"We will host a dinner a week hence to celebrate." His father's obvious aversion liquefied the word. *Celebrate.* There was nothing about this situation worthy of celebration. It was untenable that they should invite others to join the masquerade.

"There is no need to hold a dinner. None at all."

The reflection wavered in the window, then steadied. "There is every need." His father paused, his back heaving with the labor of breathing. "Stratton has asked it of us, and we will do it. The deed is done. You did not hesitate to take care of that...in every way. You will honor it. For Stratton's sake."

Nicholas waited for more, for some indication that his father understood the turmoil of his emotions. Surely he had some inkling of the depth of deception that surrounded all that was good about his love for Catherine, threatening it like a quagmire. The chimera in the glass remained still.

Nicholas surrendered. He had not backed down before an army, yet he could not bring himself to do battle with this old man. It was salt in a gaping wound, but his father was right. Nicholas must honor her. He owed it to the memory of a dream, and he owed it to Stratton, who had always treated him like one of his own.

NICHOLAS STARED AT the closed door. Hushed voices chased

slivers of light across the floor. He longed to go to her. To tell her he forgave her. That he would forgive her anything. Had she lain with another man out of loneliness, perhaps he could. But she had betrayed him in the worst of ways. She'd given her heart. And not to some distant acquaintance, or better yet, a stranger. She'd given it to his brother. How was Nicholas to move past that?

He rested his forehead against the frame. Anger warred with despair. He wanted to hit something. Instead, he threw open the door, startling Catherine and her maid.

"Leave." He focused on Catherine's face, searching for fear. There was a brief flash of bewilderment, but she recovered quickly from his abrupt entrance, her face becoming a tranquil mask. When had she perfected that art? He'd used to be able to read her like a book.

The girl hovered.

"I said leave." He fought to maintain a level voice, although fury was fast winning the battle waged at the threshold.

The girl scurried to the main door, pausing to look back.

"I'll be fi—" Catherine began.

"Now!" Did the girl think she could ignore his command? She quickly left the room, and he glared at Catherine.

"There was no need to be so rude. You frightened poor Sadie." Turning her back to him, she picked up a brush and began pulling it through her hair. It was darker in this light, all hint of red muted. Waves of silk flowing over shoulders, which were barely covered by a chemise. His wrath plummeted to his cock. Lord, he wanted her.

He took the few steps to stand behind her, recapturing her gaze in the mirror. Was she intimidated by his entrance? By his presence? Did he want her to be? He leaned in, smelling her hair, the scent of jasmine spiking his desire. She sat rigid. Unaffected. The woman he loved, immune to him. When would he accept that she was not his? Would never truly be his?

"I've just come from Father," he said.

She said nothing, just watched him in the mirror. Raising the brush, she stroked again, her hand shaking. Not so unaffected. *Did* she fear him? *Damn*, when had he ever doubted her feelings? This was not how it was supposed to be between them.

"We will host a wedding dinner in a week's time. You are the mistress of this house, so I leave the guest list and the details up to you." He turned to leave.

"No."

He paused, taking a deep breath. "No?" His throat constricted on resurging anger. "No?" He repeated it slowly, unable to believe she had the audacity to argue after what she'd done.

"It is too soon. Daniel has been gone but three months. It's not proper."

"Not proper," he bit out. "Not proper?" He placed his hands on her shoulders and stared at her in the mirror, fighting the urge to squeeze until she showed some emotion, some hint of the pain that ripped through him.

"What is not proper is that I left for the continent to fight, wanting to make the best life for us...for *you*." He paused, steadying his breathing. "What is not proper is *your* inability to remain faithful. What—is—not—proper is *you* choosing my brother. You wanted an earl. Never *me*. I was but a stepping-stone until the real thing came your way."

"Nicholas," she began, her eyes shimmering in the candle-light.

He waited, but she said nothing more. He forced his fingers to uncurl and let go of her shoulders, disgusted because he wanted more, wanted something, anything, from her that said he mattered more than Daniel or Daniel's damn memory. He strode to the door.

"I don't want this...celebration."

His sire had vilified the word too.

"Then take it up with your father." There was no satisfaction in the slamming of the door.

CHAPTER FIFTEEN

*Things without all remedy should be without regard: what's
done is done.*

—Shakespeare, *Macbeth*

CATHERINE TOOK THE laneway to the gatehouse. It was
shorter to go via the stables and around the larger of the
two lakes, but she wanted no reminders of that day at the folly.
She'd thought she would treasure the memory forever, but
instead it taunted her with what could have been—what should
have been.

No one was around as she turned from the gatehouse onto
the path that led through the woods. She had spent more of her
youth among its flora than she'd ever spent behind the walls of
Stratton Hall, chasing the three boys endlessly and always fighting
to join in their games. Sometimes they would allow it. Sometimes
she'd spent her days trying to seek them out. Either way, she had
loved being outside, adored the smell of fresh air and the crunch
beneath her feet.

She kicked at the ground and loosened some pebbles, sorting
through them quickly before deciding which one to take.
Reaching the small lake, she took the footbridge, pausing to stare
at the trout. The earl kept the water well stocked. When she'd
first realized she loved Nicholas, she would come and sit beside

him for hours while he fished. He would say little, but it hadn't mattered. In the throes of love, she'd been content to just sit and stare at him. Daniel and Laurence would inevitably show up and ruin her romantic idyll.

It was tradition to pick up a stone on the path and toss it into the lake with a wish. She fisted the one she'd snagged and held it close to her lips. "This is for you, Laurence. It may be too late for the rest of us, but you have a fresh start. May love find you again," she whispered, then kissed her fingers before throwing the stone into the lake, watching the ripples, imagining them undulating until they reached Laurence. Wherever he was.

She dawdled, not quite ready for another confrontation. Lovely crimson dianthuses were in full bloom, and she picked some, tempering the royal display with a spray of the gentler version, Sweet William. She loved to see vases throughout Stratton Hall. They brought a joy to the dark rooms. Finally, emerging from the woods, she stared at her old home.

Stratton's architecture may have dictated gloom, but only love and laughter filled its halls. It was a stark contrast to Woodfield Park, built to let in sunshine but mired in darkness. She had always hoped she and Nicholas would find a place of their own, something that reflected their abiding love. She grunted at the thought. She was here to speak with her father about the dinner gathering, to ensure it got canceled. Abiding love indeed.

The door opened before she reached the threshold.

"Miss Baring!" Edwards beamed, his dark eyes twinkling whiskey in the sunlight.

"Lady Walford now," she teased, patting his arm and handing him the flowers as she strode by.

"Ah, yes, I do apologize."

"No need to, Edwards. I am not used to it myself." She pulled sharply at her ribbon, released the bow, and tossed the hat on the table. "Do you hang about the door, waiting for new arrivals now?"

He laughed. "I was about to take in a breath of fresh air on the steps."

"Is Papa about?"

"He's in the library." He took her shawl. "I will let him know you are here."

While she would not normally hesitate to intrude on his privacy, she no longer lived here, and he would not be expecting her. She had no doubt of her welcome, but the man deserved warning. She walked over to the buck mounted on the wall.

"Well, old man. What think you of all this? You warned me to be careful of what I wished for."

"Still talking to stuffed animals?" Her father stood in the doorway, arms crossed, a smirk on his face.

"Quite frankly, I find it far easier than talking to some men."

He laughed and held out his hand. "Come, kitten. Sit with me and have some tea. Let us pretend you are ten once again and that your father knows everything."

They each took a chair by the empty fireplace. It was a fair day, and though the hall remained damp throughout the year, her father was always hesitant to waste. Yet if she were in residence, he would have a small fire burning for her comfort because she would inevitably curl up and read in this chair.

As they waited for tea, her father talked of his trip to Worcestershire, regaling her with tales of his friends' follies. She laughed until she cried. And once started, she could not seem to stop.

Her father leaned forward in his chair. "Kitten?"

"Sir?"

She lifted her head as her father waved Edwards away. Her father rose, gave her his handkerchief, then returned to his chair. Eventually the tumult slowed.

She crumpled the cloth in her hands, holding it toward him. "It seems I am forever soiling your handkerchief."

Leaning forward, he folded her hand over the cloth. "You keep that. In case I am not around when you need it next." He squeezed her fist. "Although, I will always be here. Know that."

She sat back against the stuffed chair. "Papa, there is to be a dinner."

He said not a word, just watched her.

"There is nothing to celebrate. I do not want it."

His fingers steepled, he was silent. Considering. "I want it."

So it was true. Her father *had* demanded the dinner. Even now, despite her clear distress, he wanted it to proceed.

"No…please."

He winced, and she regretted it, but she could not bear the thought of the charade.

"Kitten." He cleared his throat. "No. Catherine. You are a married woman now. I must accept that and treat you as such."

Her heart sank at the dismissal of her pet name. Did everything warm and loving need to be put aside?

"You have known your heart since you were young. You think I have forgotten when you ran into this very room and declared your love for Nicholas and swore you would run from me if I ever disapproved of it?" He chuckled. "I thought it the whimsy of a child, but you have never surrendered it. He left you when he did not have to do so, yet you waited for him. You waited year after year until—"

"Oh, Papa, it is not as it should be. I cannot stand before a room of guests and pretend otherwise."

"You can, and you must. I will not have the world murmuring speculations, wondering if you are even now increasing with child. Your marriage was rushed. You didn't even wait for your dear father to be present." He waved off her protestations. "It is unseemly unless it was the product of haste due to undying love. If I had been here, I would have forbidden it until you found peace with Nicholas. But you did not wait. And so I will proclaim true love's impatience at the dinner. I will not allow you to put forth otherwise."

"What of Daniel? It is not proper. He is not yet cold in his grave."

His face darkened, a storm of rage twisting his genial features.

"Daniel? Daniel! You dare hold that man in esteem after everything that has happened? He thought nothing of you or of your love for Nicholas. He thought only of himself!"

"That is not true, and you know it. It was an untenable situation. Daniel merely tried to find a path that would benefit all. He loved as I do, deeply. You cannot deny his love."

The bluster left him like a balloon deflated. She regretted the pain, but the words needed to be spoken. Her father had said little along the way, but he had shared her journey. He knew the truth.

"Daniel did not deserve you, kitten. None of the men in your life do, including me."

"Oh, Papa, don't say that."

He pinched the crease between his brows. "I will declare my pleasure in your union at this dinner. No one will refute it. Not Nicholas. Certainly not Lord Woodfield. I have made clear the consequences if he dares stand in the way." He wiped a hand over his face. "There are only two men left who know the truth. One of them is fighting in the Americas. God keep him safe."

She didn't want to stay for tea. Too much lay between them at the moment for idle chatter. She kissed him on the cheek. "I will do as you ask. You are a good father."

He raised his hand to her cheek. "If I were a good father, you would not be in this position."

She pulled his hand from her face and kissed its palm. "It is that same goodness that has put me here. No regrets for love, Papa. No regrets for love."

CHAPTER SIXTEEN

Play out the play.

—Shakespeare, *Henry IV*

S ADIE HAD DONE wonders with Catherine's hair. It was piled in large curls and held snuggly by a crown of pearls, but a few strategic strands fell, softening the angles of her cheeks. She peered closely, then sat back with a sigh. Her nose was too sharp, her bones too dominant. She touched her lips. They stood in stark contrast to the angularity of her face. Nicholas had used to call them lush. When he'd loved them. When he'd loved her. She shook her head to dislodge that thought and scowled at herself. They were duck lips.

"Quack!" She leaned toward the mirror. "Quack!"

"My lady?"

Sadie looked so perplexed, and the urge to laugh bubbled unexpectedly. Catherine fought it. If she began to laugh, she just might never stop. Then it would be off to Bedlam for her.

Instead, she focused on the gown the girl held. "That is lovely." It was the color of fresh grass, veiled with sheer beige.

"Yes, my lady. Your hair will be stunning against it."

"I'm afraid I can't wear it, Sadie." The maid's face fell, but it was of no account. Catherine had to leave her disappointed. "I must honor Daniel this evening. This is a house still in mourning.

Please get my gray bombazine."

Sadie sighed her regret, carefully draped the dress over the large, stuffed chair by the fireplace, and disappeared back into the dressing room. Catherine rose and walked across the room. She lifted the skirt and ran her fingers over the satiny fabric, the candlelight shimmering on the green beneath the gauze. Sophia had a wonderful eye for color and cloth. Catherine would never have chosen something so rich, so soft. Her friend had argued for every piece in Catherine's trousseau. Only one item had been worn so far. She tucked away that memory. It was too sad to contemplate.

Despite the long week spent wandering the estate, and the endless lonely nights waiting for a knock that never came, she tried to hold fast to the memory of her wedding night. Nicholas was not a shallow man. He could not make love to her and feel nothing. Surely more than desire simmered beneath his cool exterior. But even that was a starting place she would welcome. Someday she would breach the barricade. She clung to that thought for courage. With a room full of people waiting below, she needed all the fortitude she could find.

She spritzed her neck, sniffing at the sweet, floral scent infusing the air. Sadie stepped out of the dressing room with the drab gown held high. Catherine stepped into it, shifting to allow Sadie access to the long row of buttons at the back.

When Sadie was finished, she tucked a cream fichu around Catherine's neckline, completing the somber look. "Oh, my lady, I so wish you would wear the green, but you are stunning nonetheless. Ever so elegant."

Catherine smiled at the kind words and glanced in the mirror. "Quack," she mouthed before following Sadie to the door.

Sadie stood in the doorway, waving when Catherine hesitated at the top of the stairs. She envisioned going back, grabbing the girl, and dragging her down the stairs. A champion by her side would be nice. Instead, she straightened her shoulders, lifted her chin, and descended the steps. Conversation hummed from the drawing room. She should have been there to greet the guests, but she feared she could not pull off the pretense of a happy newlywed. Dinner, at least, would provide a distraction.

She stood at the base of the stairs, feeling disoriented, the cold marble seeping through her slippers. Laughter burst from the room, light spilling out in invitation, but she could not bring herself to move toward it. Nicholas had not talked to her for a full week. He left before she arose and returned long after she had gone to bed. His father had not emerged from his rooms. Stratton Hall might be odd, with its assortment of animals staring from the walls, its halls dark and cold, but it was filled with life. With love.

"My lady." Fredericks greeted her quietly. "There are many who have asked for you."

He stood rigid and proper, with his shoulders hunched only slightly from age, and that shock of white hair that was Fredericks. He was such a mainstay. His eyes exuded considerable warmth and caring. Shades of Stratton Hall. Tears prickled.

"Hush, girl," he said softly. "They have come to support you. To celebrate you both."

He scooped her elbow gently and steered her toward the room. "Child, I have watched you your whole life. You have a stiffer backbone than many a man. Don't shy away now. You have earned this moment. Go in there and take hold of your life."

Fredericks squeezed her arm and then stepped through the doorway and announced her arrival. Her chest tightened as talking ceased and everyone looked her way. Oh, she could not do this. She began to turn.

"Catherine!" Sophia pulled Catherine into a warm embrace, and the binding around her chest loosened a little.

"I was so happy to hear of your nuptials. Oh, that is an outright lie. I have been over the moon. It's as if *my* dreams of love have come true!" Sophia gushed loudly, then grabbed Catherine firmly by the shoulders and held her away, Sophia's lovely dark eyes piercing but her smile unchanged. "Truly, I'd begun to think

I'd be helping you pick out widow weeds with the man away so long at war. Instead, you get your fairy-tale ending." She sighed dramatically. "I concede that true love conquers all!"

Sophia released Catherine and looked at the gathering. "I must confess, I am green with envy." Light laughter rippled around the room, and the murmur of conversation renewed.

Catherine kept her smile in place, but her head was spinning. She had deliberately excluded Sophia from the guest list. Catherine had not seen Sophia since Daniel's death, nor had Catherine spent the effort to make the long ride to Sophia's estate. The betrothal was behind Catherine, and it seemed some things were best left unsaid. Aside from Catherine's guilt about keeping secrets, she had not wanted Sophia to be a part of this parody. Sophia was always straightforward and despised facades. Catherine didn't want her friend to see her for the fraud she now was, pretending this was the marriage of her dreams. Nicholas's disappointment in her was enough to bear without shouldering Sophia's too. Yet here Sophia was, and Catherine found herself grateful for it. She just might get through this evening after all.

"Thank you for coming. You cannot know how much it means." She clasped Sophia's hands and squeezed.

Sophia's back now to the room, her expression sobered. "*Che cosa, il mia amica?*" she murmured.

Catherine's sight glazed with the threat of tears. *My friend.* Oh, how those words made her weak. She needed a friend, and she had one in Sophia. Solid and true, unfettered by doubt.

"Nothing. We'll talk later. Just, please, stay by my side and keep the attention on you." As she was bolstered, the tears receded, and her back stiffened with new strength.

Sophia's face lit as she pulled Catherine close, kissing each cheek. "*Mia amica,* how happy I am for this union. You have loved each other for *so* long." Her voice had risen again so that all in the vicinity could hear her.

She hooked her arm in Catherine's, and they moved into the room, Sophia chattering frivolously and Catherine smiling, although she was not truly listening. She was too busy studying people's faces to see if they sensed the truth. She and Sophia paused in front of the beautiful woman who had stood at her marriage.

"Lady Thornwood," Catherine acknowledged, wanting to slip under the carpet in embarrassment.

"Lady Walford," Lady Thornwood responded, reaching out and touching Catherine's gloved fingers. "Do please call me Elizabeth." She squeezed her hand. "I have few friends, and I would so like to count you among them."

Sophia placed her hand on top of theirs. "Then it is done, *bella*, for I adore you both and cannot bear it if you do not feel for each other as I do for you."

Another muscle eased in Catherine's shoulders. Lady Thornwood—Elizabeth—had not judged her. Nor had she disclosed the horrible circumstances of her wedding to Sophia despite their obvious friendship. Catherine had allies.

"Ladies," her father said, joining their little circle. "While you make a lovely bouquet, and no doubt have much to talk about, I fear my little kitten has made us wait long enough." He pressed a kiss to her temple, softening his chastisement.

"Countess Tessaro, thank you for gracing me with your presence." Her father held out his arm. "If I may?"

Sophia looked delighted as she winked at Catherine and tucked her arm in his. Catherine stared at them as they moved toward the door. Sophia was chatting away, leaning toward her father, no doubt colluding further, and Catherine felt her first genuine smile of the evening. She suspected her dear papa was responsible for Sophia's presence. Catherine must remember to thank him later.

"You are mistress of this house. Our guests await your direction." Nicholas smiled at her courteously, but his hissed whisper in her ear was anything but polite. Heat rose to her cheeks. Her father was breaking protocol by leading Sophia to the dining room. He was a mere baron. She glanced quickly around the room, assessing rank. Oh, she was no good at this. She had created the guest list through consultation with Fredericks and Nan and had thought pairings through meticulously, but her father had undone her plan. He never stood on ceremony. Now how was she to orchestrate the exit?

"Lord Woodfield will make a good pairing at dinner for the Dowager Duchess of Middleton, don't you think, Lady Walford?"

Catherine turned to find Elizabeth smiling encouragingly.

"I would be delighted if your husband would care to escort me to the dining room, and mine will provide your escort." Elizabeth named the rest of the pairings quickly. "Both your father and Sophia are known for their…eccentricities." Her smile broadened, and she laughed, creating the illusion that they had been sharing an amusing moment. Then she nudged Catherine toward the waiting guests. "Everyone will see it as charming that the two of them left first."

NICHOLAS SETTLED LADY Thornwood to his left, pleased Countess Tessaro sat to his right. It was clear she had more than a passing acquaintance with Catherine. Perhaps the countess could shed some light on the missing years. Fredericks's troupes placed the soup, and Nicholas made polite conversation with Lady Thornwood in between sips, fighting the urge to lift the bowl and drink it down. He was anxious for the next course so he might speak with Countess Tessaro.

He glanced across the table at Catherine. She was engrossed in conversation with Thornwood. He scanned her attire, his blood boiling anew. When she had walked into the drawing room, he had struggled with the urge to drag her out. How dare she think of Daniel on this night! Nicholas pulled at his too-tight cravat, his anger simmering as a footman removed his bowl. When the man laid the next course, Nicholas focused on the countess.

"May I?" He lifted the platter of cutlets. She nodded politely, yet playfulness sparkled amber in her dark eyes.

He offered her several dishes. She tipped her head in acquiescence to each one but said not a word. He tore at the cutlet, shoving it in his mouth. She had chattered like a magpie with Catherine. He swallowed, and the meat lodged in his throat. Grabbing the wine, he gulped it down, and a footman promptly refilled his goblet.

He glanced at the countess. Her countenance had shifted. She now appeared concerned and, unexpectedly, sympathetic.

"It must be difficult after all these years to reacclimatize to civilian life. When one has lived through trying circumstances…" She let the statement hang, patting her lips as though she were the one fighting the rising bile.

Was that what she thought was going on? She was either not as close to Catherine as he assumed, or she had not yet had the chance for a tête-à-tête.

"They are certainly two opposing worlds," he responded, reaching for the beans and spooning a small pile on her plate before adding to his. He speared a small stem before turning to her again. "It is quite difficult to reconcile the past four years with my long-held vision for the present."

She tilted her head to one side and studied him. "Some things in life are simply too good to wait for, no? I, for one, was not surprised by your hasty nuptials. Over the few years I have known her, Catherine has talked of you—endlessly, I might add—with such a light of love in her eyes. It is no wonder you were swift to act upon this union when you arrived home."

"And what of my brother? Did she speak of him as often?"

Countess Tessaro appeared genuinely baffled. Then her face lit with understanding, and her already rich coloring deepened with a blush. "I am sorry, Lord Walford, for your loss. It is insensitive of me not to consider the weight of such pain despite the joys of love. It is just that my heart is so happy for my friend. I did not mean to be crude."

He focused on his plate, moving a bean around. It was as if the woman did not understand his insinuation. Surely she knew? There was no mistaking the relationship she had with Catherine. He swallowed the bean, its coarse sides ripping at his throat. He slammed down his fork. *Damn.* Was there not even to be pleasure in the food this evening? He reached for his wine as Stratton pushed abruptly from the table, drawing Nicholas's attention. Although his father-in-law did not look his way, he felt his censure. Stratton was clearly trying to distract from Nicholas's poor manners.

"My friends," Stratton began, gesturing around the table. "Well, in truth, I know so few of you I should say 'my acquaint-ances.'"

Laughter tinkled gaily; faces were jovial. Nicholas was certain his angry clattering of cutlery had gone unnoticed.

"Well, friends, old and new, my good neighbor, dear friend, and now family member"—he tipped his glass toward Nicholas's father, and Nicholas wanted to roll his eyes—"has agreed I should do the honors of welcoming the new couple to the fold."

Lord Woodfield's face remained impassive, revealing neither pleasure nor disgust. Did the man feel emotion? The dowager leaned in, murmuring in his ear, covering his hand as she spoke. Nicholas had had no idea they were close.

"Catherine," Lord Stratton began, staring at her with such fondness Nicholas fought jealousy. What was it like to know a father's enduring love?

"Catherine," he repeated. "You burst into the house, at the ripe old age of six, declaring your love for young Nick. Despite my many attempts over the years to veer you from your course toward this young scoundrel..." He paused, at last staring directly at Nicholas. The ensemble tittered approvingly, but he didn't miss the dead seriousness in Stratton's eyes even if the others seemed oblivious.

"...you could not be dissuaded." He held Nicholas's gaze for another painful moment, then turned his attention to Catherine.

"You were right, and I was wrong." Stratton walked around the table and stood behind Catherine, touching her locks lovingly.

Irrational resentment reared. Nicholas gripped the tablecloth at his lap, fisting it, twisting it. That was *his* Catherine. He longed to claim such an unaffected familiarity.

"You saw love," Stratton continued, "knew it for what it was and claimed it." He glanced around, settling on Nicholas across the table. "If we could all be as wise as that young girl, life would be rich indeed." Stratton raised his glass, holding Nicholas's gaze.

"God bless this love. The years have thrown unforeseen obstacles in its path, but never has a girl been truer. Her love for all is pure." Finally releasing Nicholas from that penetrating stare, Stratton waved a path around the table with his glass.

"I regret their haste. However, I remember it well. Just so, I loved her mother." His eyes softened, and he pressed a kiss to Catherine's head. "You make her proud in all you do." He tilted his glass and tipped back the contents.

Nicholas unclenched his fingers, letting go of the cloth, a wave of guilt washing away anger. The women were teary-eyed. The men smiled fondly. He was surrounded by a sea of emotional people sipping libations. The toast had definitely been heartfelt. He respected Lord Stratton. He'd always been the warmth to Nicholas's own father's cold. The baron had been a part of Nicholas's life for as long as he could remember. So had Catherine. Nicholas threw back his wine. Stratton paused behind the chair and placed his hand on Nicholas's shoulder as the guests began to talk once again.

"I consider you a son," he said, so quietly the exuberant table could not possibly have heard. "I expect you to behave accordingly."

CATHERINE AVERTED HER gaze from both men, looking down at her lap. Her father made a high demand. He of all people should realize Nicholas had the right to be angry, to be unhappy with the state of their marriage. The fault for everything wrong lay on the home front.

"Lady Walford?" Mr. Randall held out a plate of beans, his eyes twinkling merrily in the candlelight, his dimpled cheeks exuding pleasure.

"Yes, please." Some of Catherine's strain lifted at his welcoming face, and she found it easier than she'd expect to smile in return. He had been included tonight because he was a guest of Lord and Lady Thornwood. He and his new wife were enjoying a country visit. When they'd drawn up the list, Fredericks had mentioned the man had recently surrendered a commission.

"I understand you were once with the army, Mr. Randall?"

"Yes, cavalry officer"—he lowered his voice and inclined toward her conspiratorially, his voice a stage whisper—"now turned pirate."

"Christopher!" His lovely, young wife leaned into the table, reprimanding him. Her dark eyes warmed at his grin.

"What, Mrs. Randall? Is that not why you fell for me so quickly?"

Catherine tried not to resent the sweet teasing between the two. It was how she had imagined married life. Mrs. Randall now contemplated her plate, her cheeks flushed.

"I do, of course, jest, my lady," Mr. Randall said. "I own a shipping company, and it keeps me busy on the waters during this time of war with the Americas. Many consider the profits made by merchants privateering."

Nicholas had dreamed of such enterprise before he'd left, despite his father's disdain of anything mercantile. He'd had plans for their future, one day dreaming of architecture, the next of building a profitable business in commerce. Now he was to be an earl. His path had changed, and he would not travel the road of his choice. Catherine had not thought of what that meant to him.

He'd always been fiercely independent, had needed to be. Now he had a responsibility to the estate and its tenants. How did he feel about the unexpected burden?

"Were you on the continent, Mr. Randall?" Nicholas interrupted, clearly listening in on their conversation.

"I was, my lord."

"Your rank, sir?" Nicholas's voice was clipped, almost challenging. She knew he was as displeased as she about the dinner, but had he lost all manners in the last years?

Mr. Randall's placid expression grew serious. "Captain, my lord, cavalry. My final stand before resigning my commission was the Battle of Fuentes de Oñoro, a year ago."

Nicholas still sat rigidly, but his tone softened. "Wellesley talked of it. You lost a lot of men."

Mr. Randall cleared his throat, glancing at his wife, who was now deep in conversation with Lord Woodfield. "Perhaps we can discuss it after dinner?"

Nicholas looked at Mrs. Randall, then nodded, and the tension between the men seemed to dissipate. Mr. Randall turned to the dowager and took up a conversation, while Nicholas renewed his talk with Lady Thornwood. Catherine touched her temple, her pulse thrumming madly, as she stared at Nicholas. She did not know this man, this soldier who interrogated a guest at the dinner table. Perhaps she never had.

CHAPTER SEVENTEEN

How bitter a thing it is to look into happiness through another man's eyes!

—Shakespeare, *As You Like It*

T HE NIGHT SEEMED endless. Despite Nicholas's persistent prodding, the countess gave no indication that she knew much of Daniel beyond his relationship as Nicholas's brother. He had no doubt she was both socially clever and a protective friend.

Exhausted and defeated, Nicholas bid goodbye to the Dowager Duchess of Middleton, who had lingered far past the others. When Fredericks at last closed the door, Nicholas braced himself to escort Catherine up the stairs only to find she had already left. Her dark dress swayed as she crested the top stair and skirted to the right. Red fire lit his dulled senses, fury coursing through his veins, giving him new life. She could hardly wait to get away from him. *To the devil with her mourning!* He took the stairs two at a time and sped along the galley, managing to block the door to her chamber just as she moved to close it.

"Nicholas?" She sounded weary, and he hesitated. Shades of blue tinted the pale skin beneath her eyes, her flesh ghostly in contrast to her gown. The damn gown. It mocked his sympathy. The heat of anger rose again, and he shed the cloak of guilt that threatened to settle upon his shoulders. She had made this bed, not he.

"How many people were privy to your plans?" He moved into the room, and she took a step backward when he kicked the door closed behind him. But she didn't look afraid. Instead, her brow furrowed, her forehead wrinkled as though she was confused. She had become the consummate actress since he'd left.

"Who knew you were to marry Daniel?" he asked.

She whirled from him but stumbled, and he grabbed her arms, pulling her upright. Her perfume wafted. His balls tightened. *Damn.* He did not want to want her.

"Who?" he demanded.

"Our fathers. Laurence." She paused. "No doubt the servants. There are no secrets in our homes." A smile flitted, quickly replaced by the now familiar forlorn downturn of her lips. "We had not yet formalized our agreement. Had not made it public."

He fought the rush of pleasure. It was irrational. Bloody stupid. Her reticence to share with others had no direct correlation to her love for Daniel. And certainly nothing to do with her love, or lack thereof, for him. Elation was foolish. Anger spiked again.

"You didn't tell your friend Sophia?"

"No. Nor any other guest in the room tonight."

A calm washed over the ire, cooling its flame. He felt less the cuckold. It was ridiculous, but his pride smarted at the world believing he now had Daniel's seconds. He knew, in his heart, he was her first in all ways. Yet perception was reality in society. He rolled his shoulders. When had he begun to care about the opinion of society?

"Is there anything else…my lord?" Her pause, her bland tone, reignited his waning wrath. Did she think he would use his role to demand compliance? Did she not know him better than that?

"No," he growled, turning and walking toward the door.

"Well, happy wedding celebration to you, then…my lord."

Gone suddenly was the wane girl with tired eyes, although a

flush creeping up her neck was the only sign of emotion. Oh, she was all woman now, glaring at him. Only she could get under his skin like a tick. He would scratch with a harsh word, but her insinuation was pervasive. He could not easily rid himself of it.

Three quick strides, and he towered over her. "Do not make me the villain in this dark gothic drama."

"Nor am I the fragile miss awaiting her hero!" Her green eyes sparkled, challenge accentuating her set features.

His rage bubbled, fully surfacing. Grabbing her, pulling her close, he inhaled deeply. Her scent spurred him on. He took siege of her lips, nibbling, sucking, biting until the taste of blood made them both moan.

He pushed her away, holding her at bay, trying to calm his need. Her eyes were closed, her carefully coiffured hair tilted awkwardly to the side. God, he loved her. He moved nearer, breathing her in. He had smelled her in his dreams when he'd lived in the depths of hell. Muck and mire softened by the memory of jasmine. He inhaled again. His Catherine. He caught sight of her silken gray shoulder, the fabric glimmering in the candlelight. No, not his. Daniel's. He pushed away from her, flinching as she stumbled again, her confusion clear.

"Get rid of those weeds," he barked. "I don't ever want to see them again. You are a wife, blast you, not a widow."

She glowered, her eyes a darkening forest. "Then prove it."

His rampant pulse echoed in his temples. She dared goad him to verify his virility? The moment hung, suspended. He faced her, determination tightening her angular cheekbones, defiance sharpening her gaze. Prove it?

He roared as he crossed the few steps to her and seized the dress with both hands. The ripping of fabric was quickly replaced by the sounds of their breathing. She did not cringe. She stood, her chest heaving, a cold Venus in a chemise. That goaded him on more than the gauntlet she'd thrown at his feet.

"Damn you." He scooped her up and threw her on the bed, giving her no chance to scurry from him. The light undergarment bunched above her hips, trapped there, her dark chamber exposed, a luring invitation. He fell upon her, spreading her legs, nuzzling.

"Damn you," he repeated before he lost himself in the taste of her, the feel of her, the sweet ambrosia of her response. She pressed against him, mewling, crying. Her release was deep satisfaction. He lay his cheek against her stomach, his heart pounding in his chest. Had Daniel given her this pleasure? *Damn and double damn.* He pushed away and sat up.

"Nicholas?" Her voice was raspy, satisfaction and confusion muffling its tenor.

"Go to sleep, Catherine. It's been a long day."

Not waiting for a response, he adjusted his painful erection and strode to the door before closing it gently. He stared at the sitting room. It was supposed to be a place of shared tranquility. He guffawed bitterly. Would this house ever know serenity? He heard rustling beyond the far door. The popinjay was about. Nicholas could not face Isaac's colorful countenance right now. After pulling open the door to the hall, he quietly descended the staircase and stood at the bottom of it, oddly disoriented. On the battlefield, life had been linear. He had forgotten how circular it was here. Just when you thought you'd made headway, you were back at the beginning.

Pausing at the billiards room, he contemplated entering. It would pass the time, but it would provide no relief. After strolling quickly past it, down the hall, he pushed into the study. Daniel's study—his study now. *Bloody hell.* Sitting at the desk, he stared at the darkness beyond the window. Had Daniel ever sat here in the night to ponder life? To think about Catherine?

Nicholas lit the candle, yanked open the drawer, and stared at the bundles. He had not been to the room since finding the letters. He'd been too busy with the estate. He was lying to himself. The estate had not kept him from the room. He'd been using work as an excuse to avoid Catherine and to escape thoughts of Daniel. Was he finally ready for more revelations?

Lifting out the next packet, he placed it on the desk, running his hand over the papers. Daniel had written these. Addressed them to Nicholas. He owed it to his brother to read them. Surprisingly, Nicholas's hand shook as he pulled the ribbon.

My Dearest Brother,

I live in fear of news from the continent. I know it is in your nature to take charge, to see to everyone's welfare, and I fear it will lead to no good end in such an environment. I don't know what I would do if I lost you. Damn this war for stealing you away.

Father is solemn and speaks very little when he deigns to join the table. When he does, it is to exalt your role in the future of England. He says Wellesley has great plans for you. He pontificates your virtues, and oddly, I believe his genuineness. How sad he never shared his admiration while you stood before him in the flesh.

His father spoke highly of Nicholas? He could not remember a word of praise from the man's mouth, yet Daniel had written of esteem. Daniel, ever the optimist, had no doubt been projecting his own goodwill.

I am still hesitant to speak with you of my happiness when I know that you are enduring endless hardship. But I have no one with whom I can share my joy. And, dear brother, I know that you know love and will recognize my earnestness.

Nicholas rested the letter on the desk. This was the one. He grabbed it, crumpled it, and pivoted awkwardly toward the fire. The cold, empty hearth mocked his attempt. There would be no escape. He swiveled back, lay the paper on the mahogany surface, and methodically pressed his hand across the wrinkled page, trying to flatten his nerves as much as the parchment.

We walked in the woods today, hand in hand, acquainting ourselves to this growing affection. We spoke of you and our mutual esteem for all you do, both wishing we could exemplify your qualities but knowing that you will forever be beyond our ilk. Despite that, we agreed we admire you immensely and love you deeply.

Our own love is still fresh, new, and unexplored. We recognize it is not proper, that we are betraying many by indulging in it, including you, but we are having great difficulty fighting its pull. Our pleasure will result in so much pain. It is distressing to think upon it. Perhaps there is a solution not yet clear.

I will keep you apprised, dear brother, of developments. For the one thing I have never doubted in this life is your support—and your love.

He read quickly through the sheaf of paper, but Daniel made no more reference to his blossoming relationship. Nicholas slammed his fist against the desk. *Damn.* They had fallen for the same woman. Could he blame Daniel? After all, his brother had stood alongside Catherine, begging Nicholas not to go to the continent. He had left the two of them together, foolishly thinking he'd be gone a year, two at most, and that Daniel would watch over her. Well, he certainly had. That and more.

Then again, if not Daniel, another may have stepped into the void Nicholas had created. Perhaps he should be grateful it was his brother. Satisfying pain rippled as the second pounding on the hard wood vibrated up his arm. He had asked Daniel to care for her, not to…care for her? *We recognize it is not proper, that we are betraying many by indulging in it, including you, but we are having great difficulty fighting its pull.* Were they to blame that he had left them to find one another? He rested his head on the cool mahogany. Dear Lord, he thought he'd left the insanity on the continent.

"My lord?"

"Go away." Could he be more childish? Raising his head, he twisted to face Isaac.

The man eyed the pile of letters, sympathy deepening the cherub's lines. "My lord, he was a good man. A kind man. A man who loved deeply."

Nicholas felt defeated. Clearly the relationship had not been a secret. And despite poaching from his own brother, Daniel had earned the devotion of this egocentric dandy. Because Daniel *was* a good man. Had been a good man. Nicholas knew that. He'd always known that Daniel was decent to the core. A kind soul. *For the one thing I have never doubted in this life is your support—and your love.* Nicholas ran a hand down his face, trying to wipe away the image of Daniel's sincerity, his belief that Nicholas was an equal man. Memories swirled like leaves in the wind.

"My lord, morning is nigh. A few hours of sleep may restore your equilibrium."

Nicholas blew out the candle and followed Isaac up the stairs. Nicholas had never been more discouraged.

CHAPTER EIGHTEEN

She's gone. I am abused; and my relief must be to loathe her. O curse of marriage.

—Shakespeare, *Othello*

IT WAS A two-hour ride to Sophia's estate. Catherine had told Fredericks she might not return this afternoon and not to worry. It was not unusual for her to spend several days with Sophia, so the countess would not be entirely surprised to see her even though Catherine had not taken the time to send word she would be coming. After last night, there was no reason to hurry back to Woodfield Park.

She watched the countryside roll by. It was her favorite time of year, the greens ripe in a quilt of harmony. When had she last felt accord? The child in her had hoped her father's demand would pull Nicholas in line, that he would realize he was integral to a larger family and would do his part. He adored her father, so she'd hoped that might tip the scales in her favor. She'd been angry when she'd challenged him, but when he'd risen to the occasion, she'd foolishly believed he'd wanted her and craved her as much as she longed for him. His abrupt departure had dispelled that illusion. She had been left reeling, bereft, and abandoned.

She could make no sense of it. How could he want her one moment, then discard her the next? Sophia was a woman of the world and might be able to shed light on the matter. Catherine so needed guidance in this. She also owed Sophia some truth. About last night. And about Daniel. She had lied to her through omission. Things had spiraled quickly out of control in those weeks before Daniel's death. There'd been no time. In truth, she wasn't sure she would have shared with Sophia even if she'd been nearby. It had been all such a mess she wouldn't have known where to start.

She blew out a long breath and turned from the window. It seemed so cloak-and-dagger in retrospect, almost dirty. No, never dirty. Love, true love, was never dirty. And there was no doubt Daniel's love was the truest kind.

The clanging of the wheels shifted to a more muted clunking rhythm as the carriage slowed to a halt. Catherine adjusted her hat and smoothed her skirt, suddenly unsure this was a wise idea. Perhaps her secrets should remain that. The footman opened the door and helped her to the ground. She stared up at Château Nouveau, renamed by Sophia from its original staid English name to the more optimistic French one. Its majestic stairs wound in invitation.

"Leave my valise," Catherine said to the footman, speaking with a confidence she did not feel. "You may return to Wood-field. Countess Tessaro will see me safely back."

The driver and footman tipped their hats as a trill filled the air. *"Amica bella!"*

All doubt evaporated, and Catherine grinned at the exotic specter on the landing. Swathed in crimson, her dress and her hair flowing in the wind, she held out her arms in welcome. Sophia was stunning, and her warmth was irresistible. Grabbing her skirt, Catherine quickly climbed the stairs. Breathless when she reached the top, she gratefully accepted Sophia's embrace, hugging back with equal vigor. Catherine had grown up with men. Sophia had introduced her to the purity of a woman's love and the security of a true friend's support. Support she dearly needed now more than ever.

Sophia grabbed Catherine's arms, holding her at arms' length, staring intensely. *"Amica bella.* You have much to share, no?" She kissed each cheek, then pulled her to the door. "Do give me a moment."

Sophia disappeared into the drawing room, closing the door behind her. Antsy, Catherine strolled around the large foyer, admiring the collection of paintings that were as bright and vibrant as Sophia herself. Many were portraits, but Sophia said that none were of family, that those remained in her family home in Italy. These had been selected solely because of their beauty, although she claimed to have befriended each and every one of the subjects…in her imagination. Catherine had loved that. It had somehow made talking to the stuffed heads at home seem more charmingly eccentric.

The drawing room door opened, and Catherine caught a glimpse of a man she didn't recognize, before Sophia closed it.

"I'm sorry, Sophia." Heat rushed to Catherine's face. She hadn't even considered that Sophia might be entertaining. Catherine was aware Sophia had a reputation as a widow who did what she wanted, but Catherine had never actually seen her with a man. As a safeguard to her own reputation, Catherine never attended Sophia's renowned socials, and Sophia was always alone when Catherine visited. "I didn't mean to interrupt."

Sophia waved her off dismissively. "You have interrupted nothing, *bella.* Simply some business that can wait." She hooked her arm in Catherine's. "Come."

They ascended another set of stairs to Sophia's private suite. The inner sanctum, she always jokingly referred to it. Catherine knew it was Sophia's private quarters and few crossed its threshold.

Settling on the sofa, Sophia patted the seat in invitation, and Catherine sank onto the plush tapestry. Before either could speak, a tap at the door signaled the arrival of refreshments. She had only been here a few minutes, and the servants were prepared. Sophia was a marvel of hospitality. Or had Catherine interrupted more than a business meeting down below? No matter; she was grateful Sophia didn't seem to mind. Catherine needed her too much right now to graciously return to Woodfield Park.

Sophia poured them each tea from the steaming silver pot. The warmth was a comfort, bracing in its familiarity. Sophia sipped, eyeing Catherine over the cup but saying not a word. Catherine squirmed uncomfortably. Now was the time, but how much should she, could she, share?

"Last night's dinner was…interesting," Sophia said with the raise of an eyebrow before taking another sip.

Interesting? Catherine could not imagine what it must have looked like to their guests, never mind to someone who had received a covert invitation from her father.

"I didn't mean to exclude you." She had refused to invite Sophia because Sophia was too genuine for such a charade. How could Catherine tell her that without fully betraying the farce that was now her life? Yet wasn't that why she'd come?

Sophia waved away Catherine's excuse. "*Amica bella*, there are no apologies between friends. Only honesty."

Catherine cringed. Sophia may be Catherine's only friend now, but she was a good one. She had pulled Catherine from her lonely world and pointed her toward her future, shopping and laughing, and had encouraged her to dream. Sophia had also held Catherine's hand when fear for Nicholas had grown dark and the wait had become agonizingly long. Did Catherine really wish to lie to her?

"I didn't want you to be witness to the masquerade. To my sham of a marriage," Catherine said.

Sophia contemplated her as she set down her cup. Then she grabbed Catherine's hand and held it tightly. "No, *mia amica*. No fraud exists." She squeezed, then released Catherine's hand before heading to the sideboard and pouring small amounts of wine from a barrel-shaped crystal decanter. Sophia returned and gave a glass to Catherine.

"*Salute.*" Sophia raised her glass before taking a sip.

Catherine stared at the ruddy liquid. Blood had been shed on both sides of the continent. Metaphorically and physically. She felt that hers was seeping slowly from her body. She took a too-large drink of the Madeira. Sweetness clogged her throat, but she managed to swallow. It instantly soured in her stomach.

"No charade, my friend, despite what you may have to tell me. He loves you. That truth is clear. He's confused, but he loves you."

Catherine's eyes burned. Oh, how she wanted to believe that.

"He questioned me deeply about his brother. I believe he thinks I have the brains of a sparrow, but even had I wanted to, I could not answer his questions." Sophia arched her eyebrows, expectant.

"I was to be betrothed to Daniel. He died before it could be announced." Catherine swirled the remnants of wine, waiting for the questions, the revulsion. She had made of mockery of Sophia's championship of the love between Catherine and Nicholas.

"Ah, *mia amica.*" Sophia sighed, shaking her head solemnly, then grabbed Catherine's glass and elegantly strolled back to the sideboard, her crimson skirt swaying with each step. Sophia slipped back onto the sofa and handed over the full glass, sympathy clear in her gaze. "Loneliness can make us do foolish things, no?"

Catherine shook her head as she gulped the wine. Her head spun a little. She was not used to libation, certainly not midday and with little food in her body. Sophia's eyes darkened, her brow wrinkling with concern. It would be so easy to leave it at that. Simply a case of loneliness. But Catherine knew she must be honest if only to unburden her own soul.

"Perhaps you are right. Daniel's love was profound. I must confess, it caught me off guard. But when he spoke of it, I felt its depth, its sincerity, and I ached for his longing. The more he talked of it, the more I knew I must surrender my dreams. He was the golden boy. He was always hard to resist and almost impossible to say no to."

"I understand the appeal. I met him but once, and he lingers with me still. A beautiful man."

"Yes, a beautiful man. Inside and out." Catherine took another generous sip before continuing. "When he proposed marriage, I could not deny him. Nicholas had been gone for four years. I began to feel he might never come home. Daniel needed me. Needed me as Nicholas never had." She choked on the remaining wine. "As Nicholas never will."

"*Amica bella!*" Sophia opened her arms.

Catherine moved into Sophia's embrace and surrendered to her warm arms, to her caring, to her own pathetic self-pity.

CHAPTER NINETEEN

Eating the bitter bread of banishment.

—Shakespeare, *Richard II*

NICHOLAS PACED THE sitting room. It had been three days since she'd left. Left without a word to him, instead telling Fredericks where she was going and not to worry should she not return. Fredericks. Not Nicholas. No words for him at all. He hit the doorframe to her room. Should she not return? He hit it again, pain rippling up his arm. Had she left him? He licked the blood on his knuckles. A dog licked his wounds for succor. That was what he was. A dog. A lowly cur. It was his fault she'd left. He had driven her off.

He'd kept busy continuing traveling around the estate, making note of each complaint, each need, entirely appalled by the neglect. Where the hell was Brownlee? Surely he should have responded to the demand for his return by now? How bloody far away did his family business take him? Nicholas didn't know who to direct his anger toward. The steward? His father? His brother? One missing in action. One in ill health. And the last dead. *Damnation.* Had Daniel not realized people were dependent upon him?

Nicholas ran down the stairs swiftly and, not hesitating this time, headed directly into the study. He lit the candle and pulled out the next bundle. He tore at the ribbon, yanked it from the packet, and spread out the first sheet. He was done toying with the past.

Dear Brother,

Father is incapacitated, laid low by a failure of the heart. The doctor is not sure when he will recover, or if he will recover. I am panicked. I do not have the wherewithal to assume his place. Were you here, I've no doubt you would relieve me of much of the burden and take his stead in all but title— although, I would gladly grant you that as well. Instead, you are lost to me somewhere on the continent, and I stand here alone this abysmal night, staring across the desk at the darkness, wondering if I can rise to the role of earl.

Nicholas gazed out the window. The flame's dance reflected in the glass, obscuring the night. Daniel had sat here full of angst too.

While you lead battalions, I fear I cannot even direct my own emotions. I am a failure. You would be ashamed of my trepidation. I but hope our father's stubbornness reigns and he lives to see another day.

Nicholas scanned the next letters detailing his father's confinement and slow recovery. The last missive ended with a celebration of his father's certain rally. He shoved the packet back into the drawer. He wanted to hate Daniel as a traitor. Dismiss him as irrelevant. Yet the thought of doing so did not sit well. He could hear Daniel's voice as he read each word, feel his rising and falling anxiety. Nicholas empathized with Daniel's sense of being overwhelmed and filled with self-doubt. Daniel had always been able to wrap around Nicholas's heart.

He grabbed the last bundle and stood. He did not want to read his brother's final words in this cold room. He clutched Daniel's last thoughts to his chest as he took the stairs.

The cherub opened the door before Nicholas reached the landing. "There you are, my lord. Should I prepare a bath?"

"Get out."

"I beg your pardon, my lord...have I done something to offend?"

None of this had anything to do with the man. Nicholas's anger sputtered. It felt too much like kicking a pup. "No, Isaac, nothing. I just wish to be alone."

Isaac spotted the bundle, and Nicholas dropped his arm, but it was too late. Isaac's eyes watered as he smiled. "Of course you do, my lord. Of course you do." He strode out of the room, gently closing the door behind him.

Nicholas tossed the packet on the bed. The small ivory pile stood stark against the crimson spread. Like a man shot down in battle, his life seeping into the ground. Like his brother lying in the woods in his own blood. Nicholas ran a hand through his hair, shaking his head, trying to dislodge the image. *Damn*. He still could not bring himself to read the final letters. The last words Daniel would ever share with him.

Turning from one pain to face another, he stood in front of the fireplace, grabbing the edge of the mantel as though it could anchor his thoughts. Three days. The chasm between them was so great, even when standing side by side. What did it matter if she was here or not? *Bloody hell*. She was *his* wife now, and that mattered. That meant something. Her place was at Woodfield Park, whether she liked it or not. Whether she cared for him or not.

Perhaps she had returned, but gone to Stratton Hall? He had no hope of recovery if that was her choice. Her father would protect her against Nicholas's...against his what? His love? He growled, not knowing what to call it anymore, only knowing he ached to have her near.

A slight sound pierced his anguish. Hushed voices, the closing of a door. He stepped into the sitting room. A trace of light wavered beneath the door, and there was more muted talking.

The band around his chest eased. He took a deep breath, then slowly blew it out. She was back. She was not staying with the countess indefinitely. Despite all the reasons she should not, Catherine had come home.

He laid his forehead against the door that stood between them, his heart pulsating in his neck. He had felt fear in his life, and this had been as keen as any he had known. He pressed harder against the wood until stars radiated. She had come home.

He walked away from the temptation that lay beyond the threshold and returned to his bedroom. The letters remained silent on the duvet. They would wait another day. He set them on the side table. After discarding his clothing, he climbed into bed, suddenly bone weary.

Catherine was here. A room away. For tonight, that was enough.

CHAPTER TWENTY

Go to your bosom; knock there, and ask your heart what it doth know.

—Shakespeare, *Measure for Measure*

NICHOLAS ROSE AT first light, dressing quickly before Isaac burst through the door. Nicholas was not up to facing the man's enthusiasm this morning. Or worse, his sympathy. Nicholas had slept for a few hours, then lay staring at the door, finally coming to a decision. Today he would face all demons, strip the past of deceit, and reveal the truth. It was far past time he behaved like a man and the future Earl of Woodfield Park.

He descended, one deliberate step at a time, counting them as he had when he'd been a child, when Daniel had blindfolded him for some foolish game they'd been playing. *Daniel.* Nicholas paused at the study and patted the packet in his jacket. *I will hear you. I will listen. I will deal with it today. For better or for worse. Today.* He turned the corner and headed down the narrow hall. The smell of fresh biscuits wafted, a scented path to one of his favorite destinations.

Nan was setting down a platter when he entered. He walked to the long trestle table and grabbed one, tossing it between his hands. It was definitely fresh from the oven.

Nan clucked, pushing a plate at him. He dropped the biscuit

onto it.

"Sit, child, sit." She grabbed some fruit preserve and set in on the table as he dropped to the bench.

He tore apart the soft bread and let it cool a moment before slathering it, sniffing it, and then savoring each bite. The strawberry jam was as familiar to his tongue as the bench was to his backside. He smiled as Nan placed a steaming cup of tea in front of him. She'd always been around, welcoming him into her domain, knowing his needs before he did. She sat down across from him, wrapping her hands around an old, chipped cup. It belonged to his mother's set and should have long ago been tossed in the trash. Nan always said it brought her comfort, that it reminded her of the love that had once filled these halls.

"You are up and about early, my lord," she said.

He'd gone from child to lord. He grinned. Nan had manners when she wanted to use them.

"I'm off to Stratton Hall to tend to some business." Well, that was the truth. "I've got some ideas about increasing the flock, but we need more grazing land. Stratton has some fallow meadow. Thought he might be interested." The bit about increasing the flock was truth too, but he'd no intention of discussing sheep this morning with anyone.

Nan lifted her cup and gazed fixedly at its contents. "I remember when you took an interest in the flock. You and Daniel were bird-witted with excitement about the ewes that were about to breed. The two of you would leave in the morning and go stare at the sheep, waiting." She chuckled. "Came home disappointed each day 'cause it wasn't happening fast enough. You were a lad of four if this old mind remembers rightly."

She blew at the steaming brew, and he sugared his tea while waiting patiently for her to continue.

"One day you burst through the door, stumbling in with a bloodied, little lamb, crying for your old Nan." She set the cup aside. "The herdsman was gonna kill the lamb 'cause it was black. The mark of the devil. Had to hold you and that slimy lamb both, just to calm you down some. Then you got angry. No way were you going to let that happen."

He laughed at the memory. "And you asked me what I was going to do about it. Told me if I was going to save it, I better be prepared to take care of that black sheep, since no one else was going to."

"And you did." Her hand covered his. "You've always cared for those who could not defend themselves. Have always known that each life on this earth deserves a place to call home, to feel the warmth of acceptance, despite differences."

He covered her gnarled hand, relishing the familiarity of each ridge. "Nan, you make me feel like a small boy again. It's a good feeling. Thank you." He gave a squeeze and then stood.

"Have a care, child. As you did when you were young. Everyone deserves to be accepted."

He stared at her. Old Nan was never cryptic. Did she fear he would not embrace Catherine? Nan loved her as dearly as she did him. He kissed her on the cheek in assurance. Whatever the outcome of today's revelations, he would always take care of Catherine. Nan should have no fear of that.

⇒⟫⟩⟨⟪⇐

NICHOLAS STARED AT Stratton Hall, the red sandstone fading to pink in the early-morning sun. Light glinted amber on the glass of the second-story window of the left wing. He could almost see Catherine standing there, waiting for him, anxious for their daily ride. All had been right in his world in those days.

The house seemed quiet. His knock on the door was the only sound he heard. He knocked again, and this time, he could hear movement beyond the threshold. He pulled at his jacket and adjusted his cuffs.

"My lord, it is good to see you," Edwards said.

"And you, Edwards." He stepped into the hall, glancing at the array of beasts displayed on the walls.

"Lord Stratton is in the study. I shall let him know you are here."

"Thank you."

The hall was Nicholas's favorite room in the house; he had passed many hours here with Daniel and Laurence. They'd made some of these grooves in the well-worn table. He traced the etching of three swords, each with a set of initials on the handle—his, Daniel's, and Laurence's. The three musketeers. They'd thought they were invincible back then.

He strolled around the room, a cloud settling over the fond reminiscence. They had ceased being the three musketeers many years ago. About the time he'd discovered that spending time with Catherine was far more pleasurable. He stopped in front of the big buck. "I bet you know all her secrets, don't you?"

"Nick! Good to see you. Come. Come. Share a cup of tea with a lonely, old man," Stratton said.

Nicholas followed him through the door, into the study. A fresh wave of memories washed over him. These richly paneled walls had closed in on him when he'd come to ask Lord Stratton formal permission to court Catherine. How the man had laughed at that. "As if she would allow me to forbid it" had been Stratton's response. Nicholas had been so relieved.

Lord Stratton had stood by the window when Nicholas had come to announce his commission. Stratton's shoulders had stiffened, and he had not turned. "Does she know?" Then when Nicholas had come to say goodbye that rainy night. Stratton had pulled him close, hugging him tight before releasing him. "You are a son to me, Nick. Stay safe. For all our sakes."

Nicholas sank into the chair by the fireplace, wiping a hand over his face. He was sweating, though no fire burned in the grate. He was certain Stratton held the answers, but Nicholas didn't know where to start. He revered this man. They loved the same woman.

"Sirs, your tea." Edwards entered, setting down the tray on the table between the two chairs. He poured, splashing a little milk into Stratton's tea, leaving Nicholas's black.

"Anything else, my lord?"

"No, that will be all, thank you." Lord Stratton eyed Nicholas, raised the cup, and sipped. Then he shifted his attention to the empty grate.

"So, Nick, was the army everything you hoped it would be?"

The army? Nicholas had not come here to talk of his time in the military. Of course, Stratton didn't know that. It made sense that he would ask about his time on the continent. They'd not had an opportunity to talk one-to-one since he'd come home to Woodfield.

"It was nothing that I hoped. The threat from Napoleon is a stark reality, and we must fight his aggression. I'm proud to have done my part." He paused. If he was truly proud, why did he feel sick when he thought of it? He stared at Stratton's profile. He might understand. "But the actuality of war, sir, is death and destruction." Nicholas thought of Badajoz—all those lives wasted.

"It is a young man's folly to believe war will make him a better man or lead to his elevation in society. For a few, perhaps. Wellesley comes to mind. Although, I would not have been able to convince you of that. You were too busy trying to prove yourself worthy."

Nicholas left his tea untouched. Catherine and her father were exceptionally close. She would not have agreed to a betrothal with Daniel without Stratton's permission. Here sat another layer of betrayal. Why had Nicholas not thought of that before? Unexpected anger bubbled.

"You knew she had agreed to become Daniel's wife."

Stratton's profile hardened, and he nodded.

"How could you allow that? You love her, you love both of—" He choked on the words.

"You were gone a long time. Things change. Life unfolds." He looked tired as he faced Nicholas, his eyes that dark forest of emotion so like his daughter's. "Have you ever stopped to wonder why, Nick?" He shook his head and waved away the words. "Of course you have. But have you ever asked her?"

CHAPTER TWENTY-ONE

If you have tears, prepare to shed them now.

—Shakespeare, *Julius Caesar*

NICHOLAS INTENDED TO avoid the folly. He should have taken the path by the gatehouse, but his feet chose otherwise. He'd been so proud of this structure, so cocksure that his talent lay in architecture, in designing imposing edifices and, perhaps, dabbling in shipping to ensure the best of materials for his projects. His father had mocked it all, making a particular point to ridicule any mercantile aspirations. Nicholas had had no choice but to join the army. It had been his only sure alternative, the only way to guarantee a place in the world. A place far from his father.

He mounted the steps but paused at the door. Catherine's scent lay beyond it. Her look, her touch, her memory. He clung to their first lovemaking, for sanity. He could not taint it with the letters. Daniel did not belong past the threshold.

Instead, Nicholas sank down onto the step, and his tense muscles eventually relaxed against the warm stone. It was a beautiful summer day, and he wore no overcoat nor gloves. Even so, it was becoming uncomfortably warm. He shrugged from his jacket and laid it across his lap, staring out at the water sparkling in the morning sun. He had taught Catherine to swim in this lake.

As Daniel had taught him.

But have you ever asked her? Stratton's words hovered like a heavy fog. Why had Nicholas not? He clenched his fist, then relaxed it one finger at a time. Because he did not want to hear it, was unwilling to face the bald truth. For Catherine would not deny it. It was not in her to lie. He knew in his heart that she had not been clamoring for a title, would never do so. No, she would speak of her love for Daniel, and it would tear Nicholas apart. He had not asked her *why*, because he was a coward.

He pulled out the packet and laid his jacket aside. Setting the bundle on his thighs, he stared at the ribbon that kept it bound. Daniel's last words. His brother's words. To Nicholas. Here lay the truth. *...and you will know the truth, and the truth will make you free.* The book of John? He couldn't quite recall.

Resting his head back against the door, he closed his eyes and let the warmth wash over his face. A dove cooed. Its mate responded. The wind rustled restlessly as birds fussed. Their call was low, melodic but insistent. So mournful.

He sat upright and shifted so his back was fully braced. He pulled the ribbon and carefully unfolded the first letter. He didn't know if he could ever bear to hear Catherine proclaim her feelings for Daniel. Perhaps his brother's words would provide the bridge.

My Dearest Brother,

We hear of your exploits. It seems Father has a childhood relationship with your commander. He sends brief updates, laced with lauds of your accomplishments, declaring that you make Father proud. While it would kill the old man to acknowledge that sentiment, I have noted he shares these missives with all who will stand still long enough for his pontification of your virtues. I would laugh if I did not fear so for your safety.

Nicholas scanned the next few letters. They were reiterations of his movements on the continent and a review of their father's improving health. He unfolded the second-to-last one from the pile. Maybe Daniel had never shared the truth? He would surely have known the pain it would cause. Daniel had been a kind soul and might have tried to avoid that.

My Dearest Brother,

Forgive me. I told Father of my love tonight, despite the certainty he would be furious. It was sheer insanity. I knew it then as I know it now, but I needed him to understand why he should place his faith in you for the future. Father would not accept it. He has decried a pox on our family if I do not produce his heir.

It darkens further, dear brother. He swears he will share, with the world, the perversity of his son. His words, not mine, I assure you. Although, I cannot argue that I do not feel adrift in my longings. Perhaps his words are more truth than my heart wishes to hear. Catherine says I am not to dwell on it, that we do not get to choose whom we love and it should not be repudiated. As livid as Father is, I cannot believe he would tell all and sundry, but he is our father, and I have rarely seen the grace of humanity light his face.

He demands an expeditious marriage. I do not have your fortitude. Forgive me, for I know you lose far more than you will gain. However, if I do not deny my love for Laurence, then there will be no life for any of us, including our beloved Catherine. You know the world will decry it, that shame will fall upon both families. She is in agreement and comes to the marriage with full knowledge of all that is at stake. It is her love for all of us that fortifies her choice. It keeps us all strong.

Forgive me, dear brother.

Nicholas reread it twice, and his skin grew clammy as he registered its full import. He shifted quickly, and bile mixed with Nan's biscuits splattered the climbing shrubs. The putrid, acidic smell mingled with the sweet fragrance of roses, and he heaved again in response. Then again. Finally he slumped back against the door.

Daniel. Laurence. *Bloody hell.*

He sucked the air until his lungs filled and his breathing

calmed. Laurence. Catherine. And him. Daniel had loved them all. *Blast and damn.* He fisted the paper, crumpling it into a ball. No one need ever know. Except Catherine. His father. No doubt Catherine's father. *Have you ever asked her?*

His head ached. He had assumed the worst of her. But how the hell could he ever have known this was the root of her betrayal?

The lake flickered, sparkling in the sunlight, shimmering with joy. Daniel holding Nicholas's hands as he floated like a dead man. *I've got you, Nick. You're safe.* Catherine's legs wrapped around his body as he treaded water, too excited to speak. *I feel safe with you, Nick.*

The sky stretched, an endless blue. Endless. He squeezed his eyes tight, trying to block out the images. If only it were true, but the blue was not limitless. Nor was life. Both were finite. Especially life. He'd seen that firsthand. He'd seen that it was absolute. His gut wrenched. How could this hurt so much after his witnessing all that?

Unfolding the final letter, he smoothed it gently. His brother had not betrayed Nicholas as he'd thought. Daniel had not stolen Catherine's heart. She'd been a sacrificial lamb. Anger simmered, then quickly calmed as Nicholas's racing pulse slowed. Not her heart, and that mattered most of all.

My Dearest Brother,

I find myself at a crossroads, unable to make a clearheaded decision. How I wish you were here, my younger only in years, certainly not in wisdom. You were born an old sage. You would have prevented this situation I have allowed to develop, made me see reason. It will come to no good end for any of us.

Of one thing I am certain. I cannot let Catherine make this sacrifice. I love you all too deeply to allow for such a pretense. It is unbearably painful in thought. I cannot imagine how horrendous the everyday reality would become. For all of us.

I am to meet Laurence in the woods in the morning. For all our sakes, I will end this farce today.

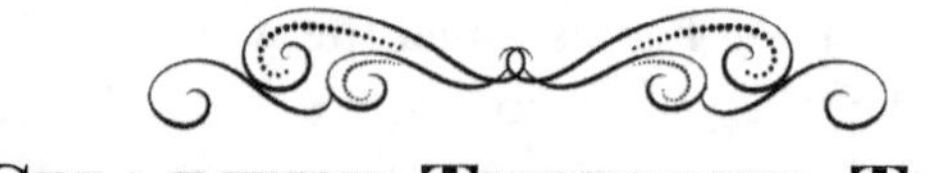

CHAPTER TWENTY-TWO

Well, every one can master a grief but he that has it.

—Shakespeare, *Much Ado about Nothing*

CATHERINE PACED THE drawing room. She had resolved to speak honestly with Nicholas, but he'd left so early she'd had no chance. Now she was doubting the wisdom of such candidness. Did he need to know the truth? What was to be gained? It was still betrayal. She had been willing to forsake their love for another. What if he could not accept it? What would happen to Laurence?

A small breeze rippled through the open window. It was hot, even for July. She loved summer, when the light lingered long into the evening. She stared out at the fountain, its endless splashing audible. A memory of Nicholas teaching her how to swim floated through her mind. Would she ever feel so free with him again?

She'd actually found some peace during her visit with Sophia. The distance had removed her from the undercurrent of drama. Unable to suppress the emotional turmoil, she'd finally released a mass of pent-up frustrations.

Sophia had embraced Catherine as she'd sobbed her sorrow and anger. She'd held nothing back, had told Sophia everything. When Catherine had calmed, she'd feared Sophia's censure.

Catherine shouldn't have doubted her friend. Sophia's face had conveyed no judgment, only concern.

"*Mia amica,*" she'd murmured, brushing Catherine's hair from her face. "You are the noblest woman, besides my mother, that I have ever known." Sophia had leaned in and kissed Catherine's forehead. Sophia's amber eyes had darkened, glimmering with tears.

"While I understand why they asked it of you, it was not right that Daniel and your brother requested such a sacrifice." She'd lifted her fingers to Catherine's lips when she'd tried to defend them. "Hush. I have listened to you. Now you must listen to me.

"I have learned much in this life, *mia amica.* Too much, I feel some days." She'd chuckled, but there had been real pain in her eyes. "There is no recourse for you but truth. It can do no more damage than has already been wrought. It may do some good. The truth may not make us free, but we cannot be free without it. Profound, is it not?" She'd laughed lightly. "I read that somewhere."

Sophia had nurtured Catherine throughout the few days. They'd eaten, walked, talked. Sometimes, they'd simply sat quietly together, each with a book in hand. Although, Catherine had not read a word. She'd been too busy considering how to tell Nicholas the truth. When she'd left, Sophia had hugged her, then held her by the shoulders, her smile beaming and encouraging. "Now go home to that man you dreamed of for four long years, and *diamine*, give me a happy ending!"

Home. Would Catherine ever consider this mausoleum her home? It seemed impossible. She watched a robin on the edge of the fountain, more shadow than bird in the fading light. It dipped its beak into the waters, then pecked at its feathers, executing its bathing ritual, its cleansing. That was what she needed. In truth, she needed full ablution.

Once again resolute, she turned from the window and strolled to the door. Fredericks carried a food tray, heading toward the stairwell.

"Fredericks?"

A smile lit his face. "Yes, my lady?"

"Is that His Lordship's dinner?"

"It is."

"Then he is up and about. Feeling well?"

"Yes, my lady. Last I saw him."

"Then carry on. I shall come and keep him company during his meal."

She followed Fredericks to the door that was discreetly hidden behind the stairwell. She braced herself—the lion's den. She should have faced the man long ago. Fredericks opened the door and stood aside.

"Just lay it on the table." The old hand waved in dismissal.

Despite the warm evening, a small fire burned. Lord Woodfield sat before it, a blanket pulled over his knees, a paper resting on his lap. He stared at the flames, his sagging skin sallow in the dim light. She thought of his once strong profile, his daunting presence. Sympathy welled, but she pushed it back down. He was no melancholy hound dog despite his appearance.

"Let me, Fredericks," she said, loud enough for Lord Woodfield to hear.

"As you wish, my lady." Fredericks smiled in encouragement before he disappeared, closing the door softly.

Setting down the tray, she took the chair on the other side of the small table and stared at the fire, not knowing how to start, not knowing where to start. Perhaps she should let him begin. A spark snapped. She waited, trying not to clasp her hands, focusing on suppressing the urge to wring the stress through them. A slow hiss fizzled from the grate.

"Come to gloat, gel?" he finally said, not bothering to glance in her direction.

Anger, long simmering, began to boil. "Gloat, sir? Gloat?" The man was insufferable. "What am I reveling in, Lord Woodfield?"

He turned to her, his breath rattling in his chest. She might have felt concern, but he was glaring at her, his pale-blue eyes piercing, his mouth drawn in disdain.

"You've managed to catch an earl after all."

An earl? An earl! Did he honestly believe that was all she cared about? That Nicholas would someday be the earl? Yes, of course Lord Woodfield did. He had offered her money, after all, believing wealth and position were her goals in life.

"Yes, I have caught myself a fine earl. An earl who cannot bear the sight of me. An earl who wishes he were back on the continent, facing the enemy rather than sitting across the dinner table from his wife. An earl who believes I have betrayed him in the worst possible way."

The lines around his mouth deepened, but his face showed no empathy. Blast this man! He was the head conductor of her misery, yet he scowled at her as though she herself had orchestrated the demise of her dream.

This man had manipulated them all. He'd demanded Daniel marry. Lord Woodfield had offered her money to make that happen. She'd not said yes to Daniel because of money. Yet despite the fact that she had refused Lord Woodfield's insulting offer, he'd treated her like a paid whore. How dare he!

"Yes, let me rejoice in this most excellent of situations," Catherine said. "I have lost my brother, my best friend, and my only love. I get to wander this crypt of a house, remembering it was once filled with hope, but it will never be again. Let us invite the neighbors over to celebrate. We can raise our glasses of fine champagne and toast to a future that will not be."

"Sarcasm does not become a young lady. And you will hold that tongue while you live under my roof. I am still the earl, and this is my house, and you best not be forgetting that." He shifted in his seat to stare her down, his cheeks mottled with anger, his threat lingering in the air.

"Or what, sir? Or what? You'll tell Nicholas?"

The color drained from his face, and the light left his eyes. Sympathy warred with anger. No! She could not let this man win. It was untenable and could go on no longer.

"Lord Woodfield, you tell him, or I will."

"Tell me what?"

She bolted from the chair. Nicholas's face was ashen against the storm brewing in his eyes. How much had he heard? He took a step toward her, holding her gaze.

"Tell me what, Catherine? About these?" He shook a fistful of papers at her.

"I know not—"

"You—know—not?" He advanced until he stood before her, nostrils flaring. "How dare you," he growled. "You knew all. And told me none."

The rage that had bolstered her seeped away, and her courage withered. The crumpled foolscap said it all. He knew the truth. The pain in his eyes stood testimony to that.

"Nicholas." She reached for him, but he recoiled from her, redirecting his anger toward his father. "And you! You play the role of fragile, old man well, but you've not changed. You are as controlling as you have ever been."

"You watch your mouth, boy." Lord Woodfield's face was bright red, but his heart was not in it. The man seemed to shrink before his son's fury. "I have only done what needed to be done. Your brother drove me to it. He was...unnatural." His shoulders caved, and he shifted back toward the fire, shutting them both out.

Nicholas stared at his father's profile for a long moment, then turned to her. She wanted to weep at the desolation haunting his eyes, wanted to touch him, to soothe him. Instead, she stiffened, waiting for the final blow. She knew him too well to believe that the truth would set them free.

"How could you?" His voice was gruff, but he stood ramrod straight, a military man facing the enemy.

"Nicholas." She stopped herself. She refused to plead. If he did not understand the depths of her love, then so be it. "How could I not?"

His gaze lingered, washing her with his pain. Then, without a word, he walked past her and out the door.

CHAPTER TWENTY-THREE

There is occasions and causes why and wherefore in all things.

—Shakespeare, *Henry V*

NICHOLAS GASPED FOR air, leaning back against the door. It was true. All of it. Daniel had not been writing fanciful fiction. He had been confessing. To Nicholas. His stomach churned, and he pushed away from the door.

He had known men in the army like this. But not his brother. Surely to God, not his brother. He could not reconcile the playmates of his youth with reality. He'd thought his father would deny the truth, but he hadn't. It lay blatant, splayed like a whore at a brothel and equally disgusting.

He paused beneath the staircase. *God's blood!* He leaned against the cool stairwell, trying to calm his body so he could mount the stairs and get away from the truth that lay behind him. In front of him. All around. He straightened, grabbed a vase, and slammed it against its pedestal. Shattered fragments flew. The piece that remained in his hand had sliced his palm, and blood dripped on the floor, marring the white marble.

"Master Nick?" The voice was quiet, unobtrusive, and entirely welcome.

"Fredericks." Suddenly drained of all emotion, it was all Nicholas could manage.

Fredericks pulled the handkerchief from his inside pocket and wrapped it around the cut. "Come on, son. Let's get you to your room."

⟫⟫⟫⟪⟪⟪

CATHERINE LEFT LORD Woodfield as she had found him, staring morosely at the fire. She had tried to provoke him, to see if he would speak with Nicholas, but he'd refused to respond. Frustrated, she'd finally given up.

A young maid quickly stood when Catherine exited Lord Woodfield's chambers.

"My lady." She bobbed, a rag in hand.

"You're working late tonight," Catherine said, taking in the scene. The pedestal stood empty with a bucket of broken china at its base. Had Nicholas run into it in his hurry to get away from them?

"Not so late," the girl said, drawing Catherine's attention back to her. "I'm always ready to care for my lord," she said, adding, "no matter the hour."

"Thank you. I have no doubt Lord Woodfield appreciates it."

She left the girl to her task and moved to the entrance hall, staring up the stairs. He was in his chambers. He was hurting. She wanted to go to him, to ease the ache. An ache she herself had nursed alone. But he didn't need to heal the wound by himself. She could tend to him. Did he want her to?

Ignoring the stairs, she headed down the hall, toward the kitchen, too unsure of her welcome to head up straightaway. She needed to gather her wits. Nan would help her figure it out. She always did.

Nan took one look at her, wiped her hands on her apron, untied it, and laid it over the back of a chair. She sat before the fire and picked up her knitting. Catherine hesitated.

"Come, child. Sit with me. Just like old times."

Gratefully, she took the other chair. Nan's needles clacked rhythmically, calmingly. The world turned, life went on, and Nan's knitting remained ever constant. Catherine closed her eyes, listening to the soft clicking, remembering the eternity of years she had done so in her life. Where would any of them be without their Nan?

"A cup of tea, lass?"

"Not tonight. I but needed to see you."

Nan laid aside her wool and stared at Catherine intently. "He knows the truth."

Catherine fought tears and nodded.

"It is for the best. You know that, love."

Nan reached out, her warm hand covering Catherine's cold one. She could only nod again in response.

"A man hurt is a wounded animal. He must be tended. While it may be fraught with danger, when he is healed, you will have his loyalty for life." Nan squeezed her hand. "Have no doubt, lass, he loves you. He has loved you for too long for that to be extinguished because of your brothers' folly."

Catherine stood.

"That's my girl. Go remind him about the gold he mined long ago."

Nan. Catherine's champion. A champion of them all.

She leaned in and kissed Nan's cheek. "I love you, wise, old woman."

Nan's gnarled hands cupped her cheeks. "And I, you, lass. And I, you."

NICHOLAS RELAXED AGAINST the counterpane. After much fussing, Isaac had finally left. Still feeling overheated and clammy, Nicholas lay back against the pillows, flexing his hand. The cut was shallow and had stopped bleeding. Where to from here?

Neither Catherine nor his father had denied his accusation. Where the *hell* to from here?

A light tap sounded at the door. When Fredericks realized Nicholas had not eaten since the morning, he'd said he would bring up a small plate. Perhaps this fog of disorientation would lift with a little replenishment.

"Enter," Nicholas said.

A dark-haired girl paused in the doorway, staring at him. Well, not exactly at him. At a certain part of him. The heat of embarrassment warmed his cheeks, and he flicked the edge of the coverlet over his lap. *Damn.* He had thought Fredericks was bringing the food. Nicholas must mention to the man not to send maids to his room for service.

"My lord?" She seemed to hesitate, a slight flush climbing her cheeks.

"On the table by the window…" He faltered. She looked familiar, but he couldn't recall her name. He must add to his ever-growing list of things to do to familiarize himself with all the household staff.

"Kate, my lord. Kate." She set the tray on the table, then sauntered to the side of the bed. "Is there anything else, my lord?" She traced the curve of her lip with her tongue.

He remembered her now. She was the chit from his wedding night, and it was clear, once again, what she was offering. His cock twitched in response. Those were long, lonely years on the continent, and there'd been little respite on the home front, so he could not blame the poor, neglected thing. It would be so easy to bury all his pain in her. But this was not what he'd waited for. He had not abstained for four years to end up demeaning himself by dallying with the help.

"No. Thank you…Kate. That will be all. For now. For always."

She frowned, petulance painting her face. "Are you sure, my lord?"

She placed a knee against the bed and reached beneath the

cover, stunning him with her audacity when she grasped his cock and pulled its length, with an experience reflected in her knowing expression. But he had stayed the hands of many a whore on the continent.

He covered hers with his. "I am sure."

"I…uh…apologize for interrupting…" Catherine stumbled over her words, her face ashen, her hand on her chest. "…my lord." She turned and disappeared into the sitting room.

He wrenched the girl's hand from his crotch, staring as the door closed. *Bloody hell!*

"Get out." He pushed the girl from the bed. "Get out now." He needed to go to Catherine.

The girl's eyes lit with excitement. "Oh, but, my lord, I can pleasure you far better than your—"

"Wife? My *wife*, you little fool! *Your* mistress!"

She grinned. "As I could be yours, my lord."

The girl moved quickly, pushing the cover from his waist, exposing his failing cockstand. Her tongue pursued its length. He froze in disbelief. Cold anger shivered down his spine, and he grabbed her mobcap, hair and sundry clasped in his fist, lifting her away. She reached for his hand, trying to lessen the pull, her eyes wide in shock.

"Get out of this room. Get out of this house. If ever I see your face again, I will bring you before the magistrate for solicitation." He wanted to fling her across the room. Instead, he willed each finger to release its grip.

She rubbed her head, anger sparking from her dark eyes. "Oh, my lord, I so hope you do. For there is much I should like to share with the magistrate."

"Get out!"

At last the chit heeded the command and headed for the exit. The light from the hall spilled softly into the room as she opened the door. She wheeled around and glared at him. "I shall leave this house. But make no mistake, sir, if I do not receive a good reference and severance"—malice darkened her eyes, although her sneer softened—"I myself will seek out the magistrate," she finished almost sweetly.

For the third time this night, a door clicked closed, the sound echoing ominously in the room.

CHAPTER TWENTY-FOUR

Wisely and slow; they stumble that run fast.

—Shakespeare, *Romeo and Juliet*

CATHERINE FELL TO the floor, pulling out the chamber pot just in time. She had not eaten since breakfast, so there was little relief in the dry heaves. Her arms wrapped around her waist, she sat rocking. Nicholas had been…he was… She could not finish the thought. She'd believed they could bridge the gulf, but it seemed she was wrong. He did not need her in any way.

Pain ripped across her stomach, and she toppled onto her side. The dank smell of the wool rug mixed with the stale smell of the pot that sat inches from her nose. How had it come to this? That he could hold another when she was but a door away? He knew the truth, knew she had not abandoned him for love of Daniel. At least, not the kind of love he had presumed. Yet he allowed another woman into his chambers. To…to… She pulled her knees tight to her chest.

She needed to get away, far away, from him. But she was his wife now. Would always be. Although, he'd made it clear in the past few weeks that he did not need her by his side, and it would now seem, he did not even require her in his bed. Her last hope of a hold on him had disappeared with those lusty ministrations by the maid.

He did not need her. Did not want her. She could not undo the marriage, but she refused to sit idly by and suffer endless humiliation. Let him keep a slew of doxies. She would not stand witness to it. There was still someone who loved her, someone who would care that she lived, felt, hurt.

She sat up, glancing at the shadows in the room. A single candle burned on the mantel. She ran her hands down the flimsy nightgown she'd donned, foolishly believing she would be soothing Nicholas this night, that he would have need of her care and body.

Her legs shook when she stood, and she took a moment to steady herself. Numbing calm began to suffocate the hurt. She did not deserve this and would not stand for it. Sudden decisiveness renewed her strength, and she marched to the bellpull. She would not wait; she had no wish to see the smug face of the maid in the morning. *I am always ready to care for my lord, no matter the hour.* If she had not witnessed that spectacle herself, she would not have believed it. While she knew the foibles of others, she had never doubted Nicholas's integrity. It seemed she never really knew any of the men in her life.

Sadie tapped, then entered, glancing around the room, no doubt looking for Nicholas. Catherine was surprised to see her so quickly. She must not have settled in for the night, for she was in full dress.

"I was just about to have a warm milk with Cook," Sadie said by way of explanation, straightening her cap. She spotted the chamber pot, and her eyes narrowed. She darted to Catherine's side. "Oh, Miss Baring…my lady…what ails you?"

Catherine fought the urge to surrender to a sympathetic ear, but this could not become the gossip of the servants. At least, not through her. No doubt that maid would be busy spreading rumors.

"I'm not myself and have a strong desire to return home. To be with my father."

If Sadie was shocked, she did not show it. "I will see every-thing ready for the morning."

"No. Now."

This time, Sadie could not hide the surprise.

"Please help me get dressed. You can come back tomorrow for my things."

Sadie moved to the fireplace, lit a candle off the one flickering its meager light, then ducked into the dressing room. Catherine paced, trying to quell any second thoughts.

Sadie reentered with an armful of clothing and laid the pile on the bed. "Are you sure, my lady?"

She could only nod. Half an hour later, they stood in the atrium.

"I shall get Fredericks to get the carriage ready," Sadie said.

"No, we'll walk."

Sadie stared at her, plainly thinking Catherine had lost her mind.

She squeezed the girl's arm. "It will clear my head. I could go through these woods blindfolded. You know that."

Sadie's smile was sad. "Yes, miss, many a night you have wandered it. I thought those days were done."

"As did I." Catherine looked at the imposing front door. Through it lay her past and now, once again, her future. She pivoted and headed down the hallway, toward the kitchens. "Let us say goodbye to Nan. I cannot leave here without a word to her."

Nan still sat in the chair before the embers in the grate, her knitting resting on her lap, the soft sounds of her breathing filling the empty room. A lone candled flickered on the table, soon to extinguish in the puddle of wax. Catherine could not wake the old woman. She worked so hard and deserved her rest. Catherine could not resist a light kiss against Nan's hair. Nan always smelled of fresh bread. Catherine would miss her, but she could visit discreetly. She blinked back tears.

"You be careful out there in the dark."

Catherine covered Nan's hand with her own. "I will. I'll be back to see you."

"He loves you, child. Don't doubt that."

She pressed Nan's hand to her cheek. "As I love you, Nan. Thank you." She could say no more or her tears would spill over.

It was a warm night and the quarter moon exceptionally bright. Neither she nor Sadie said a word, the soft sounds of their footfalls blending in with the noises of the night. The walk through the woods was, as expected, uneventful. Catherine had spent countless nights wandering through their lands without fear. Quite the contrary. The darkened forest always brought her peace, so she was reasonably calm again as she approached the doors of Stratton Hall. Here she was safe. Here she was truly loved. Sadie pushed open the door, and they stepped inside, trying not to disturb anyone.

"I shall go up and ensure your bedding is fresh," Sadie said, taking Catherine's shawl and bonnet and heading through the doors, toward the stairs.

Catherine moved into the old hall, drawn, as always, to the buck who held dominion over the room. "Well, what say you, old man? Gloating, are you? Did you know it from the start? Know that I was a green lass in love with a fantasy?" He said nothing, his shape barely visible in the moonlight shining through the windows. "Come on. Nothing to say at all? About the fool who loved a man who…" She choked, unable to finish.

"Catherine?"

Her father's silhouette stood in the doorway, blocking the light from the hallway beyond.

"Catherine?" he repeated, his baritone voice deep with concern. The dark shape shifted, and his arms opened wide.

"Papa," she cried, running into his embrace, his strong arms enveloping her, wrapping her in love. Love she needed so desperately.

"Oh, kitten. Hush now, hush." He brushed her hair with kisses. "You're home now."

She relaxed in his arms and released the flood of tears. Home. Just not the home of her dreams.

CHAPTER TWENTY-FIVE

Anger is like a full-hot horse, who being allow'd his way, self-mettle tires him.

—Shakespeare, *Henry VIII*

NICHOLAS WAS DUMBFOUNDED. He'd just been threatened by a maid. Was this to be Daniel's legacy? Surely Daniel had not been so indiscreet as that? His letters indicated he'd chosen to abide by his father's wishes and not live beyond the pale. The chit was guessing. Or simply grasping at straws. Nicholas felt sure of it. The audacity! He ran a hand through his hair. *Damn.*

He swung his legs around and slipped off the bed but stopped short of going through the sitting room door. What had Catherine seen? Stupid question. Enough. Enough for her to fumble and leave. He could easily imagine what the scene had appeared to be. Why had the chit chosen now? Chosen him? He doubted Daniel had ever encouraged it. His father? Nicholas cringed at the thought. The man might be many things, but a lecher he was not.

Nicholas slipped his arms into his robe and jerked at the line of loops. He should go to Catherine, but what was he to say? "I'm sorry you saw a maid fondling my cock"? "I'm sorry you have not been doing the same thing"? He groaned and sat back down on the edge of the bed. "I'm sorry you did not trust me enough to share Daniel's truth"? His head ached. He didn't know how to fix it. Any of it.

A rap sounded on the hall door. Surely the girl was not so bold as to try to come back? Well, she would not regain entrance into his chambers. He jumped off the bed and marched to the door before opening it abruptly.

Fredericks lowered his hand, obviously about to knock again. "My lord, I do apologize for disturbing you—"

Fredericks suddenly stumbled to the side. "My good sir! You were to—you cannot just—"

"Langdon!" Nicholas cut off Fredericks's angry sputtering, his own grin reflected on the face of the stout man who had just boldly shoved Fredericks to the side.

"Sinclair!" Langdon reached out and grabbed Nicholas's hand, pumping his arm up and down. "It's right good to see you, Sinclair, that it is!"

The weight of the last twenty-four hours slipped from Nicholas's shoulders. An ally at last.

A not-so-discreet cough interrupted his elation.

"Fredericks. All is well. This is my man, Langdon." Nicholas turned to the ruddy, freckle-faced, red-haired man, who beamed in pleasure. "Langdon. This is Fredericks."

Langdon stuck out a hand. "Ah, the man who taught Sinclair how to be one. It's a pleasure to meet you." He grinned toward Nicholas, then back at Fredericks. "You did a good job, old man. That you did."

Fredericks blushed at the praise. The man actually flushed a bright red, but his milky blues twinkled, and he surely fought a smile. "A pleasure to meet you...Langdon. I will leave you two to your reminiscence."

"Come, come." Nicholas ushered Langdon into the room.

His friend shuffled in a circle, whistling slowly through his teeth. "Well, Sinclair, you've not done badly for yourself. Thought I'd die of exhaustion coming up that grand staircase." He chuckled, throwing his cap on the table. "The old man wanted me to wait downstairs, but I declined his fine offer. Told him I'd seen you in your clothes as well as out of them and did not care what state you might be in." His expression grew serious. "That was unless you were otherwise occupied." He held out his hand again. "I understand congratulations are in order. You waited a long time, sir."

Nicholas's newfound elation burst, a balloon deflated. He had waited a long time and, after this day's events, may remain forever in the wings of his own life. Things were certainly not unfolding as he'd planned. But then, neither had the road been smooth for Langdon. The man's lower sleeve was pinned up neatly, hiding the stump beneath the rumpled jacket.

"So you fought the devil and won." Nicholas could not resist a grin, despite the drag of personal despair. This man had stood at his side during the foulest of times, cleaning his clothes, tending his wounds, talking him back to sanity.

Langdon waved his stump, sparring like a pirate. "The fiend did not stand a chance." He chuckled, then suddenly sobered, his hazel eyes darkening. "Badajoz took all the devil's energy. He had none left to chase me down."

Nicholas's rising spirit was now fully dampened. Badajoz had taken its toll on all good men. War was a burden to bear, but what had happened after the success of conquering that town was too dark for a man's soul to hold. He pushed it away. "Langdon, I am glad to see you whole."

The man waved his vacant sleeve again.

"Well, almost whole," Nicholas amended, throwing his arm around Langdon's shoulder in a quick embrace, glad to feel solid flesh beneath his arm. Langdon had surely won his health back. It was too warm to light the fire, but Nicholas lit a few more candles on the mantel after pushing Langdon into a chair. Moving to the side table, Nicholas poured two hearty glasses of cognac. Tonight why pretend in increments?

Langdon sniffed appreciatively, then threw back half the contents, sighing in response. "Fine stuff, Sinclair. Mighty fine."

Nicholas sipped, the fiery liquid burning a smooth path. He had never shared a drink with Langdon. Until Badajoz. Then they had obliterated reality together. Langdon waiting for someone to tend to his wound, and Nicholas trying to block out the grotesque injustice happening all around them. They had toasted each other, believing they would never sit together again.

He shook his head. That was then; this was now.

"I'm happy to see you well, my friend," Nicholas said.

Langdon looked at him over the brim of his glass, then lowered it. "Yet I sense it is not happiness you are feeling." The glass rested in his lap as he eyed Nicholas. "Tell me, Sinclair. My lord," he corrected with a crooked grin. "What has you so down in the mouth when the world has unrolled at your feet?"

Where to begin? Should he begin? Langdon had pulled him from carnage when others had seen him as a forfeit of war. Langdon had nursed Nicholas back to health, had stood by him through each and every skirmish. They had shared their childhood memories, their dreams. Langdon was here not because he had to rejoin his officer but because he wanted to be here. Nicholas pushed aside doubt and shared everything that had happened since returning to Woodfield. Everything, including the debacle an hour ago. It felt good to tell someone the naked truth.

Langdon tossed the long-held remnants of cognac and stood. "Well, my lord. I do believe you have more important business to see to than this old soldier." He saluted. "I shall go find your man Fredericks and see where he would like me to park this tired carcass."

Nicholas stood, grinning at Langdon, who was swaying before him. Not a man used to drink, Langdon wobbled precariously.

"We'll sort you out in the morning. Take my bed tonight." Nicholas paused, contemplating the adjoining door, finally ready to take action. "I don't intend to use it."

Langdon saluted again. Nicholas strode to the exit, stepped into the shared sitting room, and pulled the bedroom door closed.

Darkness blanketed him. No candle sat aflame, no fire burned. No light shone beneath the opposite door either. He moved cautiously toward it, his heart beating a staccato rhythm. He did not deserve her, but he wanted her anyway. He hoped she still wanted him.

He knocked lightly on the door, pressing his ear against the panel. Silence. He stayed like that for a full minute, but there was no stirring. Perhaps she was sound asleep? He pushed open the door. The room sat in utter blackness. He moved cautiously toward where he knew the bed lay until his legs made contact with the frame. Then he stood perfectly still, sure she would sense his presence, register his breathing. His own breath whispered back at him.

Carefully he climbed the bed. He did not want to startle her or even disturb her. He just longed to be near her. If he could curl up close, he would deal with the explanation in the morning. Gingerly stretching out on the bed, he reached across, anticipating contact. His hand fell to the coverlet.

He inched toward the center of the bed. Nothing. He sat up, patting the mattress as if she was a small animal that might be balled up in some corner. She was not here. *Where the hell was she?* He knew the answer before he finished the thought. She'd left him. She'd gone to Stratton Hall. He lay down and pulled his knees to his chest, hugging them tightly. Gone. As she should be. As he deserved.

HE LAY STARING at the ceiling as dawn lightened the room. The night had been long, but he was now resolved. He would fetch Catherine. She had no right to hold last night against him after all her lies. His transgression was an unfortunate circumstance; her offenses were blatant and numerous. They must put it all behind them and make the best of it.

Throwing back the cover, he hopped off the bed and pulled his robe tight. He wanted no more incidents. He strode through the sitting room, pausing at his own door. He leaned his head against the frame, fighting a rush of defeat. Why was it all so complicated? If he didn't love her…

He pushed open the door just as Langdon was closing the one to the hallway. He grinned when he caught sight of Nicholas.

"I just chased some coxcomb pecking at your door. He wanted to attend to your toiletries. Told him I'd be seeing to you from now on. He said he would hear it from His Lordship's mouth. I told him he would hear it from my fist if he didn't leave straight away. He puffed up like a peacock but scurried quick enough." His chuckle faded. "You didn't want the dandy to stay, did you?" He ran his hand through his hair, the red bristle standing on end. "Sinclair?"

"She's gone."

"She's—?" He brushed across his crown again, understanding dawning and widening his eyes. "Oh, I see." He dropped his hand. "It's sorry I am, Sinclair. Sorry."

Langdon's pity jolted Nicholas from his misery, and he shook his head. He was decided. She was his wife, and she would live under his roof whether she wanted to or not. "As am I, Langdon, but she will return."

"Right, sir. Let's get you dressed, then."

Efficient as always, Langdon reached for the clothes he had already laid out. He grabbed the breeches, holding them awkwardly as Nicholas stepped into them. Nicholas bit back impatience at Langdon's slowness. *The man is learning how to work without a hand, for God's sake!* After successfully shrugging into the shirt Langdon held, Nicholas began tucking it in as Langdon grabbed a freshly ironed slab of cotton. He stood there staring at it, his brow furrowing in frustration.

"Never mind, Langdon. I hate the damn things anyway." Nicholas sat down and pulled on his Hessians before the poor man realized that that too was beyond his range of abilities now.

Langdon threw the cloth on the chair, then stared at Nicholas's boots, his face crimson with anger. "Sinclair. Sir. I do believe I am of no use—"

"No use? Because you can't tie a piece of cloth or pull my boots up?" He stood. "Get a grip, man. You were never just a valet. You know that. I need you for far more important things than holding my trousers."

Langdon's brow creased in doubt, but the blush receded from his cheeks.

"Not saying I don't want you about to make sure those trousers are ready. Just don't need you to be holding them." Relieved to see the man's shoulders relax with a slight chuckle, Nicholas put his arm around his comrade, his ally—his friend. "Get Fredericks to show you around. Tell him you'll be my man in all things." He released him and strode to the door. "Oh, and make sure you drop into the kitchen and let yourself be known to the cook. Nan is the most important person to have on your side in this house. Not to mention she makes the best biscuits."

He left Langdon and headed down the stairs.

Fredericks paced beneath them. "Brownlee awaits you in your study."

Now? The man chose now to return to the estate? Unfortunately, Nicholas could not ignore the steward; the estate needed tending. Irritated, Nicholas marched to the study. Anger ignited at the sight of one of Daniel's letters in the man's hand. Nicholas had carelessly left the pile on his desk.

"Brownlee?" He hoped his look was as withering as his voice. He stared pointedly at the man's hand.

Brownlee had the civility to flush in embarrassment. "Sinclair...my lord. I thought to tidy while I waited." He laid the paper on the desk.

Nicholas moved forward and scooped up the pile of letters. "I have needed your presence, Brownlee." He pulled open a drawer and dropped the papers into it. "It seems it is a condition of stewardship to be available for discussion and planning of the estate." He closed the drawer slowly, anger still simmering. This man had let the land and its tenants fall by the wayside. "Yet you have been noticeably absent."

"I have been weighing my decision to return at all." Brownlee shifted uncomfortably, then straightened, his shoulders visibly tightening, a growing defiance hardening his expression. "I returned only because you are now the person I would answer to."

"As opposed to my father?"

"As opposed to your brother. I work for men." Brownlee's nostrils flared like a bull's when ready to charge.

"What the hell does that mean?" Nicholas asked, although he was certain he understood the implication.

Brownlee narrowed his eyes pointedly at the closed drawer. "Do not pretend, Sinclair, that you are unaware of your brother's…penchants."

Nicholas fought for restraint. The vein at his temple pulsated, and he rubbed it, trying to calm the growing storm. "No, sir, I do not believe I am." He wiped a hand across his eyes. This could not be happening. "Please—" He paused, trying to swallow the rising fury. "—enlighten me."

The man had guts; Nicholas had to give him that. Brownlee did not back down. In fact, he seemed even angrier than Nicholas.

"It is my position, sir, to edify you with regards to all that goes on." Brownlee's nostrils flared. "While you have been defending our country, your brother has been…" His voice trailed, and he appeared uncertain for the first time.

"Has been what? You only work for men; be a man." Nicholas's voice was far more placid than he felt.

"Busy with your wife's brother." Brownlee made a rude gesture as Nicholas stepped toward him. "I do not work for sod—"

Nicholas heard the splinter of bone before he could stop his fist. Brownlee fell to the floor, the blood spurting from his nose, spraying across Nicholas's clean trousers.

"Get out." He calmly wiped at his legs, only smearing them

further. What a mess. He pulled his shirt from his trousers and wiped his bloodied hands on the cotton. "Get out before I truly lose my temper."

Brownlee haltingly stood, holding his nose, his eyes blazing. "I will see that all know what goes on behind these doors. Perhaps the brothers Woodfield are painted with the same brush!"

Nicholas seized Brownlee's lapels, lifting him off the floor, surging forward until he slammed the man's back against the wall. The echo of the contact rippled down Nicholas's spine with satisfaction. "Any accusation you make, I will ensure it reflects upon you. Think of me as your mirror. Your very powerful, moneyed mirror." He knocked the man's head against the paneling, then dropped him before the rage surging through his blood could encourage more. He took a deep breath. "Get out of this house. Get off my lands. I'd better not hear a whisper of your name again."

Brownlee staggered to his feet, bracing himself against the wall, glaring at Nicholas. "Money doesn't buy clemency for everything, Sinclair." Brownlee turned and stumbled out the door.

Nicholas weaved across the room and grabbed the edge of the desk, holding on until the room stopped spinning. *Dear Lord.* Would it ever end? He moved around the desk and opened the top drawer. There lay the key. This was not a house of confidences. It had never harbored secrets. There'd never been a need to securely store anything from prying eyes. He locked the drawers. He should burn the letters. He shuddered at the thought. Daniel's last words going up in flames. Words meant only for Nicholas. From his brother, who'd trusted him. He pocketed the key and strode from the room.

Fredericks, standing at the ready outside the study, gasped. Nicholas wondered how much he'd overheard.

"Sir, you're bleeding."

"Not my blood, I assure you Fredericks. No worries, not

mine." He had no time for Fredericks's fussing.

"Brownlee…?" Fredericks asked.

"The man is to gather his things and leave at once. Tell him a stipend will follow only if he agrees never to set foot on this property again. And remind him that if I ever hear he has so much as mentioned Woodfield Park in passing, he will pay."

"Yes, my lord. With pleasure."

Thankful to have someone he trusted ensure Brownlee's departure, Nicholas headed back up the stairs for a change of clothes. He had no patience nor time for the likes of Brownlee. He needed to find Catherine and make something right in his world.

CHAPTER TWENTY-SIX

Truth hath a quiet breast.

—Shakespeare, *Richard II*

THE BUCK STARED blankly back at Nicholas. It stood witness in this hall. Catherine had once told him she confided in it all the time. Too young to appreciate the trust in sharing her secret, he'd rolled on the ground, laughing at her. Indignant, she'd claimed it was a far better companion than he was and had stomped off. Sadly it seemed she was right.

"My lord." Edwards gestured toward the doorway.

Nicholas moved past Edwards and went directly to the study. Stratton stood by the window, his back to Nicholas. Catherine was not in the room. He swung around to address Edwards. "I expressly asked to speak with Catherine."

Edwards looked pained. "Yes, my lord, you did."

"And I have denied your request…for the moment," came Stratton's voice.

Nicholas swung around and glared at Stratton's rigid back, frustration growing.

"Leave us, Edwards," Stratton said quietly. The door discreetly closed, and Stratton faced Nicholas. Shadows darkened the skin beneath Stratton's eyes, and the lines around them were deeper. It seemed he had aged overnight.

They stared at each other while Nicholas waited for an explanation. Waited for Catherine to come through the door. But it seemed neither was forthcoming. Frustrated, he broke the silence.

"I did not come to speak with you. I came to see Catherine. To bring her home."

"No."

"No?" His anger flared, spiking hot, prickling his cheeks as he fought to keep his voice level. He'd had more than enough today already, and his self-control was hanging by a thread.

"You heard me, Nick."

Heat rushed through his body. The lingering tension from his encounter with Brownlee reignited, and Nicholas's shoulders stiffened in response as he drew up to his full height. He would not cower before Stratton, father-in-law or not.

"She is my wife," Nicholas bit out, wanting to roar and charge.

"For God's sake, Nick, I'll not deny that. Sit down." Stratton's stern posture collapsed as he pointed to the chair opposite to the one he sunk into. He ran a hand over his face. "Come, Nick. Sit. I am not the enemy."

Nicholas complied, a spark of sympathy tempering his anger. How could that be? This man may not be Nicholas's foe, but nor was he on his side. Stratton had colluded with Nicholas's father. Stratton had deceived him alongside Catherine. If he looked the worse for it, well, it was no one's fault but his own.

"I just want Catherine to come home," Nicholas said.

Stratton's green eyes stared intently, so like his daughter's it hurt Nicholas to look into them. "To what?"

What the hell kind of question was that? To him. To her husband. "To me." He managed to maintain a civil tone, but irritation still hummed below the surface.

"You," Stratton repeated, "and your judgment of all that has happened in your absence? Your condemnation of Daniel? Dismissal of *her* brother?"

"So you are fine with Laurence's..." Nicholas's fury sputtered as he floundered, looking for the right word. He respected this man, yet Stratton had knowingly betrayed Nicholas, had condoned unacceptable behavior. Worse, Stratton had allowed his daughter to become party to the inexcusable.

"Of course not. I don't like it. Truth be told, I detest it. But...he's my son." He stared down at his hands, then looked up again, holding Nicholas's gaze. "He's my son, Nick. And Daniel your brother. Both good men with good hearts."

Nicholas could not bear to witness the pain in Stratton's eyes, the plea for understanding. He got up, strode to the side table, and poured himself a brandy without asking. He whirled the contents and lifted it to his nose. *His son. My brother.* He threw the glass at the empty grate, the shattering a violent explosion, enveloped by the ensuing silence. A wave of shame washed over him. *His son. My brother.*

He left the room without a glance at Stratton, without another word, and stood lost in the hallway. What now?

"My lord?" Edwards had clearly heard the noise.

"I would see my wife, Edwards."

"My lord, she left early this morning."

Nicholas's heart plummeted to his stomach, its leaden weight pulling him down. She had left him, truly left him. Remorse entwined with the shame.

"...so I do not expect her back until dinner."

"I beg your pardon?" He held his breath.

"She took a picnic with her, my lord. She always stays away for a good length of time when she does that."

Nicholas exhaled, his spirit soaring erratically, a pendulum swinging to the far side. He could have kissed the man. She had not left. She'd taken a picnic. Nicholas strode to the entrance hall, going directly to the buck. "We both know where she is, don't we, old man?" he said, feeling an odd congeniality with the stuffed animal. Sudden doubt crowded the room. *Please let her be there.*

CATHERINE SAT ON the steps of the folly, leaning back against a pillar. The fragrance of roses tickled her senses, taunting her with the beauty of life. The lake shimmered, incandescent in the morning sun. There was so much for which to be grateful. So many people in this world never knew her comfort or the splendor of her surroundings. Yet she could not seem to draw peace from them today.

She leaned over and pulled at a rose petal, pressing its softness to her nose, closing her eyes as she inhaled its sweet perfume. Where to now? The wind stirred the trees, but no answer moved with it.

"Catherine?"

Nicholas stood at the base of the stairs. His eyes, catching the reflections of the sun and the lake, twinkled a startling blue. Oh, how she loved those eyes. He placed a foot on the bottom step and then paused, his forehead creasing in concern. She could not look away, but she would not help him out. Was there truly anything left to say?

"The girl…," he said, then looked up, taking a deep breath before returning his gaze to hers. "The maid. She was forward…I did not invite…" He ran a hand through his hair. "It was nothing…*hell*…I mean, nothing happened."

She stared past him at the lake, memories rising from its depth, as she digested his words. "We played here so much as children." She could see them there, romping and shouting with no adult to tell them to do otherwise. They had had so much freedom. It had all been so simple then.

"Remember when I was six and the three of you put me in a barrel and told me I was Moses floating down the river? 'Have no fear,' you shouted, 'you will live with royalty!' I cried out when the cask filled and the water reached my chin. Our brothers stood laughing on the shore, but you jumped in, swimming to my side.

You grabbed me as the barrel submerged, treading water, holding up my face. It wasn't until that moment that Daniel and Laurence ceased their snickering enough to realize something had gone wrong. They swam out and made quite the show of saving me." She met his gaze again. "But it was you, Nicholas. It has always been you."

His eyes washed a pale blue, pooling with moisture. Did he feel as she did? The hurt, the longing, the hope?

"You never forgot that moment on the lake," she continued. "You hounded me for years to learn how to swim. I was too afraid. Until the yearning to feel your arms around me out-weighed my fear of the water. Then I allowed you to teach me. But only so you would hold me."

He stood still. Was he appalled by her wanting? By her bla-tant need?

"You are under no obligation," she began.

"Hush," he said, taking the stairs two at a time, then sitting by her side. He grabbed her hand and pressed it to his mouth. "Hush," he repeated.

Her heart pounded relentlessly, suffocating her chest. Did he not want to hear her words? Did he desire conciliation? Or did he just wish to stop her from humiliating herself further?

"I want you, my love," he said.

She melted at the words as he kissed her hand again and again. He pressed it against his heart, staring at her, his gaze penetrating. His eyes darkened, and he leaned in, kissing her with a ferocity that was unnerving and exhilarating. Suddenly nothing mattered but them. Not family, not doubt, and certainly not the maid. She nipped him, wanting to swallow him whole.

He growled and scooped her up effortlessly into his arms before pushing through the doors of the folly. He strode purposefully, smoothly laying her down on a settee. He stood still, staring down at her, pensive and intense. Then he dropped to his knees, grasped her hands, and held them tightly in his. "Tell me, Catherine. Tell me the truth about your love."

She freed a hand, tracing her fingers down his sharp cheek-bone, following the line to the dent in his chin. Her dream. Her man. She replaced her finger with a kiss on his cleft, then lay back against the bolster, drinking him in.

"The truth is I love you. I always have. I always will. God forgive me if it's sinful, but I cannot lie. It is you, Nicholas. It has always been you."

Not a sound followed her confession. Was he regretting her emotion? Did he wish to somehow undo their union? She hated that doubt was swiftly creeping back in between them.

"You unman me," he finally said gruffly.

She sighed in relief as he rose and lay upon her, his weight the comfort she sought. He inhaled deeply, then kissed a path from her neck to her mouth, softly, gently, and oh so tenderly.

He stopped and propped himself up on his elbows. "No more lies between us. Or half-truths. Promise me. Give me your word."

She couldn't give her word. Not yet. She released her breath slowly through her mouth. He deserved her honesty. Full disclosure. It wouldn't serve anyone to hide anything anymore. Her vision blurred. Dear Lord, why did it have to be her to tell him?

"Is it so hard to guarantee?" His voice softened with sadness.

She pushed at his chest, and he shifted, sitting up. She sat beside him, wiping angrily at her tears. Enough. It was time to end all subterfuge. For all their sakes. Where to start?

"I came daily to the folly when you were away. I could feel you here and would know in my heart you were still alive. I knew for certain that were you not well, here is where I would sense it." She might as well start at the beginning. He took her hand in his, squeezing in encouragement.

"I was sitting on the steps here, dreaming of you, when Daniel asked me to marry him," Catherine said.

He stiffened beside her.

"Oh, Nicholas, it was not like you're thinking," she said quickly before she could lose courage to continue. "None of it is like you think.

"Daniel didn't want it nor did he deceive me by pretending he did. He shared with me his deep love for Laurence. I must confess I was not entirely caught off guard. Their affection for one another has always been clear for all to see."

He grunted and shifted.

She ignored his discomfort. "Yes, even to you, if you would but put aside your personal hurt for a moment and think on it. It is not such a stretch to believe they loved as we do."

"It is unnatural—"

She cut him off. She'd heard enough slander about Daniel and Laurence from his father, and she refused to allow Nicholas to become his father's son. "Judge not lest ye be judged," she said quietly.

He did not respond, but he still held her hand in his. That was good, was it not?

"Your father was pressuring Daniel to marry. He selected a fine girl, Isabella Whittington. I've met her. She is lovely, although I'm not sure she knew Lord Woodfield had handpicked her for his son. I think Daniel might have enjoyed her fine spirit." She shook her head. She had thought this too many times. What if Daniel had just agreed to that marriage? Could he have found happiness? But was that not the same as asking her if she could have found happiness with a man other than Nicholas? Once love has been discovered, can it ever be forgotten?

"Daniel had had far too much to drink when your father last approached him and informed him he had made arrangements for Daniel to ask for Miss Whittington's hand. Daniel erred gravely. He told your father of his love for Laurence. Told the earl he would never marry, that your father had best get used to it and resign himself to counting on you, Nicholas.

"Daniel knew that with me, he would not have to fulfill his husbandly duties. And the fact that he wasn't acting as a true husband would never come to light. Still, I refused Daniel that first time. There was too much deceit in the whole concept, and I could not reason beyond my love for you." She looked directly at Nicholas for the first time since beginning the sordid tale, twisting her hand so that she now held his. "I turned him down for love of you." She raised his hand to her mouth, kissing it reverently. "I could not imagine a life without you by my side. Worse, I could not imagine watching you live your life by the side of someone else."

He tried to pull her to his lap, but she resisted.

"No, Nicholas. This story does not continue as you think." If he wished to hold her when all was revealed, then she would revel in his embrace. But she couldn't continue the hurtful tale if he held her.

"Your father summoned me the next day. He asked if I knew that my brother was unnatural."

Nicholas's intake of breath soothed her resurging acrimony. He was nothing like his father.

"I did not dignify the question with a response. I was almost free of his lair when he declared that if I married Daniel, the world need not know what my brother was."

Nicholas stilled beside her but said nothing.

"I was furious. How dare that man!" Her heart beat as though it was happening now. "I told him if the world knew of my brother, then it would know, too, of his son."

"I offer you the position of Lady Woodfield. Marry Daniel, and I'll not say a word." The man's heart had failed him but not his tongue. Wrapped in a blanket by the fire, he was as intimidating as he'd been in her youth. She'd always avoided him. But she refused to cower before him.

"I'll not marry Daniel for a title, my lord."

His nostrils flared, and his cheeks mottled with anger. *"Name your price, gel, name your price."*

"There is nothing that can induce me to marry Daniel. You know fine why that is." She turned once again to leave.

"Nicholas." Woodfield's voice was low, more a growl.

She spun around and faced him. *"Yes, my lord, Nicholas. The son you seem to have forgotten. The man fighting for our country, believing his family is hale and healthy, the man anxious to return to it—" She paused, feeling triumphant. "—and to me, Lord Woodfield. I wait for him even if you do not."*

The old man's face twisted, bitterness making his taciturn expression pinched. "I will expose both boys and ensure Nicholas is blocked from inheritance. I will leave him in penury while you watch the two deviants swing from ropes." His smile was evil, victorious. She was afraid he would hold true to the threat. Dear Lord, what choice did she have?

Nicholas pulled her close, holding her tight to his chest. "Oh, Catherine. I'm so sorry." His voice was hoarse as he stroked her hair. "You should not have been put in such a position." He continued his caresses, brushing kisses across her crown.

She wanted to wallow in his empathy, to lie languid in his arms. He'd requested honesty. No half-truths. She was not yet done.

She pushed from the succor he offered. "There is more."

CHAPTER TWENTY-SEVEN

*When sorrows come, they come not single spies but
in battalions.*

—Shakespeare, *Hamlet*

NICHOLAS FOUGHT HIS rising temper. It was not what Catherine needed. He'd had no idea she had been pressured so. From everyone. His father the coarsest of all, but the others had applied their own, he had no doubt. He now knew why Stratton had allowed the betrothal. It had been too great a gamble to bet on any leniency from Lord Woodfield.

"Catherine," he began but was quickly cut off.

"No. Let me tell you all. I fear my courage will fail if I do not persevere now." Her eyes glistened. "Please."

He swiped his thumbs, wiping away the drops that pooled, then trickled off her eyelashes. He wanted to pull her close and make it all go away, but her eyes begged him to let her continue. Willing his strength to fortify her, he pressed his forehead against hers and then let her go.

She took a steadying breath and continued. "I agreed to marry Daniel. There seemed no other choice, for any of us."

He concurred. It had been an untenable situation. He reached for her hands, holding them tightly. "I understand."

She pulled away a hand and wiped at the tears that sprung

anew. "Thank you," she whispered. "But there's more. Oh, Nicholas, there is so much more."

What more could there be that could be any worse than the transgressions already committed against her? His family had compromised his and Catherine's relationship, not Catherine. She hadn't stood a chance against their powerful influence.

"More," she repeated, the blood leaching from her cheeks, her moss eyes wide.

"Hush, my sweet." He pushed back a stray lock of her hair, caressing the silken strands, luxuriating in the touch he longed for. "I understand."

She straightened, pushing away his hands. He recognized the determination. This was Catherine when she knew what she wanted. This was the strength in her, the woman who could stand by his side in good times and bad. Lord, he loved her. How could he ever have doubted it? He fisted his hands at his side and sat back, resisting reaching out. Letting her speak. It was so hard when he all he wanted to do was hold her close until the last four years disappeared.

"It was no accident." The words hung, suspended, a mist that hovered, then slowly condensed, dripping down his spine. He shivered. It had been deliberate?

"Are you implying murder?" He could not wrap his mind around the idea.

"No, no." She shook her head vehemently. "Laurence didn't kill Daniel. Accidently or otherwise."

He shifted until he could look directly into her eyes and saw only truth. "But? What? How?"

"I'm still not sure what truly happened that day." She touched his hands with hers, and he grasped them. "Laurence was decided. We had talked late into the night, and he refused to allow me to be a pawn in your father's games. I tried to talk him from it, tried to convince him he need not deny his love, just live discreetly, but he was determined to leave for the colonies. He loved Daniel but knew it could not be. He thought time and distance might ease the pain. He sent a message in the wee hours of the morn to Daniel, saying to meet Laurence in the woods."

Her voice caught, and he squeezed her hands, little comfort for the pain that stormed her eyes.

"Shortly after he left, a message arrived from Daniel for Laurence. Edwards was reticent to give it to me, but when I pleaded, indicating Laurence's well-being was at stake, he relinquished the missive. It requested Laurence meet Daniel, that he could not go through with present plans and wished to discuss the future. It was obvious Daniel was not going to pursue the path of matrimony." Guilt darkened her eyes. "Perhaps if I had readily agreed…"

"No!" He squashed the anger that rumbled like thunder in his chest. Catherine had been a victim of men. With the exception of his father, men she'd known and loved. Family. Friends. "No," he repeated more quietly, sick that he had been a party to the persecution.

She smiled, its small shine dissolving quickly, darkened by the cloud of emotion that swept her face. "I knew where they would meet. The same place we found love. Somehow I just knew I needed to get to them."

A visible tremor rushed her body, but he did not intervene, did not stop the tale.

"I heard a shot. It seemed odd, but it was not the first time poachers had been in these woods." She pulled her hands from his and wrapped her arms around her waist, rubbing up and down. It was a warm day, and she could not possibly be cold. Still, he resisted the urge to warm her and, instead, nodded in encouragement. A shot. She'd heard the final moment of Daniel's life.

"I was approaching the folly when another shot rang out. My skin hummed with warning." Her hands moved more quickly on her arms, and she looked past him, over his shoulder, witnessing something he could not see.

"I ran toward it, knowing in my heart something was wrong." She started to rock. "Laurence was cradling Daniel, crying." Her voice caught, and she paused, breathing deeply, while the portrait she painted became vivid in his mind.

"I watched as Daniel's lifeblood seeped into the ground. I watched my brother's twisted torment. His despair as he kissed his dearest love goodbye for the last time." She stopped rocking and stared at him. "They loved, Nicholas. They loved. I do not care what judgment is passed in this world. Their love was as honest and true as, well, as..." Her voice wavered, and she drifted, seeming lost.

"Nothing you have told me explains what happened." He rubbed his forehead, trying to make sense of what she was saying, trying to erase the image of Laurence and Daniel. "I don't understand."

If possible, her look saddened further. "Nor did I." She reached out and touched his arm. "When Daniel had...passed—" She swallowed the sorrow. "—Laurence became frantic. He picked up a pistol and tucked it into his shirt coat. Then he took Daniel's rifle, pointed it to the sky, and shot. He was crying as he said, 'Please, Catherine. For love of us. Do not tell the truth. I could not bear for him to lie at some crossroads, denied by all. Let him leave this world with dignity.'"

Good Lord! Daniel had taken his own life. No wonder the world had been cryptic since Nicholas's return. His brother was steeped in the two worst sins of society. Nicholas's stomach rolled. He couldn't believe it. Perhaps Laurence had—? Nicholas could not even finish the thought but had to ask.

"Laurence?" he started but knew not how to phrase the question. How did he ask the woman he loved if her brother might have killed his?

"He never mentioned the pistol to a soul. I know now that the second shot I heard was him firing his rifle when he knew Daniel was dying. He was adamant that Daniel die of a hunting accident. He fired Daniel's rifle, too, to ensure it appeared as though they were on a hunt." She crumpled before him. "The first shot was...well, it was..."

Daniel taking his own life. *Damn* their father. *Damn* Daniel for being a coward. Rage burst through anguish. And *damn* this woman who let them all do as they would without a thought about herself…or Nicholas. He stood abruptly.

"Excuse me, but it seems I need a moment." He strode from the building, ignoring the gasp that filled the air behind him, bouncing off the chamber walls and echoing hauntingly in his ears. Her pain was a knee to his gut, but his wounds were an agonizing knife to the heart—they reigned now. *Bloody hell.* Daniel had willingly said goodbye to this life. Nicholas choked on rising emotion as he descended the stairs. *Damn you, Daniel. Damn you!*

He took the path back to Woodfield, marching furiously, until he was drawn toward a clearing by the dancing rays of sun on the small glade. Was it here? Was this magnificent corner where Daniel had chosen to end his life? He saw Daniel laughing, falling down with glee, then awkwardly standing, pressing a pistol to his head. He growled, rushing toward the image. It disappeared, disseminating in the sparkle of sunlight. He sank to the ground, wrapping his arms around his updrawn knees. "Daniel. How could you?" He fought the pain, wrestling it until he grew numb. "How could you?" he murmured to the clearing where Daniel had stood, an illusion now gone.

The sun was setting before Nicholas could will himself to leave the meadow. He plodded toward Woodfield. There lay the hypocrisy of his life. Those walls would now be his one day. Would they forever enclose secrets?

He stole quietly into the empty kitchen, like a young lad, and stood beside the smoldering embers. Here a fire always burned. A hearth. His home. He stared at the glowing cinders. Here he had only known tenderness. Acceptance. Warmth. The evening remained tepid, yet he held his hands before the grate, seeking that warmth. He turned to the large trestle table and sank to the bench. How many meals had he shared here with Daniel?

Nicholas laid his head on the table. So weary. So damned

tired.

"Child, it grieves me to see you suffer so." Nan's hand brushed his hair back, and he took comfort like a small child. She pressed a kiss to his head and patted his shoulder before shuffling away.

He remained still, weighed down by worry. By fears. By regret. This was not how life was supposed to unfold. While his path had never been clear, he knew it had never been this. This abomination. This blasphemy of all that should have been.

Nan sat beside him on the bench, the warmth of her old hand enveloping his, her clasp tight. "Lad, stop being angry because your brother disappointed you. There are far greater treacheries than loving another, despite what the law may say." She released her grip and tapped his hand lightly. "Cease your ire and grant him, if not your understanding, the peace of your compassion. It's in you to give, eh? And for heaven's sake, forgive that lass. Absolve her of both brothers' sins."

Sorrow welled. He was embarrassed by his tears, appalled by their ferocity. Nan wrapped her arms around him and pulled him to her chest as she had done years ago. He choked, then clasped her small frame tightly and let wave after wave course through his body, easing his heart and cleansing his soul.

CHAPTER TWENTY-EIGHT

From her shall read the perfect ways of honour.

—Shakespeare, *Henry VIII*

NICHOLAS SHOULD FEEL shame. Instead, he felt purged of all the filth—the years on the continent, Badajoz, Daniel. He'd not wept since he'd been a child. It was both exhausting and euphoric.

He turned at the top of the stairs and headed for his room, pausing at its entrance. Two doors down was Catherine's chamber. Obligation and debt. He rested his forehead against the doorframe. And love. *By God, he loved her.* As did everyone else in this insane spectacle. Yet they'd all abused her affection. How was he ever going to show her that his love was genuine? That he would never again ill-treat her so? Could he possibly convince her to live under this roof again?

He pushed open his bedroom door. Several candles flickered light over Langdon's frown as he pushed to his feet, using his one good arm.

"Sinclair. Welcome home." Langdon eyed him and hesitated. "Is everything well?"

Nicholas shook off the man's concern, having had more than enough empathy from Nan. "All is in perfect accord, Langdon," he lied. "I would like a hot bath and a small bite to eat before I retire."

Langdon saluted and disappeared, and Nicholas sank into the abandoned chair. There was something unnerving about staring at the empty grate. Home and hearth and all that. The black cavern mocked him. Apropos, he supposed.

A parade of men interrupted his dark contemplations. He glanced at the steaming pails, then returned his gaze to the fireplace. He had men at his beck and call. Few people would refuse his bidding now. Catherine hadn't bowed to his father. Luxury would have been hers as Daniel's wife—more than she could ever have hoped for as his. Yet she'd been willing to wait.

"Your bath is ready…Sinclair?" Langdon said.

Nicholas stood, immobile and mute, as Langdon stripped him. Then Nicholas grabbed the robe Langdon offered and strolled naked into his dressing room. He tossed the silk banyan over the chair and sank gratefully into the warmth of the copper tub. Lying back, he closed his eyes.

Time for reconnaissance. Daniel had written to Nicholas of his love. Laurence had been that love. It was not just unacceptable in the eyes of society; to act on that love was a capital offense. Nicholas ducked beneath the water before surfacing with a shake of his head. His father had demanded the unthinkable of Catherine. She had agreed, not for love of Daniel but for love of all of them. Nicholas stared at the crimson jacket that hung in stark contrast to the newer wardrobe, its pride belied by the small tear and the thread that dangled where his badge of honor had once sat.

He slipped under again. Resurfacing, he wiped the water from his eyes and stared once more at his jacket. He'd done what was best for his battalion at Badajoz—secreted them to the side, waiting, despite the cries of battle. Finally, taking advantage of a lull, he'd rallied them forward, and his division had breached the impenetrable wall. He was ashamed of the aftermath, but he was proud of his strategy and his courage during the siege. Proud he'd been decisive, with an eye to the survival of all his men.

He stepped from the tub and reached for the drying cloth, drawing it slowly down his chest. Catherine had faced the same dilemma. Sit idly by or make a decision. She had been strong and decisive, had sacrificed her dreams for the sake of others. No, not for the sake of them but for the very safety of them. He did not doubt she loved him, although she had sacrificed their love on the pyre of their brothers' recklessness. Still, he could not fault her for it. If possible, he loved her all the more for her loyalty and compassion.

He tossed the towel to the floor and strode back into his room.

"Sir? I'll grab your robe," said Langdon.

"Leave it, Langdon. That is all. Go have some dinner with Nan."

Langdon raised an eyebrow but said nothing before obediently leaving. Nicholas stood in the middle of the room, lost for a moment. Then, coming to a decision, he pulled open the door, strolled through the sitting room, and tugged opened the next room's entrance. He paused, taking in the hint of jasmine that lingered, then he pushed the door quietly closed.

If she was truly his, he would abolish this room and demand she share his. He inhaled deeply. He could smell her. She'd made incredible sacrifices for her brother, for his brother, for him; he knew he didn't deserve her. The room was dark, but he was familiar with where the bed sat. If he could lie with her scent upon the sheets, perhaps he could sleep this night.

His knees softly hit the frame. He pulled back the coverlet and crawled in. Stretching out, he rolled onto his side, holding the pillow tightly and breathing deeply. "Oh, Catherine, I love you so," he said quietly, longing for her.

"Nicholas?"

CHAPTER TWENTY-NINE

He is the half part of a blessed man, left to be finished by such as she; and she a fair divided excellence, whose fulness of perfection lies in him.

—Shakespeare, *King John*

THE FOG OF sleep blanketed her body. *Mmm. Nicholas?* He whispered words of love. *I love you too.* A sob caught in her throat. Oh God, how she loved him. If only it were enough.

The mattress dipped. Her heart pounded as she rolled toward the valley. "Nicholas?" She panicked, surfacing to reality, trying to squirm back, but warm arms caught her, pulling her close. She inhaled. Nicholas. She hadn't been dreaming.

She relaxed against his chest. "You came home."

His lips brushed the top of her head. "I thought you might need me." He paused his kisses. Was she too presumptuous? She had needed to be near him, unable to bear leaving him entirely alone this night. Not after all she had revealed.

Pulling her hands free from where they lay trapped between their bodies, she ran them down his stiff back. "I am so sorry. So sorry for everything." And she was. If she could change it, save him from the hurt he had faced since coming home, she would.

He lay still, saying nothing. Then she felt a slight rise in his shoulder blades. She caressed them softly. His chest heaved, and he shuddered. She held him, murmuring her own words of love, grateful he would share such raw emotion with her. It was a tempest quickly spent. He calmed, then rolled onto his back, pulling her with him, tossing the sheet over them. She rested upon his chest, listening to the cadence of his breathing, feeling the stark beat of his heart upon her cheek.

He pushed strands of hair from her face, curling them over her ear. "I have much to apologize for. So many regrets."

Holding back her own rising tide of emotion, she forced herself to lie still. He continued stroking her hair, the methodic rhythm soothing.

"I judged you. I did not trust you. Trust us."

She tried to lift her head, but his hand held her cheek firm against his chest.

"No. Do not grant me clemency. Not yet," he whispered. "For I, too, have confessions to make."

He was silent for a moment before continuing. She knew he was weighing his words, but could not fathom what he was about to tell her.

"I saw many things while at war. Glimpses of heroism. Some regrettable moments. Mostly endless, mind-numbing days of planning and vigilance. And waiting. Until Badajoz." His hand rested heavily upon her head.

"It was a long siege. Weeks of digging trenches in wet, cold weather and planning our attack. I must admit, when the order to advance was finally given, I prayed to the heavens and said my goodbye to you. There seemed no chance of success."

She held her breath. He'd thought he would die. *Thank you, God, for keeping him safe.*

"I watched the slaughter as man after man fell trying to take the walls. I held back my men, though they were angry with me, feeling betrayal of their comrades. It was the longest night of my life." His hand resumed its gentle stroking in stark contrast to the tension she could feel in his body. "Finally I spotted a diminishment on the west wall defenses. We took the wall and helped turn the tide to victory."

She could not imagine the life he'd lived while she'd roamed restlessly, safely, about their two estates. She'd no idea how he could have borne such hardship.

"Nicholas," she began, but he pushed her head back down, holding it close to his heart.

"Langdon was wounded. When success was imminent, I pulled him from the trenches, back to my tent. The surgeon was not sure Langdon would live."

She was surprised by his chuckle, his chest rumbling beneath her cheek.

"I knew he would. The man is driven. And stubborn. Never left my side even when I ordered him to. You'll like him."

His tone changed abruptly, his clasp on her head tensing. "I held Langdon down while they severed his arm. He glared at me while he bit down on the leather, no doubt willing me to hell, but he didn't make a sound. I wanted to weep for his loss, but I could not. If he could be that brave, then so could I."

His gentle strokes resumed, but she could not relax. The pictures he was painting were horrific, and his body was rigid, his tale not yet done. If this was not the worst of it, dear Lord, what was? She caressed him softly. What had her Nicholas seen? Lived through?

"We were triumphant that day. We took Badajoz. I nursed Langdon, feeling vindicated at our success. Until the reports began rolling in." His hand stalled again. "Our men went...insane. There is no other word for it. They sought revenge for their losses. Pillaged the town. It wasn't until later that night, when the cries of women, of children, echoed across the lands, that I realized the depths of their claims, of their depravity. I met with fellow officers, but there were so few of us and so many of them. I offered to go in and try to calm the men. I did but was met with derision and violence. I was lucky not to be torn apart, such was their state of mind. They were mired in grief and drunk on their own survival."

He fell silent.

She didn't know what words to offer, couldn't even begin to imagine how dreadful it must have been. His pain pulsated. He'd already been full of anger and hurt before he'd even crossed the threshold of Woodfield Park. How could she help him find healing? And would it be the remedy for their relationship?

He traced a finger along her jaw, pressing it against her lips, and she kissed it.

"Word of Daniel's death reached me the next day. It was release from hell, this family obligation. At least, I thought it was, until I got home." He snorted. "Hell has been losing you."

She raised her head and shifted forward, feeling for his lips, tracing them with her fingers, then brushing hers softly against them. She pulled back, wishing she could see his face. "You haven't lost me. Have never lost me. I've always been here. Waiting for you."

She leaned in and pulled his bottom lip into her mouth, sucking sensuously, her moan a mixture of mourning for his losses and the joy of tasting him once again. He groaned in response. She pushed the sheet fully off and crawled on top of him, luxuriating in skin upon skin. After Nicholas had left her at the folly, she'd known he would need her. She had not gone back to Stratton. Instead, she'd sent a missive to Sadie, telling her to join Catherine in the morning. There were no amenities in the room. Sadie having followed Catherine's direction strictly, everything had been quickly removed to Stratton Hall. So she'd undressed herself and slid under the covers as God had made her.

Nicholas's hands roved her body, cupping her buttocks, pulling her close. His erection pressed against her abdomen, and she squirmed in response. He groaned into her hair as he thrust against her.

Her body responded. Emboldened by his need and her own, she reached between them, grasping him firmly. This was the game they'd played before he'd left for the continent, and she was familiar with the feel of him in her hand. His silken flesh shifted over his hard length, and she crested it with her thumb. A shiver ran through his body.

"Catherine?"

She couldn't see him but recognized his need and knew for certain he wanted her. She kissed his nose, then licked a slow path down its slope, over its peak, to his lips. She teased with soft kisses before deepening them, pulling at his tongue as though her life depended on it. Her body responded in anticipation.

He shifted quickly, and she was beneath him instantly. He groped frantically, then oddly calmed, leisurely tracing a path, his fingers feeding the flame already ignited. "You want this. You want me."

"Only you, Nicholas. Only you. It's only ever been you. Surely you know that in your heart."

He stilled for a second, then entered her. She bit back tears as he took her. This was how it should be. How she'd dreamed it would be. He was relentless. Emotion and desire overwhelmed her, and she struggled to catch her breath. Finally he slowed, his rhythm methodical and tantalizing, release just out of her grasp.

"You," he said and thrust again. "Kept me sane." He dove deeply. "You." He pushed several times, and her body fought to keep him close. "If I did not have you, I might have lost my mind. Lost my mind and given up like Dan—" He choked, then gave one last forceful thrust.

She pulled him close as he let go. She didn't join him in his release. Instead, she held him tight, keeping him safe, a haven in the storm of his emotions. He lay heavily upon her, his breathing deepening. She stroked his damp back. Nicholas was finally, truly home.

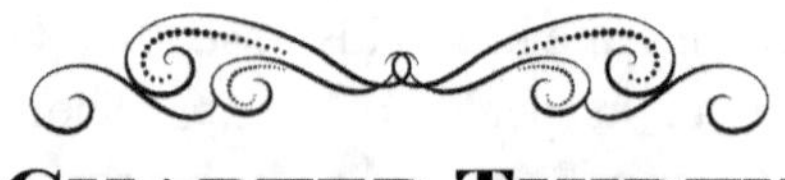

CHAPTER THIRTY

*If after every tempest come such calms, may the winds blow till
they have waken'd death!*

—Shakespeare, *Othello*

S HE LAY ON her back, relishing the weight of Nicholas's leg tossed over her thighs. His steady breaths streamed across her cheek. She fought the urge to caress him, wanting him to continue his slumber so that she might remain wrapped tightly in this bliss. Shapes became furniture as the room lightened. She sighed. She'd been right to come back. He *had* needed her.

For the first time in a long time, her world felt right. Nicholas had forgiven her. No. Much better than that. He understood why she had done what she'd done. They could move forward, begin their lives together.

He stirred, and she could no longer resist touching him, rubbing his back, tracing his spine to the dip at its base.

"Mmm." He arched against her. "Mmm," he murmured again.

Shifting so that she faced him, Catherine was rewarded with his hard length pressing against her thigh. Pushing the dark rebel locks from his forehead, she gazed into those azure depths. "My lord, you are finally fully awake." She glanced down, then back up, grinning at her audaciousness. "Yes, definitely, fully awake."

She laughed, and he growled, rolling her onto her back, nipping at her chin. He peppered her face with kisses, and she giggled with pleasure as he nibbled the end of her nose, then rubbed his nose gently back and forth across hers. He paused and drew back. Holding his weight on his elbows, he stared at her. The intensity of his gaze created an urgent pull in her womanhood.

"And you, my lady? Are you fully awake or are you yet to rouse?"

She lifted her body to his, rotating her hips, the girlish giggles receding. She felt every inch a woman with him now. His pupils dilated, darkening his eyes. Cupping his buttocks, she pushed against him, feeling daring and bold. He reached between them, tracing an enticing path.

"Indeed, my lady. I do believe you are ready to face this morn." He maintained eye contact as he adjusted his position, swiftly entering her until he was firmly nested. He leaned in to rub noses again. "*My* lady."

Tears welled. She couldn't help it. This was what she had longed for.

His smile tightened, then relaxed as understanding lit his face. He knew her so well. These tears were drawn from a well of joy.

He kissed one eye. "My love." He kissed the other. "My life."

She knew he meant it. Her entire being gurgled with happiness, the tears escaping.

"Catherine?" He drew further back, suddenly unsure.

"I'm just so happy. So incredibly content." She wiped at her eyes, laughing at his confusion.

One corner of his lips tweaked in a wry smile, although his eyes were still lined by worry. "Ah. Perhaps this is one of the mysteries of what separates man from woman?"

"There is *nothing* separating this man and woman." She thrust up her hips and rotated indolently.

He cupped her face, stilling. "Nothing?"

She knew what he was asking and couldn't blame him. He

had faced nothing but lies and half-truths. She'd been party to the worst of those. He wanted no shades of gray in the light of day.

"Nothing, my love. Nothing."

He slumped over her, his forehead pressing against hers. "Then I, too, have no bounds on my happiness."

Languidly, leisurely, lovingly, his body began to move, sweeping them both along the path of forgiveness until neither could hold back. Together they surrendered to sweet release. Two became one, as they were meant to be.

⋙⋘

NICHOLAS WAS STARVING. He'd not eaten since breakfast yesterday. Trailing his fingers across Catherine's cheek, he swept back her hair. He loved her hair. Pulling a strand gently, he let its silky length slip through his fingers. A fine claret. His stomach rumbled.

She rolled toward him and kissed his skin. Unbelievably, his body stirred anew at the press of her lips. He pulled her up onto his chest, kissing her crown, luxuriating in the floral scent mingling with that of their lovemaking. She laughed at his grumbling stomach.

This was his Catherine. Free and joyful. She was back. He was back. He grinned down at the top of her head. They were back.

"I fear I missed dinner." He kissed her again.

She looked up at him, her eyes washed to a pale moss in the morning sun. "I'm afraid I did too."

He barked with amusement when her body released a ferocious growl of its own. Setting her aside, he brushed back her locks and kissed that pert, little nose.

"As the great provider, I must find us sustenance." He traced a path down her neck, lingering at her breast, her soft flesh tantalizing. *Lord, but she was beautiful.* Although he wanted to replace his fingers with his lips, he instead reached for the coverlet and tucked it around her. He shifted across the bed and hopped off. "I shall not return until I am able to nourish you fully."

She wickedly perused his naked form. "Oh, I believe you are capable of that without leaving this room."

He leaned across the bed, kissing her quickly, tempted to surrender. "You naughty, little minx." He nipped her nose, then pulled back, stood rigidly straight, and saluted. She rolled onto her side with merriment. Chuckling, he headed for the door to the sitting room. He felt young. He was in love, and the world was once again filled with possibility. He laughed at his own whimsy.

He startled Langdon with his abrupt entrance. Langdon jumped to his feet, the optimistic rise of his eyebrows a reflection of Nicholas's much-buoyed spirits.

"I am ravenous, Langdon." He moved to the bed, where his robe lay, and slipped it on. "As is my lady." He felt like a fool, but he could not suppress a grin. His lady. Finally *his* lady in every way.

"Sinclair!" Langdon's smile mirrored his own. "I mean sir...er...my lord." Red splotches marred his face. "I am right pleased to hear it, my lord." His face blotched further and his brow furrowed as his lips pursed in concentration. "That you are hungry, sir...my lord...and your lady." Then his face split with another grin, the man's eyes twinkling with delight. "Ah, hell, Sinclair, right pleased I am."

"As am I, my friend. As am I." Nicholas clasped Langdon's shoulder and squeezed, their camaraderie too established to change with the shifting tide of Nicholas's position. They'd been through too much together to allow his newfound rank to erase their connection. He'd offered to keep Langdon as his man not out of sympathy but because he valued and respected him. Langdon's core was true and honest. Nicholas had learned much on the continent, but perhaps the most valuable lesson of all was illuminated by his relationship with Langdon. One could not woo, cajole, or buy loyalty. It must be earned honestly, and when it was given, there was nothing to equal it. He knew Langdon felt likewise.

"Now, how about some food?" Nicholas said. "Oh, and Catherine loves chocolate. Get Nan to warm some for her. The rest I leave to Nan's talented hands. Tell her she was right and all is well."

Langdon beamed and quickly departed. The bed was tightly made, everything in neat order. Hollow walls, empty of feeling. That was about to change. Nicholas would convince Catherine to forgo separate chambers and share this room with him. She could decorate it as she pleased. That would erase his father from it. Although, all he cared about was falling asleep with her in his arms and seeing her bonny face each morning when he awoke.

He strolled into the dressing room, staring at the now empty tub. He'd had more baths since returning home than he'd had in a year on the continent, yet he was tempted to call for another one. But visions of Catherine draped across the bed, that saucy gaze of hers, that enticing smile, called to him stronger than a warm bath. A pitcher of water lay on the stand. He poured some into the basin, took the cloth, and dipped it in the cool water. Dropping his robe, he quickly washed, wiping away the residue of sex, lingering at the task, mourning the eradication of Catherine from his body. He would just have to ensure she washed it once again with hers.

Quickly donning his banyan, he strolled between the rooms, not pausing to knock at hers, far too anxious to see her once again. She was exiting her dressing room, drawing closed a beautiful green silk dressing gown. His heart soared when her face lit with a smile. He closed the door behind him.

"Nicholas."

His name. Simple. Plain. It was not a question, but he heard insecurity. He would eradicate that.

He held out his arms. She ran to him, and he enveloped her in his warmth and love, kissing her head. He inhaled deeply. God, she smelled good. Arousal chased her scent. She opened the lapels of his robe, running her hand across his chest.

"Catherine," he warned, but her hands caressed a path downward, her fingers circling the fastenings. She tugged free the small loops, pushing the robe from his shoulders.

"Hellcat," he growled, losing all restraint, delighted she was unrepentant and persistent.

He lifted her, and she wrapped her legs around his thighs. Her robe joined his on the floor. She was already damp with need, and he was desperate to bury himself deep within her once again. He pressed her back against the sitting room door and pushed, her warm depths inviting. He nestled close, then stilled, holding on to the moment. *His.* As he was hers.

He wanted to wipe away all her uncertainty. Doubt he'd created. "Catherine," he started but choked on welling emotion. He withdrew slowly, then pushed back quickly, trying to refocus, to shake shattering sentiment. "It's just you."

She looked so beautiful…and so vulnerable.

"And me." He pulled back gradually, holding her gaze, willing her to trust him. "Us." He thrust to the hilt, shivering at the depth of connection.

Her eyes shimmered.

"Us," he repeated, then told her with his body that he meant every word. He did not cease until they were replete, her back pressed to the door, both of them damp and sweating.

When his body calmed, he relaxed, easing her downward until her feet hit the floor. He pulled back, drinking in her face. Her cheeks were flushed champagne pink, and her pupils were dilated, creating a dark forest where glistening moss had stood but moments before.

"Do you believe it?" he asked.

She hesitated, pulling in her bottom lip, her teeth grazing it erotically. Then she reached up and ran her hand down his cheek.

"I believe." She stood on tippy-toe and kissed his nose. "I believe in us."

The tight band around his chest released, and he exhaled. He hadn't realized he'd held his breath. She believed in them too. In the sober light of full day, their love held strong.

He grabbed her hand and kissed it. "Me too."

Lingering uncertainty cleared, and her eyes lightened with her smile. Those luscious lips beckoned.

"How about we seal this with—"

A knock interrupted his proposal. Catherine jumped, ducking under his arms and moving away from the door. She flew across the room and jumped into the bed, pulling the covers up to her chin. He laughed.

"You were not so shy a few moments ago," he teased. A pillow flew across the room, hitting the doorframe. "Hellcat!" Lord, he loved her spirit. He opened the door to the sitting room.

Langdon balanced a tray on his hand, grinning from ear to ear. The heat of embarrassment washed Nicholas's face. How long had Langdon been standing there? Nicholas was grateful the door blocked both of them from Catherine. She would be mortified.

He grabbed the tray. "Get out of here, you ruddy, old goat," he growled, keeping his voice low.

"Now, that's not at all nice, my lord. After I, a wounded man"—he dropped his maimed arm, letting it dangle—"went the great length of this house to ease your ravenous lady's hunger." He positively vibrated with his amusement.

Nicholas kicked the door shut in Langdon's face, but the man's roar of laughter was entirely audible. Nicholas smiled. Langdon had a right to his glee. He'd been Nicholas's confidant in all things and knew how long Nicholas had waited for this. Catherine still clutched the blanket to her chest, her creamy shoulders as enticing as her entire body.

"Langdon," he said in answer to her perplexed look. "He's a good man. You'll get used to him." He laid the tray on the table, grabbed the two cups, and strolled to her.

Closing her eyes, she sniffed the air. "Chocolate!" She took it from him and waved it beneath her nose. "Mmm. Heaven in a cup." Then she batted those dark lashes at him. "However did you know?"

He sat beside her. "However could I forget? You whined for it every time you entered Nan's kitchen."

"You beast!"

He held his tea at arm's length while she hit him limply with a pillow, both of them laughing. He could not remember when he'd last felt this playful and relaxed.

He took the cushion and tucked it behind his back. "Careful. You won't have anywhere to lay your pretty head if you keep tossing your pillows away."

Her eyes narrowed. "I will just have to find somewhere else to lay my pretty head, then."

He chuckled, wrapping his free arm around her shoulder and pulling her close. "You have played into my hands perfectly, my lady. Directly into my hands." He definitely wanted her in his room, not two doors away.

"Oh, pray tell, sir, how is that?" She sipped her chocolate.

"Well." He took a drink of tea. "Ah, perfect," he said, smacking his lips, taking his time in responding. "Nan always gets it just right, don't you think?"

"Nicholas," she warned.

"Hmm?" He pretended distraction, raising his cup again. He truly had missed the perfection of the brew.

"Playing into your hands?" She elbowed him, and he grunted, feigning pain. She gazed up at him through her eyelashes, a smudge of chocolate on her lip.

He leaned down, licking the bitter brew, her soft flesh beneath delectable. "Mmm. That is good. In fact, too good not to have some more." He slowly leaned toward her again, eyeing that delicious pout, dying to take it between his lips and taste it thoroughly.

Her eyelids fluttered closed in response.

He grabbed her cup, sat back abruptly, and quickly took a sip.

"Oh yes. Definitely tasty."

She opened her eyes as he swiped his tongue across his lip.

"Oh, Catherine!" He laughed out loud. "If you could only see your face right now."

"You fiend!" She slapped his chest. It made him laugh all the harder. "Put down those cups. I cannot fully attack an unarmed man."

A rap sounded on the sitting room door.

"Go away, Langdon." He got up, putting the cups back on the tray. There was nothing that could not wait. Not when Catherine was poised to attack. She had thrown back the covers and lay on her side, patting the empty spot beside her. He drank her in, following the flow of her curves. A live Rubens.

The rap came again, more insistent. "I said, go away."

"Urgent" came the muffled reply. *Damn.* Langdon would not be insistent were it not important.

"I fear I must see what he wants," Nicholas said. "I'm sorry."

Catherine had already pulled at the counterpane and was sitting up. She smiled, but disappointment was written on her face. "Me too."

CHAPTER THIRTY-ONE

The attempt and not the deed confounds us.

—Shakespeare, *Macbeth*

CATHERINE PULLED THE cover snug to her chin as another knock sounded, even harder this time then the last.

"Give me a moment, would you, Langdon?" Nicholas barked at the door, then turned back to Catherine, sighing. "I'll get rid of him as quickly as possible." He dropped her robe on the bed and then slipped into his. He leaned over and kissed her forehead. "This day is ours to celebrate."

She caressed his cheek, his morning stubble a new sensation. He was always clean-shaven. "Your homecoming."

"Our homecoming," he corrected, placing a finger on her nose and tracing it to her lips. She kissed it before he withdrew.

He gestured toward the tray. "Eat. You'll need your energy." He luridly moved his eyebrows up and down.

"You are a rake, sir!" she teased back, thrilled by his endless desire.

He headed toward the door but paused before opening it, looking back at her over his shoulder, his grin mellowing to a tender smile. "I'll send up some water for a bath. I promise to return shortly to enjoy it with you."

She blew him a kiss before he left, the clicking of the closing door creating a short, ominous echo in the room. What a foolish thought. They'd shaken the dark cloud that had hovered over them since his return. Truth now lit their lives. She'd been full of fear and worry for so long it had become customary practice. Grabbing the pillow Nicholas had lain upon, she pressed its downy softness to her nose, inhaling deeply. Well, she was going to toss the practice of fretting over everything and replace it with a new habit. Nicholas. Her man.

She slid from the bed, slipped on the silk, and stood staring at herself in the vanity mirror as she snugged the tie. Did she look any different? Her hair was a wild nest, and she cringed at the work that lay ahead for Sadie, not to mention the pain for Catherine, as the girl worked to tame the mess. She peered closer, tracing her lips with her fingers, amazed at the bruising and swelling. *Who am I now? A wife. Thank the Lord above, finally Nicholas's wife in truth.* She hugged herself tight, grinning like an idiot. A well-loved wife!

A light tap at the hallway door pulled her away from her pleasant ponderings. She grabbed a shawl from the chair and pulled it on, glancing down to ensure she was decent before letting in the men with her water. "Enter."

The door opened tentatively, and Sadie's pale face peeked around cautiously.

"Sadie?" Catherine was surprised to see her so early. Sadie had much to do reversing yesterday's decision to move back to Stratton Hall.

"My lord?" Sadie's nose scrunched as she glanced around the room. Did she fear catching Nicholas in dishabille? It certainly was something they would both have to consider now.

"He's in his chambers. Do come in." Catherine strolled to the table. She grabbed a biscuit, tore off a piece, and popped it into her mouth. Her stomach gurgled in appreciation. She ripped free another morsel.

"My lady?" Sadie thrust out her hand. She clutched paper, keeping it at arm's length as though it was offensive, and she seemed on the verge of tears.

"Dear Lord, Sadie, what is it?"

"I don't know, but it bodes ill, it does. It was sitting on the side table in the hall this morning. I asked all the staff, and none put it there."

Catherine's throat thickened. Unable to swallow, she grabbed the napkin from the tray and spit the half-chewed biscuit in it. So much for new habits. Apparently dread remained a well-ingrained response, for fear was coursing through her veins. Sadie stood motionless by the door, still holding out the parchment. Catherine strode to her, took the missive, then walked over to the hearth and sank into the chair.

She flipped over the note. The neatly printed script was unfamiliar. Nothing alarming about that, yet her hands shook as she broke the anonymous seal and pulled out the paper. She glanced at Sadie, who remained stationary by the door. They were both being foolish.

"Go see about my bath. Lord Walford was to send up the men, but it seems he has forgotten." Sadie closed the door, and for the second time that morning, the sound reverberated portentously deep inside her soul.

My Lady Walford,

It is a great relief to know you have returned to your father's home. While it was my greatest desire to wish you felicitations, I found I could not. I know full well the cloud that darkens the halls of Woodfield and did not wish for it to taint your life or your soul.

The men of Woodfield deserve their fate. They have all sullied their hands. But you, you are an innocent among the wolves. I am relieved of the burden of guilt I would carry had you remained under their roof.

I admire your grace and strength, your willingness to sacrifice for another. I would not see you hurt. Please forgive me should the stain on the others' hands cause you undue grief.

Your servant, always.

Catherine released her breath. Who had written this? She flipped over the plain paper. There was no signature, no indication of its author. What was meant by "deserve their fate"? Was Nicholas being threatened? *Dear Lord!*

She pulled open the door and ran into the sitting room. His door was open, and the murmur of voices spilled out. "Nicholas!" Panic welled as she ran across the room.

He met her at the threshold, holding her close. "Catherine?"

She sobbed at his embrace. He was safe.

He stroked her head as though soothing a child. "What is it, love?"

His voice brought her back to the crisis. "This!" She pulled away, thrusting the paper at him.

He paled.

"Nicholas?"

He hadn't read the letter. He couldn't know the horrible contents.

"Nicholas?" she repeated when he released her.

His eyes darkened indigo, then the flush of anger intensified the terse line of his lips. He turned to the equally furious-looking red-haired man who stood by the grate. "Now, Langdon. No rest until we find out who has written these."

The man saluted and, after a quick nod toward her, left without a word. Langdon. They had not yet met.

"Come, my love, come." Nicholas wrapped his arm around her waist and ushered her to a large chair. He kissed the top of her head when she sat, then moved to a side table, returning with two glasses of amber liquid. She took it from him, the brew splashing in her shaking hands.

His warm hand encompassed hers, raising the glass to her lips. "Drink."

Obediently, she swallowed deeply, choking. The burning sensation was a distraction from her growing fear. Brandy. Her father loved the stuff, but she'd never partaken.

"Again."

His hand guided it once more to her mouth, and she acquiesced, grateful for the radiating warmth and the calmness that was beginning to roll over her. He kissed her again.

"That's a good girl." Moving to the chair opposite her, he sat down, throwing back the contents of his own glass. She sipped the remainder of hers, moving beyond the shock of yet another threat to their happiness.

Nicholas smoothed the letter against his leg. He growled, his gaze furious. "Who brought this to you?"

"Sadie."

He started to rise.

"Sit, Nicholas. She doesn't know who wrote it nor who delivered it. It was on the side table in the main hall at Stratton." She raised her hand to stay him, since he seemed unconvinced. "She questioned the staff. No one had put it there, and no one saw who did. Have your man cross-check if you must, but I believe her." She was feeling much more in control now, certain she had overreacted. Nicholas would take care of this threat. She need not worry.

Nicholas sat back down, running a hand through his hair. He was dressed. His shirt was still open at the collar, but he was wearing his Hessians. He wasn't coming back to her room. How had he known? *No rest until we find out who has written these.* That was what he'd said to his man.

She gasped. "You got one too."

"You working for Bow Street now?" His attempt at humor failing, he grabbed another letter from the table beside his chair, then got up, exchanging it for her glass. He nabbed his on his way past his chair and moved to the side table, reaching for the decanter. "I warn you. The person who wrote this does not fawn over my attributes as he does yours."

She stared at the paper. Did she want to read this? Of course she did. She was not some sheltered miss fresh from the schoolroom. Nicholas trusted in her strength, and she would not let him down. She uncrumpled it. The penmanship was the same.

Lord Walford,

I'll not dally with platitudes. You have been party to the un-speakable. You have had time to rectify the injustice in the eyes of man and God, but you have done nothing. Your brother should stand at a crossroads with a stake through his dark soul, yet you allow a lie to hold.

Such sin cannot go unpunished. I shall endeavor to tip the scales of justice. One hundred pounds to be left at the steps of the folly by dusk. I will use the money to erase your brother's wickedness.

As with hers, it was unsigned. She leaned back in her chair. Whoever it was, the person knew that Daniel had taken his life. The archaic burial rite cited was still often executed for those who committed suicide—the stake ensured no ghost would walk, and the crossroads were meant to confuse and diffuse the evil spirits. It was a ghoulish practice that should be outlawed.

She shivered as Nicholas took the letter and replaced it with a full glass of brandy. This time, she needed no assistance to imbibe.

"Somebody knows," she whispered.

He sat down, legs spread, his leisurely posture belied by the compression of his lips, his jaw clenched tightly. "Somebody knows," he echoed.

"But who?" She could not fathom who would come to such a conclusion, never mind attempt blackmail.

"Who does not?" He leaned forward. "The question is, who would be so bold as to hold it over our heads? Who believes they may profit from it?"

She was confused. Who knew of it?

His lips finally relaxed into a soft smile. "You said yourself that servants see everything. Hear everything. I am guessing most have come to the conclusion that Laurence did not kill Daniel."

Of course, it was true. Nan, Fredericks, and Edwards knew absolutely everything. She relied on them because of that knowledge. They had guided her through the years as much as her father had. She stiffened. Nan and Fredericks had prepared Daniel's body. They would have been faced with the truth of how close that fatal shot had been, but she could not fathom betrayal from either of them.

"You can't possibly think Nan or Fredericks could ever do anything so hateful?"

Nicholas ran a hand through his hair, shaking his head back and forth. "I no longer know what to believe."

AND THAT WAS the truth. Nicholas had left home thinking he understood his world, that he fully comprehended the workings of man. The war had put many of those principles into question. The disclosures about Daniel, Laurence, and Catherine's willingness to support both had skewed much of what he believed. He no longer knew what to think about any of it.

"The only thing I know for certain is that someone does know and is willing to use that knowledge for gain." He had been furious when he'd read the missive. How dare he! Whoever he— she might be. When Nicholas's fury had spent, he'd racked his brain to discern the culprit while Langdon had listened patiently to his rant. In the end, it had come down to two. The maid. He could not recall her name, but she had definitely insinuated knowledge of Daniel's doings and had threatened him. Then there was Brownlee, who no doubt knew about the suicide as well. Both were furious with Nicholas. He would get Langdon to root them out.

Catherine tossed back the last of her glass, tears welling. "Oh, Nicholas."

He moved quickly, falling to his knees before her. "We will find the scoundrel, and then it will be done. All of it." He laid his head upon her lap, longing for comfort, longing to comfort her.

A knock at the door interrupted the moment. He stood, his gaze lingering on Catherine's beautiful face, her eyes darkened to ivy, her hair wondrous in its freedom. The knock repeated.

"Come in," he barked, irritated by the disruption.

Fredericks stood in the open door, looking miserable. Had the entire staff heard of the blackmail?

"My lord, your father would see you in his rooms." Despite his obvious discomfort, Fredericks's voice remained neutral as always.

"Tell him I'll be down shortly."

Fredericks nodded and left.

Catherine sat up stiffly, stoic yet somehow wilted. Did she think he would shut her out? They were partners in life now. The good, the bad, and the ugly. He feared this was as ugly as it got, but he knew she had the strength to see it through. Had she not been the pillar holding up this family since his departure for the continent?

He leaned in, laying a hand upon her back, kissing her nose. "This won't take long, and I promise I'll tell you what he has to say about all this." For he had no doubt he'd been summoned because the old man already knew about the threat.

She cupped the back of his head, staying him. "I would come with you—" She hesitated, then breathed deeply. "—if I may."

He sensed fragility. She had been through so much it was no wonder she questioned her every emotion. Well, she need not question the depth of his love any longer. "I'd like to shelter you from this, if I could."

Her shoulders slumped, and he rubbed his hand in small circles on her back. He sighed. "But I welcome you by my side." A shiver ran down her spine, sparking through his palm. He released her. "Go dress. I'll wait."

She glanced gratefully at him, then disappeared through the connecting doorway. He strolled to the window. Beyond the terraced gardens lay the woods. Was the culprit out there watching the house? Whoever it was, they knew Catherine had left him, but they had not known of her quick return. He ran a hand through his hair, yanking on the ends. *Think, man. Think.*

He did not believe this was the work of a moral reformer, despite the letter's cry for justice in the eyes of God. This was about money; he was sure of it. He had paid both the chit and the steward a hefty severance to ensure they'd have no need for complaint. One of them must have grown greedy. Or could they be united in this rapacious deed?

Damn! What were the legal repercussions for suicide? He'd never considered it before. Had had no need. Thornwood would know. Perhaps Nicholas should summon him? Dare he share any of this? All this? He was sure Thornwood would be discreet. And Nicholas could do with some help to sort through this mess.

Reluctantly, he pulled away from the window and grabbed his waistcoat, buttoning it up carefully. Moving to the mirror, he grabbed the cotton draped there and wrapped it around his neck. Nothing fancy for him. "The popinjay will not be pleased," he said to his reflection, quickly securing a simple knot upon hearing rustling in the sitting room.

Catherine wore a plain yellow day dress, the humble color of the garden primrose, yet she took his breath away with her splendor. Her burgundy tresses pulled back in a simple chignon, accentuating her high cheekbones, gave her the look of a true blueblood. As regal as she was, she stood unsure, biting her lower lip—the lip already bruised and swollen from their lovemaking.

"You leave me speechless," he said.

She released her lip and smiled tentatively. He wanted to seize her, to kiss her until she no longer held doubt in her heart. He shook his head. Now was not the time.

Instead, he snatched his jacket and shrugged it on. He held her gaze as he fastened it, then extended his hand. "Come, my love. Let us beard the lion together."

She curled her hand around his arm, and they exited his chambers. He glanced over the balustrade as they made their way to the staircase. Fredericks's shock of white hair paced back and forth in the vestibule. It seemed today's events had even unnerved the ever-staid butler.

Hearing them, Fredericks ceased his striding and moved to the base of the flight of stairs, standing stock-still. When Nicholas and Catherine reached the foyer, Fredericks's face was impassive. If Nicholas had not seen the man's agitation for himself, he would believe the facade. Fredericks had seen both boys from leading strings to manhood. Of course he was disturbed by this turn of events.

"Your father is waiting," he said quietly, hesitating as though he wanted to say something further.

"What is it, Fredericks?" Nicholas asked.

Fredericks's gnarled hand clasped Nicholas's shoulder. "Lord Woodfield is a proud man. You have lost a brother. Remember, he has lost a son. He, too, suffers. Do not let his manner lead you to believe otherwise."

Nicholas covered the old man's hand with his. "I will do my best."

Fredericks nodded and opened the door. Nicholas's father sat in his usual place, wrapped in a blanket by a well-fed fire.

"Father?" Fredericks's warning had unnerved Nicholas, made him cautious.

The earl did not look toward him, but he did gesture to a chair. Catherine smiled at Nicholas, worry muting her eyes. He held out his hand, and she placed hers in it. Together they walked to the chair.

"Please, Catherine, sit," he said, drawing the attention of his father.

The earl's gray eyebrows furrowed. "The gel should not be here. This is family business."

Nicholas stood behind the chair, placing a hand on Catherine's shoulder, determined to remain calm. "She *is* family."

"Just because you foolishly proceeded with marrying her doesn't make her family." The old man glared at him.

Catherine stiffened and reached up to hold Nicholas's hand.

Fury ignited, but he dampened its full force for her sake. "You are out of line, sir. She is my wife, and you will treat her as such or you will sit alone."

She gently squeezed his hand. Seated before the lion himself, she did not cower. He had never been prouder.

His father's face went a deep crimson with the chastisement, and rather than be satisfied with his discomfort, suddenly Nicholas couldn't let it be. *Damn it!* The man had created this mess.

"Catherine is the woman who was willing to give up everything for love of both your sons. Loyalty and sacrifice. Is that not your refrain for family, Father?" He didn't even try to keep the bitter sarcasm from his voice. "Where were those attributes when Daniel needed you?"

"Nicholas!" Catherine broke into his stream of anger, and his father sputtered.

"I do apologize, sire. That too was out of line," Nicholas said.

The old man's face caved and his shoulders collapsed as he fell back into the chair and stared at the fire. "I am unable to fathom…" His father clutched the armrest. "I cannot condone…" He reached out, his hand floundering on the table beside his chair, searching, his ruddy face suddenly ashen.

A surge of sympathy impelled Nicholas to walk over and pour a glass of port before pressing it into the old man's grip. Lord Woodfield held his hand there for a brief moment, his eyes darkened with pain. The only other time Nicholas had seen such raw emotion was when his mother had died. He returned to his position behind Catherine, gripping her chair to steady himself. His father's touch, his vulnerability, had been distressing.

They both watched his father drink some port, color seeping back into his face. He fisted the paper that sat on his lap. Nicholas did not need to read it to know its contents. It was as he suspected. His father already knew. Whoever was attempting this extortion was thorough.

"Do what you have to do. I'll not have my son's name sullied." Lord Woodfield raised the glass to his lips with a trembling hand and reverted to staring at the fire. Even in this shared pain, Nicholas was dismissed.

CHAPTER THIRTY-TWO

'Tis best to weigh the enemy more mighty than he seems.

—Shakespeare, *Henry V*

CATHERINE LOOKED TOWARD the lake. Foolish, really. Even from her second-story window, dense forest obscured the water. She had dismissed Sadie for the evening, wanting to be alone with her worry. Nicholas was out there. He'd assured her he and Langdon had everything well in hand, but she could not shake the fear something would go wrong.

She paced the length of the room, inevitably drawn back to stare at the deepening shadows of the woods. Nicholas refused to set out any amount of currency for the scoundrel, although he'd made quite the show of locking himself in his father's study as though he was taking from the safe. He'd put a mixture of paper and weights in a sack so the "payment" would appear authentic to anyone watching him deliver it.

Langdon had stationed himself at the folly earlier in the afternoon. She could not imagine the man remaining undetected, but Nicholas had said Langdon was highly skilled in reconnaissance. She smiled despite her anxiety, for Nicholas had patiently explained the term to her. He was going to come back to the manse after dropping the sack, then go out through the kitchen and circle around to trap the culprit.

Movement caught her eye.

Was that Nicholas heading back out or returning? The breeze ruffled her hair as she leaned out. There, again. At that moment, the shadow disengaged, transforming into human form. Two human shapes. One of them was hurt!

"Nicholas!" she shouted at the same time Nicholas hollered, "Fredericks!"

He couldn't be hurt and yell like that. *Could he?* Blood thundering in her ears, she ran from the room and flew down the staircase. She frantically scanned the atrium but couldn't see nor hear commotion anywhere. They must have gone around back. She veered to the right, running down the long hallway to the servants' corridor before stopping at the door to the kitchen just as Nicholas eased Langdon down on the bench at the table. The man winced, his face pinched with pain.

"I'm right sorry, sir. I almost had the scoundrel, but my foot caught on something, and I tripped. Pain ripped through my arm so bad I..." Langdon looked to Nan, who was rolling up his sleeve, and his mouth tightened into a straight line. Blood seeped from the freshly opened wound. "...I cast up my accounts, sir. Cast them up." The man's head fell, his shoulders tensing, the pain from Nan's administrations obvious.

"At ease, soldier." Nicholas rubbed Langdon's shoulder. "At ease." He cocked an eyebrow at Cook. "Nan?"

"As far as I can tell through the mess, 'tis only a small section that has reopened. Won't know for sure till we stanch that bleeding."

Catherine moved to the shelf by the door, grabbing a handful of linen.

"Catherine!" Nicholas seemed surprised to see her there.

Nan glanced up. "That's a good girl. Now press here."

She held the cloth where Nan indicated.

"Don't be afraid to hold it firm." Nan placed her hand on Catherine's, pressing it down. "You can't cause him any more pain than he already bears."

"I'll do that," Nicholas said. "You should not be here—"

Nan cut him off. "Yes, son, she should. 'Sides, I need you for other things. Stoke that fire and get a kettle boiling."

Catherine would have smiled at his instant compliance if a moan had not escaped Langdon. "I don't mean to hurt you, sir. I'm sorry."

Langdon raised his head, his eyes glazed with pain. "Me too, my lady. That I let the blackguard get away. Right sorry."

"Now that's enough out of you," Nan clucked. She sat beside him and placed her small sewing kit on the table. "You've lost a fair bit of blood. You're gonna need to save your energy."

Nan held up a needle, catching the light from the fire as she threaded it. She placed the end of the string in her teeth and pulled sharply, breaking it from the spool. "You got that water for me, Master Nick?" she asked as she knotted the thread. Catherine hadn't heard Nan call him that in years.

"It's not boiling yet." Nicholas's brow creased in frustration, and he tossed more coals on the fire.

"In due time, child." Nan grunted, shaking her head at his impatience. "In the meantime, grab me some brandy and a cup."

Nan liked a nip of brandy at night when the house had gone to bed. It was the worst-kept secret at Woodfield that she hid a bottle in the pantry. Langdon shifted, his pain palpable. Well, apparently not the worst-kept secret. Usually Nan would be asking what had happened, but she did not seem surprised by tonight's events.

Nicholas poured some brandy into a mug and set the bottle beside it. He returned to his assigned position at the fire and stared at the flames, his back to Catherine. She could only imagine how he was feeling right now.

"Okay, love, you can relax for a moment," Nan said. "Let me have a peek."

Catherine stood and pressed a hand to her aching lower back. She should have sat down rather than bent over. She spread her fingers, then fisted them, trying to release the tension.

"It's slowing down," Nan declared. "How's that water?"

"Almost ready," Nicholas said.

"Good. Catherine, grab two basins and put them in front of Mr. Langdon here. Get me some more linen. Master Nick, pour some of the water in one of these bowls. Get another kettle boiling when that one is empty." Nan turned her attention back to the wound. "Mr. Langdon, can you hold this against your arm for a minute?" He did not lift his head, but he pressed the bloodied cloth against his stump. She patted his arm. "It is not half-bad, not half-bad," she murmured before dipping the fresh cotton into the water.

"I need you to wipe away the blood as I sew. Can you do that?" Nan asked, wringing the excess water from the cloth.

"Yes." Catherine nodded, grateful she was not squeamish. She'd watched Nan stitch the boys many times, although this was the first time she'd ever had to assist.

Nan glanced up, her wrinkles deepening with a quick smile, and handed her the cloth. "Good girl. Sit on his other side. You'll have to lean across. Mr. Langdon, some brandy before I begin?" She held up the bottle.

"No, ma'am," he mumbled into his chest.

Nan picked up the needle and dipped it in the cup of brandy, pulling the thread through the amber liquid. "Such a waste of a good cuppa," she muttered.

"I'll get you more, Nan." Nicholas stood behind Langdon, his hands on the man's shoulders.

"Wiping gently, young Catherine. Gently." Lips pursed, Nan bent over and pierced the flesh, pulling the thread slowly through.

Langdon tensed but did not flinch. Catherine tried not to think of his pain. She focused on wiping after each stitch, trying to keep the area visible for Nan. Nicholas kneaded Langdon's shoulders. Neither man said a word.

An eternity later, Nan inspected her work, clucking approval. "Some fresh water, if you please. We'll just get Mr. Langdon cleaned up, and he'll be good as new."

Catherine moved to the fire and grabbed a cloth to swing out the kettle with. She carefully lifted it off the spit, trying not to burn herself. This was a task she seldom performed, and the last thing they needed was another injury to care for. She set the kettle on the table.

"Let me." Nicholas released Langdon's shoulders and took the cloth from her. He tipped the kettle's contents into the clean bowl.

Nan scooted by them, then returned with a dripping cloth of her own. "Lift your head, Mr. Langdon, and lie back."

He obeyed, and Nan gently covered his pained expression with the cool cloth.

She wiped his face gently like she would that of a small child. "Better?"

He nodded. Nan dipped the cloth into the warm water and washed up as much of the blood as possible. Then she poured the remaining brandy from the cup over her handiwork. Langdon's guttural groan was hard to hear. Catherine knew it meant his pain was nearly unbearable.

"You sure you wouldn't care for some brandy, sir?" Nan asked as she dabbed at the mix of brandy and blood.

Langdon shook his head. "No, my gut can't bear the stuff right now."

"Well, mine can." Nicholas grabbed the brandy and threw back a mouthful. Catherine had never seen a man drink directly from a bottle. He eyed her, thrusting it in her direction, his eyebrows raised in question.

She took it from him and gulped some of the fiery liquid.

"Have you no couth? No respect for an old lady's supplies?" Nan stood, hands on her hips, glaring at them. Catherine held out the bottle.

"That's better," Nan said, grabbing the brandy and throwing back a fair amount before moving to sit by the fire, bottle still in hand.

Catherine looked at Nicholas and began to laugh. He joined her until they were both giddy with release.

"Want to let me in on the joke?" Langdon's eyes were lined with exhaustion. They both sobered instantly, and Nicholas stepped up to Langdon's side.

"Sorry, old man. Let's get you to the other chair. When Fredericks arrives, we'll get you off to bed."

Once Langdon was resting by the fire, Nicholas and Catherine cleaned up the table, throwing the water out back and leaving the basins to be thoroughly washed. That, at least, could be relegated to a servant in the morning. Normally it all could have been, but these weren't normal times, and they didn't know who they could trust.

Finally they sat down on the bench, the table to their backs, staring toward the duo by the fire. The comforting sound of Nan's needles accompanied Langdon's long, wheezing breaths. Hopefully he was finding escape in sleep.

Nicholas reached for Catherine's hand, locking his fingers in hers, his skin warm.

"You're an amazing woman," he said quietly. He lifted their hands, brushing them against his lips.

She smiled at him, soaking in his admiration. Her man. Who could have been the one hurt this night. Reality hit her like a splash of cold water. "Do you know who it is?" she asked in a whisper, not wanting to disturb the others.

"I did not lay eyes on anyone, and Langdon said it all happened so fast, and it was dark..." Nicholas let the sentence trail, shaking his head.

"What happened?" Catherine asked, wanting to reach out and ease the worry from his brow.

"Nothing as frightening as I fear you're imagining." He reached toward her with his free hand, his thumb smoothing the lines between her brows. She wanted to lean into him, forget this entire affair. However, it lay there still, a fresh chasm between them and the beginning of their lives together.

"Then tell me."

His locks bounced as he ran his hand through his hair. "I left the bag on the step long before dusk, then circled back as planned." He scratched the top of his mop, then leaned back, pounding a curled fist against his forehead. "The culprit must have been watching. He nabbed the bag before I got back there. It took me a while to find Langdon. I think he passed out." He yanked at his hair. "You heard him. He took chase but tripped, and it nearly killed him. If I hadn't found him in time…"

"But you did, Nicholas, you did." She squeezed his hand.

His eyes darkened, his jaws clenched. "The man did not survive Badajoz to die because of my scandalous family."

"I'm not dead, you know. I can hear the whole bloody pathetic conversation."

Nan chuckled, but she kept knitting without looking their way.

"Now take your wife to bed. On second thought, send her to hers, and you take your own. You need your sleep. We have a battle to plan, and I need you sharp." Langdon gave a long sigh and rested his head on the back of the chair, his mouth closed in a grim line now that he was done issuing his orders.

Nicholas grinned at her, his shoulders visibly relaxing. He stood, tugging her to her feet.

"I sometimes wonder who was actually in charge of my battalion." He released her to go stand by Langdon. "I'll find Fredericks and get you comfortably settled. The battle can wait until you are well."

Nicholas moved to Nan and kissed the top of her head. "Thank you, sweet nurse. I shall replace your stores tenfold, I promise." He crossed his heart like they'd used to do when taking oaths as children.

Nan's needles continued their soft clicking. "See that you do." Her gruff voice made a lie of her indifference.

Catherine smiled. All was right with the world…for the moment.

Nicholas grabbed her hand, and they headed back down the servants' corridor she had run down ages ago. He paused at his study, the breakfast room, the dining room, finally letting out a slow, frustrated breath at the billiards room.

"Whatever is wrong?" Catherine asked.

"Where the devil is Fredericks?"

"Right here, sir."

Catherine jumped at Fredericks's voice. Where had he come from? He looked more stressed than she'd felt this entire night. His usually calm facade was missing, his cravat askew and his mane wilder than usual. Her face must have shown her surprise, for he quickly adjusted his neck cloth and patted at his hair.

"Forgive me, my lady," Fredericks said as he ran a hand over his hair again. "It has been a trying night with my lord." He turned his attention back to Nicholas. "Your father has been awaiting word. It has been difficult," he repeated.

Nicholas's eyes narrowed. If she didn't know better, she would think he found Fredericks's disordered state offensive. *Ridiculous.* He'd never cared about such things and, surely, would not be concerned about it in the midst of everything else that had happened this evening.

"Your father...," Fredericks began again, floundering for words.

She'd never seen the butler so disconcerted. How horrible of Nicholas to leave him so.

"We did not catch the culprit tonight." She had to save the poor man. Nicholas had obviously not recovered from the ordeal. He would never treat Fredericks like this under normal circumstances. "But we are not yet done, are we, Nicholas?"

"No, we are not done by far."

"Good, sir...my lord. Not that you were not successful, only that...glad to hear you will not let this wastrel take advantage of this family. I shall go inform your father."

"Fredericks!" Nicholas's sharp bark rang through the hallway. What was going on? She'd never heard that tone before, certainly would never have dreamed he would address Fredericks that way.

"Langdon is injured."

Fredericks's impossibly pale skin bleached to an ethereal hue.

Nicholas locked gazes with the old servant. "He is with Nan. I would see him comfortable while he recovers."

A slight flush of color softened the death pallor of old Fredericks. "I will see to it, my lord." He turned to leave.

"And, Fredericks"—the old butler's shoulders stiffened. He stood motionless, not glancing back at Nicholas—"I *will* catch the blackguard."

The statement hung, suspended, before Fredericks scurried around the corner to Lord Woodfield's rooms.

CHAPTER THIRTY-THREE

Our doubts are traitors and make us lose the good we oft might win by fearing to attempt.

—Shakespeare, *Measure for Measure*

"WOULD YOU CARE to explain," Catherine began before he had fully closed his chamber door, "what that was about?"

She stood, immoveable, hands on her hips and brow furrowed, her eyes darkening to that rich forest green. "Why did you treat Fredericks so abominably? He is as worried for this family as you or I!"

God, she was beautiful when she was angry. He just wanted to take her to bed and forget everything. All of it. Daniel. Langdon. His father. Fredericks. Suddenly the weight of weariness settled. Surely not Fredericks.

"Let it go." He did not want to share his suspicions until he was sure.

"No, I will not. It has been a trying night, but there is no need for the tone you took with Fredericks. I don't understand why you did so, and feel I'm missing something. Your new position has not granted you permission to take leave of your manners nor to forget those who are loyal to you."

Catherine was so accommodating, always wanting everyone

to get along. But throw a bone in front of her, and she held on to it with all the tenaciousness of a terrier. It would be amusing were it not for the bloody mess they were in.

"Do you not find it odd that Fredericks did not come running when I shouted for him? *You* heard me from up here. And if Nan knew what was going on this evening, you can bet Fredericks did too. We bloody well could have used his help. Where was he as we cared for Langdon?"

She let out a long sigh, her shoulders falling, a small smile lifting her ire. "Is that what that was all about? Fredericks wasn't there when you needed help with your friend? He was with your father, Nicholas. No small task, that." She stepped to him, cupping his cheek with her warm hand. "Langdon will be just fine."

He stared at her, her eyes brightening as her indignation dissipated with concern for him.

"You are a good friend." She stood on tippy-toe and kissed him tenderly.

He pulled her close, holding her to his chest, caressing her back. Where had Fredericks been tonight? He would have heard Nicholas shouting quite easily from Lord Woodfield's suite. And, surely, his father would not have held Fredericks back from finding out what had happened. So clearly Fredericks had lied to Nicholas. Fredericks had not been with Nicholas's father. The man was ever present, ever knowing. If he had been in the house the whole time, he would have been there to assist and to relay information back to Lord Woodfield.

"Langdon is worthy of my alliance" was all he said, grateful he was at least being truthful in that. He did not doubt Langdon's trustworthiness. "Let's retire for the night. We will think on things in the morning." He rested his chin on her crown, still unwilling to bluntly share the fear that Fredericks was blackmailing him.

A SHAFT OF light snuck through the opening between the drapes, but Nicholas was hesitant to move. He had not taken Langdon's advice. He'd undressed Catherine, enjoying revealing her delicious body inch by inch as he'd slowly discarded each item. Their lovemaking had not been prolonged, but it had been satisfying nonetheless—gentle and tender, it had been a balm for his ravaged soul. Exhausted, they'd fallen asleep, still joined.

He loved the weight of her head, and her hair splayed artlessly across his chest. The beam of light cut a swath across it, washing it to a fine claret. He lifted a strand of hair, then let it fall. It was difficult to believe this was real. She shifted, grumbling, but did not awaken. So many nights dreaming of her, and she was finally his.

His old room faced north, so he'd never awakened to the sun as a child. Dust danced in the air, a drifting, showery display. He'd never fancied himself to be whimsical, but he sure had been of late. It must be love. He laid a hand on Catherine's head, holding her tight. If only it were just them. Thoughts of yesterday's events crowded out the wistful longing. Someone was trying to undo this world, and he must stop him.

He could not believe Fredericks was at the heart of the blackmail. Yet where had the man disappeared to? He'd not been in the manse when Nicholas had returned. He was sure of it. Fredericks would have come to the kitchens. The old man had been visibly agitated when he'd stepped out of Lord Woodfield's rooms. Fredericks was eternally unflappable. Something was definitely afoot. He also knew everything. Like Nan. Of that there was no doubt. Would he betray them? To what end? But if not him, who?

Langdon could find nothing about the maid, but she had certainly warned Nicholas. Was she making good on that threat? And what of Brownlee? He had been furious, taking no measures to hide his disgust. He, too, had intimated retribution. Both had received ridiculous sums for their audacity. Perhaps it had merely whet their appetites? Their? Not for the first time, he pondered the idea of collusion.

"Good morning."

Her husky voice directed his attention elsewhere. He shifted, uncomfortable, reaching down to adjust himself. There was no time to linger with her this morning. She raised her head and peered at him through a skein of burgundy.

He smiled at her sloe-eyed look, finding her incredibly erotic in her morning stupor. He could take her now. Open the drapes wide and let the sun shine through fully. It would be a magical moment in the morning light. He reached down and squeezed his far-too-attentive member into submission. With luck, Thornwood would arrive this morning. Regardless, with or without him, Nicholas had a felon to snare.

He brushed her errant locks aside and rose up to kiss her forehead. "My sleeping beauty awakes."

Her elbows planted on either side of his chest, she lifted her head, her lips tilting in the sweetest of smiles. "And are you my prince charming?"

The question unnerved him. There was no doubt he loved her, but could he promise her the happily ever after? Did he even believe one could exist?

"Is something more amiss?" She could always read him.

He traced a finger between her brows, circling gently, trying to relax her consternation. "I long to linger with you." He kissed her nose. "Unfortunately, our problems have not been put to bed."

Her worried look saddened him. After everything he'd put her through, all he wanted was to bring joy to her life. Before he could change his mind, he lifted her and set her aside with another quick kiss and then swung his legs over the edge of the bed. There could be no happy endings until this criminal was brought to justice.

"Do you have a plan?" she asked.

He took her hand in his. "Not yet. But I will. Do not concern yourself. I will." He kissed her hand, looking at her with what he hoped was reassurance. He let go and strode to his dressing room.

The battles he'd fought on the continent seemed to pale in light of the one he now faced. This one was on home soil. Their families, their way of life—Catherine—were dependent on him to see this threat disarmed. Thornwood would know the legal repercussions of their brothers' actions, but regardless, Nicholas would not stand idly by and see their families' good reputations destroyed. Nor would he allow anyone to bleed them dry. For a blackmailer saw a well, not a bucket, and demanded to dip in endlessly. He poured a pitcher of water into the basin and splashed repeatedly, closing his eyes. The cold was bracing. After wiping his face, he stared into the mirror. This was no minor skirmish. He had to play it right. And he must win.

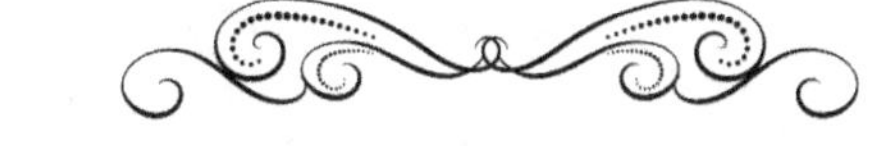

CHAPTER THIRTY-FOUR

That which I would discover the law of friendship bids me
to conceal.

—Shakespeare, *Two Gentlemen of Verona*

NICHOLAS STARED AT the terrace and the mirage of gardens
beyond. Rain pelted the glass, washing the sight away
again. Two more days had passed, and the blackguard had made
no move. The waiting was wearing.

"Nicholas, do sit down. You are doing damage to the carpets
with your pacing. You've not touched any food. Nan has sent
your favorite cheeses and bread," Catherine said.

The scent of freshly baked bread registered. Catherine sat on
the sofa, her legs drawn up under her gown, an unopened book
on her lap. Lord, but she was beautiful. The fire lit her face
golden in the dim library. August. It should have been warmer,
but it had turned unseasonably cool.

She patted the seat beside her, and the invitation was irresistible. The long days had been softened by the nights with her. She
was an incredible woman. He sank onto the sofa, leaning in to
kiss that impertinent little nose. She set her book aside. He picked
it up. *Coelebs in Search of a Wife.*

"Have you not finished with this yet?" He remembered finding her asleep in the sitting room on the night of their wedding.

He recalled the scent of her, bringing her to pleasure. His cock stiffened.

"Truth be told, I haven't started it. I am not sure I wish to read of someone else's trials in finding love." She glanced up, her eyes darkening in response to what she must surely see in his.

"We can't..." Her voice was gruff, unconvincing.

"Who says?" He shifted. Lust could be damned uncomfortable. He looked around the richly appointed library, his father's domain until his illness. *Well, damn it all*—Nicholas's domain now. Why should he not enjoy his wife here?

He ran a finger along her décolletage, exposing the smooth ivory skin hidden beneath the periwinkle fabric. A sharp rap cut the exploration short. Catherine's face fell. She was clearly as disappointed as he felt. Although, she blushed charmingly, while he just wanted to shout at whoever had knocked. They both sat up, adjusting their clothing.

"Enter," Nicholas begrudgingly commanded.

"Lord Thornwood has arrived," Fredericks said, his face expressionless.

A surge of relief washed away any irritation at being interrupted. Nicholas had many legal questions, and Thornwood would be able to answer them. Despite the surety of his title, Thornwood had specialized in law. He'd thought it would aid in his political judgments. The man had an admirable dedication to humanity. Nicholas counted on that, their long-standing friendship, and the rules of courteous form that Thornwood always insisted upon, to ensure discretion.

"Show him in."

Fredericks closed the doors before going to retrieve their guest. He seemed more himself these last few days. Both Nicholas and Langford had kept an eye on him, but there was no sign of anything untoward. Perhaps there was a simple explanation for the man's odd behavior that day. Unfortunately, there was no way to ask Fredericks about it without tipping him off, if indeed he was the culprit. More, it would be insulting. If Nicholas was wrong, he'd offend the old man. He shook his head. Some military man he was, worried about a servant's feelings.

Irritated, he stood and brushed at his trousers, then moved to the desk on the opposite side of the room. He shuffled papers around, impatience making him restless. Hopefully Thornwood would be able to guide him through this mire.

The door opened again. Fredericks announced Lord Thornwood before stepping to the side to admit him and then quietly closing the door behind him.

"Thornwood, good of you to come again." Nicholas stepped out around the desk.

Thornwood strode directly to him, taking his hand, pumping it enthusiastically. "I do apologize for my delay. It was unavoidable." He released Nicholas's hand. "I am honored you have need of me. I have let many things in my life slip and feel less connected than I used to. It does my heart good to know there is someone in need of my friendship, my company."

Nicholas was taken aback by the easy confession. Thornwood was always in control. It seemed they were all missing something, seeking something.

"I must say," Thornwood continued, "I was worried about you after my last visit." He raised his hand to Nicholas's shoulder. "The tension at both your wedding and the dinner party was tangible. It was not my business to ask, but it was clear that neither you nor your bride were happy with the circumstances. I assume that is why I am here?"

A discreet cough from Catherine caught the earl's attention. He swung around and spotted her sitting very much composed on the sofa.

"Lady Walford." His complexion deepened to a rich scarlet. "I do apologize, I had no idea…I mean…I mean…hell."

Her delightful laughter filled the room as she stood and approached the earl, reaching out to touch his arm. "No need. You are correct. The tension was unbearable, and you had every right to be concerned for your friend."

She moved to Nicholas's side. He wrapped an arm around her waist, smiling in triumph. He brushed a kiss across her hair, withholding his own laughter at Thornwood's look of surprise.

"But you're to worry no longer. We have reconciled our differences. Haven't we?" She beamed up at Nicholas, and his heart skipped a beat. It was not only her beauty that thrilled him but the truth in her words. Despite the trial they'd faced, he knew their love was finally on solid ground.

"Then may I make my congratulations once again." He bowed toward them. "And this time, they are genuine and heartfelt."

"Thank you, my lord. Your goodwill is much appreciated. Nicholas was just about to eat. Would you care to join him? The bread is fresh from the oven."

"I have never been known to turn down food."

Catherine squeezed Nicholas's hand. He followed the sway of her hips across the room to the table by the sofa. She bent over to fill a plate, the curve of her behind sweet enticement.

"Your smile borders on a leer, my friend," Thornwood said quietly, a chuckle in his voice. "This is quite the turn of events. Clearly much has transpired since I was last here."

Nicholas sobered. "You don't know the half of it."

"It can wait. I would see our guest fed first." Catherine smiled at Thornwood, gesturing to the large chair by the fire. "And *you* must eat."

Thornwood caught the concern in her voice and raised his eyebrows at Nicholas questioningly.

He waved toward the chair. "Sit, sit. Catherine is right. Food first."

Thornwood accepted the plate, sinking down into the chair. Nicholas took the proffered second plate and sat on the sofa. Catherine joined him, nibbling on a small piece of cheese. He watched her throat as she ate, wanting to lean in and kiss her long neck. His wife. She was a welcome distraction from what lay ahead.

She caught his stare, her slight flush enchanting. She reached out and rested her hand on his thigh. Heat radiated from the touch.

"Eat. Please," she said quietly, then she redirected her attention back to Thornwood. "Some tea?"

"Mm-hmm," Thornwood mumbled, his mouth full. He swallowed quickly. "Yes, please."

Nicholas pulled apart a chunk of bread. Still warm, it gummed in his hands. He popped the piece in his mouth, savoring Nan's delicious baking. His stomach responded in eagerness, and hungry for the first time in days, he worked his way through the plateful Catherine had prepared.

He watched her pour tea and converse easily with Thornwood. He had not realized Thornwood was stopping at the two boys. He had been an only child and had sworn that, when he was married, he would fill his home with a full brood. They had all changed over the years, hadn't they? Circumstances shifted, and dreams were adjusted. Or surrendered.

The fire crackled, softly lighting the small, domestic scene. He was content to watch Catherine work her magic, weaving a spell over Thornwood. The man was relaxed, sharing intimacies as if they were lifelong friends. Her engaging candidness could charm the birds out of the trees.

"Your boys sound wonderful," she said, rising to gather the plates. "You will have to bring them for a visit. Our lake is superb for swimming, is it not, Nicholas?"

Those memories washed over him again—teaching her how to swim, holding her close in the water, knowing in that moment that he must have her. Forever. And now he did.

"Nicholas?"

"Yes, you are correct. Absolutely superb."

She blushed again as Thornwood chuckled.

"Quite besotted, I'd say." Thornwood set down his cup and grinned at Catherine. "Yes, he's definitely smitten."

Catherine beamed, flushing a deeper red but looking quite

pleased. She scooped up his cup and set it on the tray. After grabbing Nicholas's empty plate, she laid it with the other dirty dishes, pulled the bell, and sat down beside him.

Fredericks was quick to arrive with a footman and efficiently cleared the mess while the trio sat silently. "Will there be anything else, my lord?"

Nicholas contemplated Fredericks. He just could not bring himself to believe the man guilty of trying to harm the family. "No, Fredericks, that will be all."

As the door closed behind the servant, Thornwood turned to him, all his earlier playfulness gone. "I suspect you did not bring me here to celebrate your newfound bliss. Your message sounded urgent."

Leave it to Thornwood to dispense with subtleties. He could talk a hound out of a round of beef when he wanted to, but one-to-one, he preferred to get straight to the point. He'd always been like that.

"I need your advice." Nicholas paused. He needed more than friendly guidance. *Damn, this is bloody awkward.* Catherine placed her hand on his arm, its warmth giving him the strength he needed to share honestly. He placed his hand on hers and leaned forward, staring at Thornwood.

"Truth be told, I need your counsel." He hesitated again. She gently squeezed his arm in encouragement. "And your discretion."

Thornwood sat pensive, looking from him to Catherine and back again. "You have both. I assure you that what you share with me will remain in this room."

Nicholas released his breath slowly, then breathed deeply again, trying to release his tension. He could trust the man. He knew it. Still, he needed fortification. It was a new habit he must consider tempering when this was all behind them.

He patted Catherine's hand, then stood. "I find I need a bit of a bracer. Brandy?"

Thornwood nodded, saying nothing, his countenance relaxed

but his eyes alert. Nicholas knew he was taking everything in, missing nothing, no nuance too small for his sharp mind. The man should have gone to the bar. He would make a fine barrister.

Nicholas strode to the table near the desk. He stared at the rich mahogany paneling and the handsomely crafted bookshelves on either side of this second fireplace. He felt like a fraud. He had helped design this room for his father, for Daniel. Nicholas had never been meant to stand in it as the future Earl of Woodfield.

He reached for the decanter, his hand shaking slightly as he pulled the crystal stopper and laid it aside. *Damn Daniel for his choices!* Splashing an ample amount of the amber liquid into each glass, he took a deep breath. *Steady. Thornwood will understand. Blast and damn, he will not! How can he, when I do not understand it myself? Any of it!*

"Nicholas?" Catherine's voice pulled him back into the room.

He shook his head, trying to shake the frustrated melancholy. What was done was done. What would come of it was what Thornwood may help him to resolve.

He strolled to the duo, handed Thornwood a glass, and took his place beside Catherine on the stiff settee. He swirled the contents, hesitant to begin.

"To friends," Thornwood began, "the people whom you choose to share your life with." He raised his glass.

"To friendship," Nicholas echoed, hoping this one proved strong and true. "It's about Daniel."

Thornwood's left eyebrow raised, but he said nothing. Instead, he waited patiently for Nicholas to continue.

"His death was no accident."

Thornwood leaned forward in his chair, a scowl darkening his calm demeanor. "You suspect foul play?"

Nicholas shook his head. "If only. That would be easier to deal with." He looked down at the floor." Suicide," he said quietly. He felt sick hearing the word aloud.

"Dear Lord, Sinclair, I had no idea!" Thornwood sat back in his chair, "I do apologize—Lord Walford now. I am just so, so…"

"Shocked?" Nicholas provided. "As were we."

"Your brother was always so positive, so energetic. Not the type at all that I would anticipate would take his own life. I heard nothing of it. Nothing at all."

"It's not public knowledge. I hope for it to remain a private matter."

Catherine's hand slipped into his.

"Is there reason to believe it might not? For, I assure you, there has not been so much as a hum about it." Thornwood was all business now, having quickly shaken off his initial reaction.

"Someone is trying to blackmail us." Nicholas handed over the letter. "It's clear they know that Daniel took his own life."

Thornwood scanned the note, then looked up, his expression riddled with questions.

"I need your legal counsel, Thornwood. What are the repercussions should Daniel's death be fully exposed?"

"Felo-de-se—the legal term for his death," he said, handing the parchment back. "Felon of oneself. Self murder." He sat back in his chair. "If he was convicted of the crime, his property would be forfeited."

"How can a dead man face conviction?" Catherine asked before Nicholas could.

"It has been done." Thornwood steepled his fingers together thoughtfully. "Were there any witnesses?"

Catherine's grip tightened on Nicholas's hand. "No one," he lied smoothly. Laurence was long gone. Besides, he had no doubt Laurence would keep the truth to himself. In that, Catherine was right. He loved Daniel. Always had. If only it *had* been like a brother. That left only Catherine. While he knew she would keep the secret, he had no wish to see her in the middle of an inquest.

"Then it cannot be proven at this point. It would be your word against this blackguard's. No judge would order an exhumation of an earl's son based on extortion, unless, of course, the blackmailer is of higher rank. Do you have any idea who is behind this?"

"I have angered a few people recently, but none of rank…that I know of."

"Still busy speaking your mind to the discomfort of others?" Thornwood smiled. "Well, no matter. It will be easily dismissed if no one of authority is making the accusation. And why would someone of standing hide behind a letter of exaction?"

"You are sure of this, Thornwood?"

"I am. Even were I not, we could prove Daniel was not of sound mind. It might not prevent the desecration of his current burial spot should they demand it, but his properties would remain untouched."

Nicholas shuddered to think of defiling Daniel's body. "I need another drink."

"I would have one, please." Catherine's request was hushed, her face pale. He was wallowing in his own agony and forgetting how distressing this was for her too.

He raised her hand and pressed a kiss to it. "Of course, my love. I am so sorry. For all this."

Her eyes shone with unshed tears. "Me too."

He strode to the table, grabbed the decanter and another glass. He topped up Thornwood's, then filled ones for himself and Catherine. The fire crackled as they stared at it, sipping quietly. Perhaps the rest need not be said? He had not heard any more from the scoundrel. Maybe nothing more would come of it? But what if it did? He needed to be prepared for all eventualities.

"I feel there is more." Thornwood broke the silence.

"Yes, there is more." This was not going to be easy. Nicholas could not fathom it himself; how was he to explain it to his friend?

"It seems Daniel was involved with another." He struggled, grasping for the right words. "He was having a liaison with another. An illicit liaison," he finished lamely.

Catherine placed her hand on his thigh, her eyes no longer shining and her determination clear. "I'll not repudiate him. Either of them," she said softly. She turned to Thornwood.

"Daniel and my brother formed a bond beyond friendship. They loved each other."

Thornwood whistled a release of breath, his shock clear in his uncensored expression. He leaned forward in his chair, his brandy cupped in both hands, held carelessly between his legs. "I would never have thought it."

"Nor I," Nicholas confirmed. "But it seems it was so." He and Catherine shared the whole tale, leaving no detail untold. When they were done, they both leaned back and stared at Thornwood, awaiting his reaction.

"Well, that certainly explains your wedding" was all he said before downing his remaining brandy. He set the empty glass on the table and moved to the fireplace, rubbing his hands together as though cold.

Nicholas waited, caressing Catherine's hand. He knew Thornwood. He was thinking, digesting the information and processing the facts.

Finally he turned around. "You fear the blackguard knows of Daniel's relationship?"

"We cannot be certain he doesn't." Nicholas reached into his jacket and pulled out the letter left for Catherine.

Thornwood read it quickly. "This is ambiguous. It is difficult to discern what is referenced. The darkened halls and sullied hands could well be referring to the lack of disclosure over Daniel's death. Suicide is considered a great blasphemy by the church as well as a crime by law. This could be the work of one of those rabid moral reformers."

"I thought that too. It's the reference to Catherine's sacrifice that has me worried. It would seem this person knows what she was willing to do for love of her brother"—he ran a thumb down her cheek, her eyes luminous in the firelight—"and mine. For love of us all." He leaned in and kissed her chastely, then clasped her hand snugly. He knew how difficult this was for her.

"Yes, I see your concern." Thornwood began to pace. "Who knows of their association?"

"My father," Catherine said.

"And mine," Nicholas added.

"Yes, yes, that was clear. Who else might possibly know?"

"Fredericks," he said at the same time Catherine said, "Nan."

"And probably every other servant if your homes are anything like mine." Thornwood smiled ruefully. "Well, the good news is no harm can come to Daniel by an accusation. His name will be sullied, but since he is no longer with us, it will not provide much amusement for long."

"My father wishes to protect him in death. Pity he had not thought to do that in life." Nicholas tasted the bitterness of his words.

"I believe he was trying to do just that with his actions," Thornwood said unapologetically, holding up a hand before Nicholas could refute the statement. "I am not saying it was the most humane approach, but it was practical. Forgive my plain speaking, Lady Walford, but what Daniel was suggesting is a capital crime. He was trying to save his son from the noose."

"Bloody hell." Nicholas ran his hand through his hair, glancing sideways at Catherine to see how she was coping with that lovely image.

She remained calm, a wave of sympathy darkening her eyes. "There is no need to shelter me. I am no innocent. Their love was no offense in my heart, but I knew what the law would say. I fear their relationship is much harder for you to discuss than I."

She was right. His stomach twisted at the thought. He had known loneliness yet had never turned to another woman, never mind… He shook his head. He did not understand it. But he loved his brother. Hell, he loved Laurence too. He would do everything he could to protect them both.

Brandy splashed in his glass. He hadn't noticed Thornwood grab the decanter.

"So," Thornwood continued as though he had not been interrupted. "The biggest concern is for Laurence. You do not want to see him charged with unnatural crimes."

"But he is safe in the colonies now." Catherine bit her bottom lip, her forehead creased with anxiety. Nicholas knew she was as worried about Laurence fighting as much as she was about this god-awful mess.

"Perhaps." Thornwood eyed her thoughtfully. "But if he has joined the army, as you say, he would not be that hard to track. And, I presume, he will need to come home someday to take over Stratton Hall, will he not?"

She nodded, still worrying her lip. "It is my father's greatest desire."

"With Daniel gone, can he actually be prosecuted?" Nicholas could not see how a charge could be laid when one of the party was dead.

"The law is a perilous landscape, my friend. He could be charged after the fact with conspiracy to commit...an indecent act." Thornwood glanced at Catherine, his look regretful.

Nicholas knew Thornwood was trying to carefully choose his words, and he appreciated it. He hoped Catherine's innocence protected her from the worst of this discussion.

"Again, I do apologize, Lady Walford." Thornwood paced anew. "If this blackguard is a peer of the realm, a charge might hold. If not, then it would be dismissed. Unless there is a witness?"

Nicholas and Catherine looked at each other. A witness to their relationship?

"No," she whispered. "Impossible."

Thornwood cocked his head questioningly.

"They were discreet. I would not know of it had Daniel and Laurence not shared the truth. Our fathers were equally oblivious."

Nicholas hoped Catherine's confidence was well placed.

Thornwood nodded, seeming satisfied. "Then, unless they have left some evidence of some sort, you might face some gossip, but little else will come of it."

Evidence? *Damn.* The letters. "Excuse me," he said, standing, fighting the urge to race down the hall to his study.

"Nicholas?"

"I'll be back in a minute." He walked as quickly as was reasonable, glancing in the rooms along the way, hoping the panic he felt did not show on his face. He was now intensely aware of the power of witnesses.

He opened the door to his study and paused. Nothing was amiss. Everything seemed as he had left it. He reached into his jacket, extracting the key. He had thought to keep it close these last few days, but had not sought out the letters. His hands trembled slightly as he unlocked the bottom drawer, his gut knowing what he'd find, despite the impossibility of it. He pulled it open hesitantly. The letters were gone. One ribbon remained. It was tied neatly around a fresh piece of parchment.

CHAPTER THIRTY-FIVE

*Think you I am no stronger than my sex, being so father'd and
so husbanded?*

—Shakespeare, *Julius Caesar*

CATHERINE STUDIED LORD Thornwood as he looked out at the
gray afternoon. He was as tall as Nicholas but leaner and not
quite so broad through the shoulders. His hair was unfashionably
long, but somehow it suited him, added an air of ancient wisdom.

He turned to her, his eyebrows drawing together. "You have
carried much weight these last months. I wish we'd met earlier,
that I could have been of some help while Nicholas was away."

She did not doubt his concern was genuine, and she smiled at
such sentiment. He was indeed a gentleman in every sense.
Nicholas was right to put their fears in his hands. "Thank you.
The support you are providing now is more than enough and is
very much appreciated."

"It is nothing," he assured her. "Where do you think that
husband of yours ran off to?"

She had no idea, but it seemed rude and ridiculous to run
after him, so she had subdued the urge. Still, she was anxious, and
clearly, Thornwood was too. "Please, do have a seat. I will ring
for some more tea."

He remained where he stood. "I find myself too restless to sit, nor am I in need of tea." He strolled to the side table and poured a healthy amount of brandy, holding up the bottle toward her in question.

She shook her head. There was still plenty in her glass.

"Even from the devastation of fire comes new growth." He held his glass high. "Many blessings to you and Lord Walford."

She raised her glass in response, sipping cautiously. She was not accustomed to so much drinking and wanted a clear head, although she did appreciate the warmth that trickled down her throat, heating her stomach.

"Walford?" Lord Thornwood took a step toward the door-way.

Nicholas, as pale as she'd ever seen him, thrust a piece of paper toward them. She flew across the room. He wrapped his arms around her, holding her tightly, and she ran her hands down his back, trying to soothe him.

She pulled back, frightened by what she saw in his face. "What's happened?"

Color infused his face, quickly replacing his wan look, and his nostrils flared as he steadied his breathing. He kissed her forehead and released her, handing the paper to Lord Thornwood. She shivered at the controlled rage that vibrated through his body as he took her by the hand and led her to the sofa, pulling her down beside him. He leaned forward, grabbed her glass, and downed the contents. Fury and sorrow warred over his features.

"Read it aloud, Thornwood. Catherine must hear it, but I cannot…cannot…" His face twisted again.

Lord Thornwood hesitated, looking from Nicholas to her and back again. She nodded, grateful Nicholas was not hiding anything from her. He leaned against the mantel, appearing relaxed if one did not note the tension in his jaw or the sharp flick of his hand as he shook the parchment, its crisp fold suspending the paper until he brushed a hand down to straighten it. He did a quick scan, and his face grew grim. She tensed as his lips tightened when he glanced at her. His deep baritone could not soften the message.

Lord Walford,

You have chosen to do this the hard way. I would have taken the initial request and fled far from your world. But you have thrown it to the winds. The injury to your man is on your head, not mine. I meant him no harm. However, if you continue to deny all that is holy, to refuse to make recompense for the sins of your household, I fear more destruction will follow.

Your brother's sins against God are too numerous and odious to recount. When your wife fled from you, did she suspect that blood runs true and that you are of an ilk with your sibling? Is that why you joined the army when there was no need? You enjoy the company of men? Is your man more than your valet? These are questions I ponder, wondering what the magistrate would think of it all.

I regret the pain I cause Lady Walford, who is always kindness itself and is once again dutifully standing at your side. I would expect no less of such a fine lady. However, no sin must go unpunished. I am your conscience, Lord Walford. Answer to me and then atone for your sins, and those of your brother, by committing yourself to servitude to Lady Walford.

Your fine has now doubled, but the directions remain the same. Leave the money on the steps of those hallowed halls of love. I expect it by dusk this eve. Do not send your man as you did before. I will be watching.

This is your final opportunity before full disclosure to all and sundry who will listen.

Catherine sat stunned. Whoever this was, they wanted to punish the brothers Woodfield. There was no doubt in her mind. Yet the person seemed to have a weakness for her. Or was that just artful deception?

"Why this leniency toward me? I aided and abetted Daniel and Laurence, not you," she said.

Nicholas raised his shoulders, releasing them along with a lengthy exhale. "I've no idea. Were you friendly with any of the maids here? Brownlee?"

"No more than any of the staff."

"Perhaps it's a red herring, meant to mislead us?" Lord Thornwood suggested.

"Fredericks," Nicholas muttered.

"I beg your pardon?" Catherine could not see any connection between what she'd just heard and Fredericks. "Surely you do not suspect Fredericks of being responsible for something so despicable?"

Nicholas ran a hand through his hair. "I cannot give credence to my suspicion, yet he was noticeably absent after the first attempt. He was not himself when we found him either."

She recalled how rude he was that evening. "Oh, Nicholas, he had just spent hours waiting with your father. That is enough to undo anyone. You cannot possibly believe Fredericks culpable of blackmail."

"No, I do not. I cannot."

"All well and fine, Walford, but I think it best we keep our plans in the confines of this room. I suggest you not even tell your father of this latest missive," Thornwood said, glancing at Catherine before returning his attention to Nicholas.

Catherine was relieved to see the hint of a smile as Nicholas stared at his friend.

"*Our* plans, Thornwood?" Nicholas asked, a full-fledged smile softening the tension in his face.

Lord Thornwood shrugged. "In for a penny, in for a pound. Besides, I haven't had this much excitement in my life since our time at Eton." His face grew more serious. "I would not leave you to face this criminal alone. Be he moral reformer or rankled employee, he is in the wrong. You've done nothing to deserve such egregious threats."

Catherine agreed. Nicholas had left to fight for his country and returned to a nightmare.

"Now tell me about these hallowed halls?" Lord Thornwood pulled a chair closer to the settee, and Nicholas outlined the structure and its location.

"So there are two paths leading to the folly, am I correct?"

"Yes"—Nicholas sat back—"two directions to come from or escape down. Unless he goes through the folly. It would be possible to get out a window, I would think. I've never tried it, but depending on how agile the bastard is…"

Lord Thornwood stiffened, looking pained.

Nicholas caught his glance and grimaced with contrition. "I do apologize, Catherine. I fear the army has loosened my verbal restraint."

"You have been cursing since you came home. I don't think this is the time for you to worry about refining your speech." She patted his arm and smiled at Lord Thornwood. "Although, I do thank you for your concern."

Thornwood's shoulders visibly relaxed, and he continued. "So three points to be covered. How is your man Langdon?"

"Better but not good enough. I will not have him wounded again."

"I can watch," Catherine offered, anxious to be part of the solution. She could not bear another evening of walking the floors.

"No."

"But, Nicholas—"

"We'll take care of it." He scowled at her. She tried to protest again, but he cut her off. "I said no."

That was it? No? Like he was speaking to some child? How could he simply dismiss her and continue to plan as though she was not even in the room? *Well, bloody hell to that!* She stood abruptly, her temples popping with swelling anger.

"I'll not sit passively by while you men work things out! You may have been fighting on the continent, Nicholas Sinclair, but I have been waging my own war here. And I am entirely sick and tired of men telling me what to do, and where to be, leaving me with no choices. Well, I've been part of this mess since the beginning, and I'll not have you shut me out now. This is my war too. My brother, my father—*my* family. I was willing to give up everything"—she shook her finger at him—"including you. I'll be damned if I'm now going to stand by and let *you men* take care of it like I am some schoolroom miss. I deserve better. I've earned it!"

"Catherine, for God's sake, not now." He ran both hands through his hair, shaking his head back and forth.

Lord Thornwood cleared his throat. "We could do with a third, Walford."

"Well, it will *not* be Catherine." He got up and walked to the window. "Time is running out."

She took a step toward him. "Then let me—"

"No, and I'll not listen to any more of this." He leaned his forehead against the windowpane. "At least the rain has stopped." He turned to her, sighing. "You can be of assistance. Go to your father. Tell him everything that's happened. Ask him to station himself beyond the folly in case the blackguard goes through the building and tries to escape through a window."

"Are you not concerned she'll be seen?" Thornwood asked, frowning at the suggestion.

"She goes back and forth frequently, so it shouldn't look suspicious. Besides, I'm banking on his apparent fondness for her and the fact that, at this late hour, the scoundrel is already in position. I assume he has done so each evening, since he could not possibly know when I would find the letter."

He moved to her then and cupped her shoulders. "Go to the stables. You won't be able to get to your father in time if you walk."

She was unable to speak, fury and fear clogging her throat. She turned to go.

"Catherine."

She paused.

"I mean it. Straight to Stratton Hall. And stay there. Take your girl with you."

It took every measure of her control not to slam the door as she left.

CHAPTER THIRTY-SIX

It is not nor it cannot come to good.

—Shakespeare, *Hamlet*

CATHERINE STOMPED DOWN the front steps, yanking on her gloves. She flicked at an irritating tendril of hair freed by the breeze and wished she had taken the time to retrieve a bonnet and perhaps a shawl for added warmth. The air was chilling against her heated cheeks, and the spray from the fountain added to the feeling of dampness. At least it had stopped raining. She tugged the cloak tighter and headed toward the stables.

She could not believe Nicholas would dismiss her worth with the wave of a hand. She'd done fine without him the last four years, thank you very much! He was not the all-controlling captain here. She didn't have to take orders from him. She had as much right to help catch this culprit as…as…well, *more* than Lord Thornwood actually! Her brother and father would suffer greatly if this miscreant exposed everything to the world.

The stables loomed, and she paused, out of breath from her fast pace and her wrath. She pulled open the doors but did not see anyone in the aisle. "Charlie," she called out but heard nothing except the rustling of the horses. She strolled between the stalls, the animals' breath misting the air as they came to their gates to greet her.

"I'm sorry, boys; I didn't bring any treats today." She stopped and patted Taurus's dark forehead. "And he calls *you* stubborn," she grumbled.

"Charlie." She called out louder this time, heading toward the tack room at the far end. Where was everyone today? The ever-present Fredericks had not been in the atrium to assist her with her pelisse. Could Nicholas's suspicions be correct? She shook her head at slipping into his disturbing doubts. Yes, perhaps gnarly, old Fredericks and humped-over Charlie were in collusion, plotting the demise of the great Woodfields. She snorted with irritation.

"My lady?"

Catherine jumped, her heart racing. Charlie stood in the doorway, cap in hand.

"Goodness, Charlie, you startled me."

"Apologies, my lady. I was just out checking the paddocks and saw the door open. Is aught amiss?"

"No, Charlie. All is well. Please saddle Star for me."

"But, begging your pardon, it will be dark soon."

Did all men think her incapable? "I am merely riding to Stratton Hall," she snapped. He was red-faced as she marched past him to wait outside. It seemed an eternity before he brought Star out, fully outfitted.

"I do apologize, my lady," he said quietly, cupping his hands together to help her mount.

Fully seated, she looked down at him, shame adding to the turmoil in her stomach. She did not bark at the servants. Charlie had not deserved her ire. "It is I who apologize."

Charlie touched his fingers to his hat in acknowledgment, and she nudged Star south toward the path around the large lake that led to her father's estate. The trail had borne the brunt of the days of relentless rain, making the going far slower than she had anticipated. She would not risk Star despite the urgent need to catch this rogue and put an end to the threat.

She rounded the end of the lake and stopped. At the north

end, out of view, lay the folly. Nicholas and Lord Thornwood must already be in place. The sky was darkening quickly. Dusk was almost upon them. She would never be able to make it to Stratton Hall in time for her father to be of any help. If she'd brought Sadie as Nicholas had commanded, she could have sent her on with word. Anger was so shortsighted.

She would just have to improvise and face Nicholas's wrath. Well, quid pro quo, she supposed. She had certainly unleashed hers upon him. Pulling on the rein, she urged Star off the main path and carefully picked through the woods on the opposite side of the lake. It would bring her to the back of the pavilion.

Stopping a short distance away, she slid from Star, not bothering to tether the horse. If she wandered at all, it would be to Stratton or back to Woodfield. The old horse was at home in both stables and knew the routes well.

"Stay here, girl." Star's nostrils flared as she snorted, then nuzzled Catherine's neck, her steamy breath comforting. "God willing, I won't be long."

Moving cautiously, Catherine glimpsed the lake through the trees. She knew the woods well. She, Nicholas, and their brothers had passed many afternoons playing here as children. In truth, it had mostly been her chasing the boys and trying to infiltrate their games.

The brush grew denser near the folly. Her foot caught a root, and she stumbled. "Oh!" She bit the tip of her tongue, slamming her mouth shut to muffle her outburst. She held her breath, listening. The wind fluttered through the trees. She shivered, swallowing the metallic taste of blood and rubbing her foot. Her short boots were sodden, the leather most likely ruined. They were her favorite pair. Another strike against the scoundrel.

She pushed cautiously to her feet and swiped at her dampened skirts. *Onward, soldier. Must make the captain proud.* She picked her way more carefully, keeping her eyes on the ground. She had no doubt Nicholas had been a formidable officer. He was certainly imperious enough. She sighed. That was unkind. He was only trying to protect her. Could she truly fault that?

"Stop where you are or I'll shoot!"

She halted abruptly at Nicholas's shouted command just as someone came flying through a bush. The wind rushed from her lungs, and pain shot up her back, her head somehow spared from smacking the ground. She looked up into the baby-blue eyes of her attacker, who looked as surprised as she felt.

"You," she whispered on the exhale, too shocked to say anything else before lying back, sucking air, each breath agony. *Dear Lord, what now?*

CHAPTER THIRTY-SEVEN

If this were played upon a stage now, I could condemn it as an improbable fiction.

—Shakespeare, *Twelfth Night*

NICHOLAS BLINKED. THE man had catapulted through a bush, disappearing beyond. Nicholas lowered his pistol, moving toward the large shrub.

"Careful, Walford. I don't hear crashing in the woods beyond. He may be waiting. He could be armed." Thornwood was right. Nicholas had not survived the war to be ambushed by some rogue on his own property. They both moved cautiously forward through the brush, their pistols ready.

"Christ's blood!" He couldn't believe his eyes. The popinjay held Catherine tight to his chest, the muzzle of an older flintlock denting the soft flesh of her neck.

"Are you all right, Catherine?" Years of training kicked in, and he managed to keep his voice calm, despite the surging rage that rippled over his body. Her mantle was filthy, and her breathing was clearly labored. She nodded, her eyes glassy with pain.

"Put the gun down, Isaac," he said.

"You know this man, Walford?" Thornwood asked.

Isaac looked frantically from Nicholas to Thornwood, then back to Nicholas. "Walford is dead. Damn you! He's dead. You are not Walford. You are not Daniel." He choked on the name.

Nicholas took a step forward. "You are right, Isaac. I am not Daniel. I never wished to be. You know that. Now give me your weapon." He held out his hand.

"Stay where you are!" Isaac cried. "I killed Daniel. I'll not hesitate to kill your lady."

Nicholas froze, stunned by the confession, but Isaac's wavering hand drew him back into the moment. Fear slid down his spine. The pistol was cocked, and the valet's hands shook, his finger closing dangerously around the trigger. He held his own pistol ready but could not fire with Catherine in the way. Thornwood was subtly shifting to the side, where he might get a clear shot. Nicholas must keep Isaac's attention from the movement.

"Why would you want to harm Lady Walford, Isaac?" Nicholas asked. "She has been nothing but kindness. You said it yourself in your letters."

Isaac's eyes shimmered with tears. "How could you allow her to be here today? What kind of a man would so endanger his wife? None of you deserve her." His hands vibrated with emotion, the pistol digging deeper into Catherine's neck.

Nicholas held his gaze steady on Isaac, but out of the corner of his eye, he could see that Thornwood was almost clear. A few more feet.

"You are right. I don't deserve Catherine. Let her go and take me. I am the one who deserves your anger, not her." He held his arms out wide, letting the pistol hang limply in his open palm. He kept his gaze on Isaac, knowing Thornwood must be about ready to make his shot. Thank the Lord Nicholas knew him to be an excellent marksman. Catherine's life depended on his accuracy.

A sudden noise from the woods drew Nicholas's attention, and he quickly raised his pistol again. Fredericks rushed forward, placing himself in the direct line of Thornwood's weapon.

"Don't shoot, my lord. I beg of you." Fredericks turned to Nicholas. "For love of me and mine, don't shoot."

Nicholas hesitated. What the hell was happening? Was Fredericks party to Daniel's death, to this seizing of Catherine? The old man stood his ground, his pale eyes a window to his pain.

"Walford?" Thornwood's voice was placid, quiet, awaiting direction.

"Bloody hell, Thornwood, I don't know."

Beyond Fredericks, Isaac still pressed his gun to Catherine's neck. She shook her head slightly, her eyes begging him to listen to Fredericks. Nicholas stared at her a long moment, then lowered his weapon.

Fredericks faced Isaac, his hand extended. "Give me the gun, son. It's done. You must face the consequences of your actions. Lord help me, but I can protect you no more."

Tears rolled down Isaac's cheeks as he looked from his grandfather's outstretched hand to his face. He threw Catherine from him. She stumbled, falling to the ground, scrambling backward toward Nicholas. He jumped forward, kneeling, pulling her into the safety of his arms. She cried out as his heart pounded its relief.

He glowered at the man who'd dared threaten her, the man who had killed his brother. Nicholas's composed battle demeanor slipped away, red anger in its place, fury flowing through his veins. He stood, pulling Catherine up, pushing her behind him. "Thornwood, take her to safety."

He raised his pistol, cocking the hammer, grasping the trigger firmly. The old man stood frozen, hand still stretched, waiting for the young valet's pistol. He was not in the way of Nicholas's aim.

"No, Nicholas! No!" Catherine's voice softened as she placed her hand on his. "There has been enough death. Enough loss. No more. I beg of you."

Her face was deathly pale, her eyes luminous with unshed tears, and her breathing labored. The sight of her, pleading on behalf of a murderer, only made him angrier.

"Daniel would expect nothing less than your mercy." Her smooth palm caressed his calloused one. "Let pity stay your hand."

He hesitated.

"Please," she rasped between irregular breaths.

"I'm sorry." Isaac cried softly, staring at his grandfather. "I'm ever so sorry…for everything."

Nicholas lowered his pistol as Isaac raised his to his own forehead.

"Please forgive me," Isaac said.

"No!" shouted Fredericks and Thornwood simultaneously, throwing themselves at the man.

Nicholas grabbed Catherine, turning her from the foray when sparks flew as the gun went off. She stiffened, trying to shift in his arms, but he pressed her head firmly against his chest, awaiting the outcome as the tumble of bodies disassembled. Thornwood staggered to a stand, seeming no worse for wear, staring down at Isaac's crumpled body. Isaac was not dead but wept as his grandfather held him, wiping at the blood that ran down the side of his face.

Catherine wriggled out of his grip, gasping at the fallen pair. She ran to them, dropping to her knees and inspecting the wound. She appealed to Nicholas. "The temple has been grazed. We need to get him to the house and have it seen to."

Nicholas stared at the trio. Isaac was a weeping pile of pathetic dung. He could lie there and rot for all Nicholas cared. Did Catherine have any idea what she was asking of him?

"I'll see to it," Thornwood said quietly, placing a hand on his shoulder. "Take your wife back to the manse, and I'll take care of the culprit. I imagine you have a lot of questions you would like answered before he's taken away."

Nicholas was grateful for Thornwood's unruffled demeanor when he himself was a boiling pot of confusion. Catherine had clearly accepted Thornwood's offer, coming slowly to a stand and brushing at her dress.

"Thank you, my friend." Nicholas was grateful to have the man at his side.

Thornwood nodded as Catherine strode past Nicholas. Was

she angry still? He was in no hurry to find out but turned to follow her. To say it had been a trying day would be the understatement of the year. And it was far from over. He would deal with Catherine and her emotions once that damned coxcomb was out of their lives.

He rounded the folly, toward the path. Catherine was walking slower now. Perhaps she wanted him to catch up? Suddenly she bent over and vomited. He was by her side in seconds, rubbing a hand up and down her soaked pelisse while she cried out at each heave. When she quieted, he gave her his handkerchief, still tracing circles on her back. She straightened haltingly and wrapped an arm around her waist, her eyes wide and shining in her blanched face.

"Nicholas," she gasped, bending over again, dry heaves causing her to cry out once more. He was going to bloody well kill that man when he got his hands on him again. *To hell with Catherine's penchant for forgiveness!*

When this bout was finished, she was flushed with exertion.

"Come, let's get you home." He draped an arm around her shoulders, pulling her close.

She flinched in response and whimpered.

"Are you hurt?"

"I'm fine," she wheezed, pushing from him, faltering on her first step.

"The hell you are. The bastard hurt you!"

She fought for breath. "He did not—mean to. Truly, he did not. It's just—he landed on me and…" She sucked the air, holding her arms tight against her chest. "I fell hard."

She stiffened when he scooped her up into his arms, holding her close to reduce bouncing her body around. Anger propelled him quickly home. That bloody man was going to pay. For everything.

CHAPTER THIRTY-EIGHT

And now let's go hand in hand, not one before another.

—Shakespeare, *The Comedy of Errors*

N AN TIED OFF the linen that wrapped Catherine's chest, then stood, tidying her apron, her wrinkled face folding in on itself with concern.

"I don't think any of them are broken, but you might have a crack." She smoothed a hand over Catherine's forehead. "Your breathing is much improved now that you're bound, so I think it is more than bruising. You must keep it bandaged for some time. Breathe deeply when you can, love. I don't rightly understand why, but it helps the healing."

She leaned over and kissed her on the cheek, then straightened. "Well, off to attend the other patient."

"Let the rotter die from shot poisoning," Nicholas said.

"Nicholas!" Catherine said at the same time Nan gasped, "Master Nick!"

Nan shuffled toward the door, stopping in front of Nicholas, who stood, arms folded over his chest—a sentinel to all who dared cross the threshold of the room.

She reached up and cupped his cheek. "She will be fine, my lord. Despite her pain, I'm glad she was there to stop something you may have regretted."

He placed his hand on her old, worn one. "My only regret is that the man still lives."

Nan patted his cheek. "We shall see, Master Nick. We shall see."

Nan pulled the door firmly closed behind her, and Nicholas's full attention turned to Catherine. He unfolded his arms and strode across the room.

"Are you in much pain?" His forehead creased with care.

"It's much better now that Nan has me bound." She took a deep breath as Nan had instructed. It was true. The pain had lessened to a tolerable ache in her chest.

"Good."

He grabbed a chair and pulled it to her bedside. His bedside. Nicholas had insisted she rest in his chambers. He'd been urging her to move into his room but had spent the nights in hers, so she had felt no need. His chamber was dark and lush, a masculine environment. Oddly, it made her feel warm and safe. Until she looked at his face.

"Why were you there?" His jaw tensed, his lips compressed. He was fighting anger. Well, it was his own bloody fault, and she told him as much.

"My fault?" His voice was low, almost inaudible. A bellow would have been better than this restrained response.

Still, she persevered. "Yes, your fault. You were willing to cut me out. To dismiss me from being a member of this family."

His face flushed. "I did not cast you from the family and well you know it." He took her hand in his, placing the other on her cheek. His eyes shone sapphire, staring into her soul. "I have spent the better part of my life, and I mean better, dreaming of you, wanting you, loving you. You are part of my family." He paused, his eyes shimmering in the candlelight. "That is a lie."

She caught her breath, then coughed at the discomfort. His hand caressed a path down her cheek until he was holding her chin gently between his thumb and forefinger.

"You are not a part of my family. You *are* my family."

Tears stung as she gulped for air, pain racing through her chest.

"Oh, my love, I didn't mean to cause you further distress." He let go of her chin and ran his hand through his hair. "What can I do to help?"

She reached up and linked her hands behind his neck, pulling him down so they were cheek to cheek. She longed to kiss him, but she could not. She could barely breathe with the emotion rattling her body. Instead, she held him close and murmured soft words of love until they both calmed.

Nicholas broke the connection, his eyes darkened with regret. He brushed stray locks from her face. "I fear it is time to go put an end to this." He leaned in and kissed her forehead.

She pushed up on an elbow, wincing as pain lacerated her chest. She took a steadying breath. "I will attend."

His brow furrowed, his lips tensed into a straight line. "No."

"Yes." She cut him off before he could ignite another fire. "Family, remember?"

He remained pensive, but his lips tilted just the tiniest amount at the edges, and she knew she had won.

"Help me get into a clean gown, would you?" Gingerly, she shifted across the bed, letting her feet dangle.

He looked at her, naked except for the bandaging. He'd even drawn off her soaked stockings while Nan had bound her chest. "I far prefer helping you from them."

She stared up at him, heat warming her face. "Well, that may be, but there are more important matters to attend to."

He sobered quickly. "Let's get it done."

CHAPTER THIRTY-NINE

*The quality of mercy is not strain'd. It droppeth as the gentle
rain from heaven upon the place beneath: it is twice blest; it
blesseth him that gives and him that takes.*

—Shakespeare, *The Merchant of Venice*

HALF AN HOUR later, Nicholas and Catherine stood at the top
of the stairs. Sadie had been waiting in Catherine's room
when he'd gone to grab a gown. He was grateful for her
assistance. As much as he knew how to undress a woman, he was
not entirely sure he'd remember all the items required for one to
be fully clothed nor where to find them all.

Catherine's head ached slightly, so she had not wanted her
hair piled. It flowed down her back, her burgundy tresses shining
after Sadie's careful, meticulous brushing. The locks far too
tempting to resist, he reached out, caressing a tendril. Love
warmed her eyes to its deepest foliage. She reached up and placed
her hand on his.

"I remember Isaac from our childhood," she said quietly. He
tried to pull his hand back, but she grasped it tightly. "You do too.
Don't deny it. He adored Daniel even then."

The thought was revolting. He yanked his hand free. "Don't
try to—"

She pressed warm fingers against his lips. "I'm asking you to listen. That is all. In memory of our youth. All of us—you, me, Daniel, Laurence…and Isaac. Listen before you pronounce judgment. Please. It is all I ask."

A single tear escaped, trickling a path down her delicate cheek. He wiped it away, then stared down as he rubbed the moisture between his thumb and forefinger. Catherine had cried too many tears, for too many men. He could halt these ones at least.

"For you, I will listen."

"Thank you." Her sigh of relief was worth whatever effort it was going to take not to strangle the damn canary.

She refused to be carried again, so he held her arm firmly while they descended the stairs, pausing every few steps to allow her a moment to catch her breath. He was as relieved as she was when they reached the marble atrium. Lights shone from the library, but it was silent. He steered her to its doors.

At the threshold, they took in the scene. Thornwood stood by the terrace windows, staring out. Nicholas had no doubt he kept an eye on Isaac's reflection in the window. Thornwood was no fool to leave himself unprotected or a man unguarded. A large fire crackled, casting ample light on the blackguard himself. Isaac heaved a theatrical sigh and lifted a glass to his lips.

Anger percolated through Nicholas. He released Catherine and stormed into the room, ripping the glass from Isaac's hand and throwing it into the fireplace. It shattered satisfyingly, and the brandy ignited a small fireball, releasing a blast of heat.

"You let the damned coxcomb drink my brandy like some guest?" His temples pulsated, ready to burst.

Thornwood turned, unperturbed. "He was incoherent. I merely sought to cease his hysterics." He looked pointedly at the man sitting passively staring at the fire despite Nicholas's own dramatics.

Embarrassment met anger, and Nicholas's cheeks heated accordingly. He strolled to the table by the bookcase, where the brandy had been amply replenished, and poured two glasses. He moved to Catherine, who had settled on the sofa. She slid off her slippers and tucked her feet under her skirts, leaning back into the corner of the settee, sitting oddly ramrod straight. She took the glass, a quick smile of gratitude softening her worried features.

He leaned against the mantel, staring at the man who had killed his brother. A bloody cherub sent from the devil. The popinjay's baby blues looked up at him at that moment. Self-pity soaked in tears.

"Master Nick," he started, his eyes watering.

What kind of man put on such a show? Well, Nicholas was not Daniel. He would not fall prey to sympathy. Where had it gotten Daniel? Dead at Isaac's hands, that was where. He could cry a waterfall, and Nicholas would remain unmoved. By rights, Isaac should lie lifeless in the woods.

Nicholas looked to Thornwood, who just cocked his head to one side in question. Apparently he was as confused by their catch as Nicholas. He sank to the sofa beside Catherine, glaring at Isaac, who sat in the chair only recently occupied by Thornwood.

"Why?" It was all Nicholas could think of to ask. Isaac did not move or indicate he'd even heard Nicholas. He simply stared at the fire.

"Why, *damn you?* Why?" His voice rose despite his desire to temper it. Catherine gripped his arm, squeezing tightly.

"Tell him," came Fredericks's voice.

Nicholas had not heard Fredericks enter. Nan stood by his side, wringing her apron. Langdon flanked the other side, his arm held tightly to his chest by a sling.

"Sit down, man, before you fall down." Nicholas gestured to the other chair, and Langdon sunk into its plush depth.

Fredericks continued to stare at Isaac, not glancing at anyone else. Nan watched Catherine, her apprehension written on her face.

"Tell him, Isaac. All of it. Let God's will be done." The old man's face remained passive, his tone neutral.

Isaac looked up from the fire, into the eyes of his grandfather.

Fresh tears trickled as he held his gaze. He visibly shuddered and then turned to Catherine.

"I am sorry, my lady, for any harm that has come at my hands."

She nodded but said nothing.

Isaac reached toward Fredericks. "Grandpapa." A single word, but the plea for forgiveness was plaintive. Nicholas looked to Fredericks too.

"I know, son. I know." Fredericks did not move toward Isaac, but his expression softened. Nicholas could feel the old man's love drifting through the room, its invisible tendrils a tangible force. He bristled, fighting sympathy. For God's sake, the man had killed Daniel!

"Tell Lord Walford everything." Fredericks held his grandson's gaze. "Everything."

Isaac shifted uncomfortably, glancing between Fredericks and the other members of the small party gathered in the library. Finally those wide, innocent-seeming eyes settled on Nicholas.

"I would never harm Daniel, ever." Isaac choked, gulping for air.

Although difficult to do, Nicholas waited without a word.

"Not deliberately."

The damn man burst into a fresh set of tears, wailing a lament fit for a funeral pyre. Thornwood crossed to the table, grabbed the decanter, and filled two new glasses. He pressed one into Isaac's hand, and Langdon leaned forward, welcoming the second. Thornwood topped up his own, then propped himself against the mantel, eyeing the weeping criminal as he sipped from the glass.

Isaac took his sweet time calming before addressing Nicholas once again. "I know you will not wish to hear this, but I loved Daniel."

Nicholas swallowed his revulsion as everyone remained quiet while Isaac sipped once again before continuing.

"I have loved him since I can remember. I was happy to serve him. Happy to spend every moment of the day that I could with him."

Nicholas swirled the brandy, staring at it. Isaac had been *in* love with his brother. *Bloody wonderful.* He raised his glass, ready to toss back the contents, begin the numbing. Instead, he lowered it. He wanted a clear head for the coming confession. For the decision that must inevitably follow it.

"I was distraught that your brother loved him as well." Isaac was addressing Catherine now. "Forgive me, but it was untenable. I loved Daniel, but he clearly was in love with Laurence." He leaned forward in his chair. "Oh, not that he ever said as much to me. No, we shared many confidences but not that one. He was the soul of discretion, I promise you." He threw back the remainder of his brandy. "But did he think me blind when he snuck out at night? When he talked of your brother with such shining joy? I may be servant-born, but I am no fool."

"So you killed him out of jealousy."

Pain and disgust flittered across Isaac's face. "Yes, my new Lord Walford. You would think that, wouldn't you? God forbid my love for your brother be true. Or his for Laurence be as pure as yours for the sister."

The cherub had the audacity to raise his glass. Thornwood lifted an eyebrow at Nicholas, then strode across to pick up the decanter. He refilled Isaac's glass. Out of the corner of his eye, Nicholas caught Catherine lifting her glass for a top-up. He would look at her, but she clouded his thinking. He needed to remain focused.

Isaac took a long sip. Nicholas glanced at Fredericks. His expression was pained, but he had not moved. Nan stared at Isaac. What did they know that he did not? Nicholas's patience was wearing thin, but it was clear pressuring Isaac would only slow the truth. And he had promised Catherine he would listen.

"I was devastated by their love; I'll not refute that." Isaac took another drink, gazing at Catherine. "When you offered yourself for them, I thought all would be well. I would never have

Daniel's affections, had always known I would not, but at least I would not be tortured by his trysts with Laurence. For I knew full well that, if he said vows with you, he would abide by them. You might think otherwise, my lady, having made kind under-the-table deals with each of them, but I know both men full well. Daniel would have honored those vows. Laurence would have abided by them as well."

Gratitude, adoration, and pain swept quickly across Isaac's features. Nicholas stiffened. Was the man playing to her sympathy?

"Then Daniel had a change of heart. I knew it in his conversations with me. He gave the letter to me to deliver that morning, instructed me to take it to Stratton Hall and ensure it got into Laurence's hands. I read it and knew he was going to renounce the betrothal. I would have to watch him pursue his love of Laurence."

The tension eased from Nicholas's shoulders. The truth at last. "So you killed him."

Isaac scowled at him, all histrionic emotion gone. "Yes, again, that would be your conclusion, Captain Sinclair. Oh, I beg your pardon, Lord Walford now, isn't it, master of all under his domain." His sarcasm dripped belligerently.

The nerve of the damn, little peacock! Nicholas leaned forward, hoping he looked as menacing as he felt, but Isaac seemed oblivious to his fury. Staring at him from under the sweep of those ridiculously long lashes of his, Isaac continued, undeterred.

"Daniel adored you. I could never fathom it. He was kindness and light. Loving and giving. Full of laughter and joy. He was twice the man you are and will ever be." He tossed back the remainder of his brandy and looked at his grandfather, who still stood rigid, Nan's hand resting on his arm. "Yet it is true. I killed him."

Fredericks stepped toward his grandson, but Nan restrained him, whispering in his ear.

"I did, Grandpapa. I'll not deny it."

"I killed him," Isaac continued, talking directly to Catherine. "But I did not mean to. Please believe me. I would never…I loved him."

Catherine leaned forward, though it clearly caused her pain, and nodded her understanding, encouraging him to continue.

"I knew they were to meet in the woods that morning." He wiped at his eyes, still staring at Catherine, telling his story to her and only her. A wave of irrational jealousy swept over Nicholas, and he bit back a response.

"I could not bear a life of watching Daniel love another. I could not." He reached out a hand toward Catherine. "I could have supported his sacrifice with you, even if he'd devoted himself entirely to loving you. I would know the cost. The price he'd paid. But I could not stand by and watch him give himself to your brother."

Unbelievably Catherine seemed entirely sympathetic. Nicholas could kill the man where he sat, yet her eyes watered with empathy.

"I delivered the missive to Stratton Hall, then went to the clearing where I knew they met regularly."

Nicholas remembered the mystical clearing he'd stumbled across when he'd been tortured by the pain of loss. Images of his brother shimmered in the light. Surely it was coincidence?

"I meant to kill myself before they arrived. I wanted them to find my pathetic, prostrate body." He smiled sadly at Catherine. "I envisioned Daniel's sorrow and his life filled with mea culpa."

She started to get up, to go to the man, but Nicholas reached out and held her arm firm. *Mea culpa* his ass. It did not explain how Isaac had killed Daniel. Catherine glanced at Nicholas. Sorrow warred with irritation. At him! She hesitated, then relaxed in his grip, settling back against the sofa.

"Go on, Isaac," she said, her tone encouraging and far more composed than his would be if he spoke. The magnetism of Catherine and Isaac's connection at the moment was undeniable. Silence hung, suspended. Nicholas modulated his breath, and his temper, and waited.

"I must admit to a fear of death. I needed Daniel to be present to face it." He shifted uncomfortably. "Daniel entered the clearing to find me with the pistol raised to my temple." He frowned at Fredericks. "Regrettably, Grandpapa, alive or dead, I would shame you."

"Son," Fredericks said gruffly. "I am not ashamed of you." He cleared his throat before continuing. "Only of your actions."

Isaacs's eyes glistened. "Thank you," he whispered before focusing on Nicholas.

"Daniel arrived to find me in that state." Isaac's head sagged, his chin resting against his chest. Everyone waited. Eventually he raised his head. "Daniel jumped me, not thinking of his own safety but trying to save me from my stupidity. The pistol fired." He swallowed a sob. "He tried to save me, and in doing so, he died. He died because of me!"

Catherine threw herself from the sofa onto her knees, exhaling sharply. Isaac startled, then threw his arms around her neck, bawling like an abandoned calf. Nicholas watched her soothe the blackguard, slowly stroking his back, and murmuring as one would with a frightened child in the night. Nicholas knew how much she must hurt right now, yet he could only watch, mesmerized by the scene and awed by her deep caring. When Isaac was sufficiently quietened, she leaned back, brushing his curling hair from his forehead.

"There is no crime in love, Isaac."

Her voice was quiet, but it resounded through Nicholas's body. Was it ever criminal to love?

"Walford?" Thornwood's voice broke through the moment. "The blackmail?"

Thornwood was quite correct. This wasn't making sense. Isaac was gazing adoringly at Catherine. It grated Nicholas's already frayed nerves.

"If you loved him so much, why blackmail his family?" Nicholas asked. "Why drag down Lady Walford to your pathetic depths?"

The cherub glared at Langdon, whose dark scowl mirrored Nicholas's own disgust. "Him!"

"Langdon?" Nicholas was thoroughly lost. What the hell had Langdon done?

Isaac's annoyance was clear. "Grandpapa convinced me you would need a valet, that my life still held purpose serving the new Lord Walford, that I could make amends by doing so. Daniel loved you, and I knew he would want you taken care of fully. In his memory, for the peace of his soul, I would do it. Then you brought him here." He scowled again at Langdon, who shot Isaac daggers of his own.

Isaac's glowering slipped away when he recaptured Catherine's attention. "When you left, my lady, I knew there was no longer a place for me here. That I could not even watch over you as Daniel would have done."

Nicholas had heard enough. "Take him away. I don't ever want to see him again." A collective gasp met the pronouncement. He looked at the people he loved. Fredericks. Nan. Most of all, Catherine. They were all aghast at his proclamation.

"What would you have me do?" he asked, looking at their shocked faces.

"Deportation?" Thornwood suggested. "With the war expanding daily, they need all hands on deck in the colonies. Perhaps you can press him into His Majesty's service?"

It was a solution that should be amicable to all. Well, all except for perhaps Isaac, who appeared distraught at the thought. Good. Nicholas glanced at Thornwood, grateful his friend was so clearheaded.

"Yes, just the thing. Fredericks?" Nicholas shook off guilt as the old man gave a subtle tip of his chin, indicating his agreement.

Catherine relinquished her hold on Isaac and slowly stood, her breathing hesitant. "Nicholas," she whispered softly as though only he could hear despite all ears attuned to her every word. "Passage and some coin. Let it be his choice to join the service, as it was yours. Let him have some say in his destiny."

He stared at her, shocked at the suggestion. The man had tried to take them down. "How can you ask it of me? This man threatened to put our families in jeopardy. He has attempted blackmail!"

"Out of fear, Nicholas. Out of love…out of loss." She gripped his arm. "Please. Do not deny him a fresh chance. In memory of Daniel, if nothing else. Daniel, who would be the first to grant clemency."

Compassion. Had Nicholas not been torn apart when none was shown at Badajoz? He could not change the course of events that led to Daniel's death, to this attempt at extortion. A man's life lay in Nicholas's hands. Fredericks's face was blanched, his eyes unnaturally neutral—a sure sign he was fighting his own emotions. Nicholas held his gaze, hoping for a signal. None was given.

"See him on the first sail to the colonies."

Thornwood nodded.

Catherine's gaze remained hopeful. Fredericks's stayed stoic. Nicholas settled on Nan. She looked at him with such love and warmth, the expectations of a mother satisfied glowing deep in her dark eyes. He glanced again at Catherine, her faith in him clear.

Thornwood and Isaac were about to exit the library. Isaac's shoulders had caved, the man's peacock pride a memory.

A sudden thought occurred to Nicholas. "The letters, Isaac. I'll have the letters before you leave."

The cherub turned, defeated. "The letters?" He seemed genuinely confused.

"My lord." Fredericks drew his attention. Reaching into his jacket, he pulled out a packet. His gnarled hands shook as he held them out. "These are the damning ones. The others have been returned to your desk."

Dear Lord, had Fredericks been a part of the scheme after all?

"I took them, my lord, that night your man was injured. I

could not find Isaac but suspected he was behind the attempt at extortion. I feared he would press you further, so I wanted to remove any leverage he might use." The old man's eyes shimmered in the candlelight, sorrow deepening his hollowed cheeks. "I should have told you. I sincerely apologize for the hurt my family has caused yours. I will leave with Isaac."

"No!" Both Catherine and Nan looked aghast at Nicholas.

Nicholas took the letters from Fredericks's shaking hand. He walked to the fireplace and tossed them in, and the flames licked the edges before the paper flared. He folded his arms on the mantel, resting his forehead against them. Daniel's words of love gone. Daniel gone...forever. The only sound in the room was the crackling fire and Catherine's labored breathing. He knew they awaited his judgment.

Suddenly exhausted, he turned to Fredericks, the man who had been a part of his life since first memory. The old servant had loved them all. Nicholas, Daniel, Laurence, Catherine. And his grandson. Could Nicholas fault him for that? Nicholas hoped that, when the time came, he would stand by his own sons and their sons as Fredericks had done.

"Your place is here, Fredericks. It is your home." He turned to his friend, waiting patiently in the threshold. "Thornwood. See Isaac with enough coin for a new life."

Thornwood smiled in approval.

"Aye, my friend." Thornwood held open the door. Isaac exited without looking back, hopefully leaving Nicholas's life forever.

Nicholas ran a hand through his hair. How was he ever to explain all this to his father? He would deal with it in the morning. He shook his head, pulling his fingers free, and turned to Catherine.

She stared at him, her eyes bright with unshed tears, then flung herself into his arms, her breath rampant with pain. He pushed her back, holding her at arm's length, aware of the agony she was feeling, both physically and emotionally. She looked at him with such love. He flushed at her uncensored adulation.

"It was all that could be done," he said lamely.

Her eyes glistened. "You could have repudiated all. But you did not. Do not think I don't understand how difficult this is for you."

She stood on tippy-toe and kissed his nose. "I love you, Nicholas. Lord Walford. Husband of mine."

His heart sang for the first time in many years as he picked up his wife, leaving the others to sort through their own emotions, and ascended the grand staircase. Daniel had not taken Nicholas's life. He had loved as purely and truly as Nicholas did. Nicholas didn't understand it, but Catherine did. She understood love in all its forms. And that was enough for him.

He kissed her forehead as he swept her up the stairs. His Catherine understood it all. Laurence. Daniel. Him.

How lucky was he?

EPILOGUE

The wheel is come full circle.

—Shakespeare, *King Lear*

CATHERINE WATCHED HER son pick petals from the profusion of roses, mumbling a song as he dropped each one on Daniel's tomb. They came here often, sharing with their son tales of their childhoods, beguiling him with stories of his uncles. He was too young yet to truly understand the anecdotes, but he'd listen and giggle, and she felt certain they were slowly becoming embedded in his memory too.

"Come, Daniel. Your grandfathers await their tea for you."

He toddled precariously toward her, his small hand warm as he slipped it into her waiting one. The other he offered to his father. She and Nicholas smiled at each other over his head. The child had done the impossible, united generations and households. When her father was in residence, he rarely missed tea with his grandson, nor did Lord Woodfield. Gone was the old man's roar. Young Daniel could get the man to practically purr like a kitten.

She looked fondly at her son, then glanced back at Daniel's resting place. He would have been a superb uncle. As would her brother. She so wished he were here. Where was Laurence now? They'd only heard from him once, acknowledging he had received word of the truth of Daniel's death. With Britain still at war with the United States, Catherine was perpetually worried Laurence would get hurt. Yet Nicholas had found no evidence that Laurence had actually enlisted as he'd planned to do. Despite that, Nicholas made regular inquiries about regimental losses but had found nothing. Nicholas assured her they would have heard if something had happened to Laurence.

Still, no word at all from Laurence himself? She could find no reason he would not contact them. Surely he planned on returning some day? Was he safe? Was he lonely? Had he found a measure of peace? If only—

"Let it be, Catherine," Nicholas said and swung Daniel up into one arm, wrapping his free one around her, pulling her close. "There are no perfect endings."

He kissed her nose, his love clear, pure, and comforting. He took his responsibilities seriously, but he'd softened in the last two years, especially since the birth of Daniel.

Nicholas whisked another kiss across her forehead and smiled. "But there are happy ones."

Daniel leaned in, kissing her nose and forehead in perfect imitation of his father. "Happy ones," he mimicked, his chubby, little hands pushing the hair from her face.

No, not perfect, she thought as she gazed into those blue eyes so like his father's. But they were both correct. It was happy indeed.

About the Author

Rose Phillips has a BA, BEd, and an Advanced Degree in Educational Leadership—none of which led to her dream of being a romance writer, but they did help pay the bills. As an educator, she worked with at-risk adolescents, so writing young adult novels seemed a natural place to start. She has three novels published in that category. While she thoroughly enjoys writing for young adults, her true love has always been adult romance, especially historical.

Rose grew up in eastern Canada, on the island of Newfoundland. She now resides on the opposite side of the country, on Vancouver Island. She enjoys kayaking, hiking, playing pickleball, and visiting the many local wineries. She long ago found the love of her life, and he continues to be the reason she believes in happy ever afters.

Twitter: @roserambles1
Instagram: rosephillipsrambles
Blog: rosephillipsrambles.blogspot.com
Amazon: amazon.com/Rose-Phillips/e/B06XB1374P
Goodreads: goodreads.com/author/show/5976526.Rose_Phillips
Bookbub: bookbub.com/authors/rose-phillips